THE BURNING TOWER

Perry Wyatt

Published by
Llyfrau Cambria Books, Wales, United Kingdom.
*Cambria Books is a division of
Cambria Publishing.*
Discover our other books at: www.cambriabooks.co.uk

DEDICATION

This tale is for anyone struggling.
Rescue yourself, go on adventures, see the world, make
friends, love hard, and burn that tower down.
You owe it to yourself to try.

CHAPTERS

One

All I had here was the view of the restless sea, the howling wind, and a monster. The latter seemed to have not made up its mind about me yet.

The Wraith of the Wastes was nothing but shadows and a fierce glare. Moonlight was streaming through a lone arched window, and its inky eyes burned into the darkness. It had no mouth or skin, existing only as a mass of shadows that moved like smoke. I didn't dare glance away.

Perhaps this was a nightmare. The Tower loomed over my childhood stories as the ultimate punishment - an ominous consequence of the worst deeds and an evil sentence befitting only the cruellest criminals.

My stomach clenched. I felt myself awaken as the spell that had kept me unconscious faded away and my eyes adjusted to the darkness. The stones of the floor were cold under my palms as I drew my bare legs in close to my body. As memories came back to me, my blood iced over.

It was all real.

Kya, the capital of Riach, the ancestral home of warlocks, wizards, and witches alike, my home, had fallen to the Horned King's armies. Trapped inside my quarters by my father, I had seen the city burn from my arched windows. The ever-busy market town – deserted; the beautiful temples to Celine – ransacked; and among the fallen, so many homes, shops, and buildings lay among the smoke as rubble. Our capital, once so full of life: obliterated.

Bile rose in my throat as I thought of my brothers, Sorrel and Abel. Had they survived? The war-worn Sorrel would go down fighting, but Abel never had the constitution for battle. Besides the Wraith, I was the only one here. Why?

"How strange," the monster said. The face didn't move – I only knew it was a face because of its shining black inkwell eyes. "I can't remember the last female sent here."

I tried to move forward, but days with barely enough food to keep a rat alive had taken a toll on my limbs. The floor was smooth beneath my feet, the stone black from dirt, time and whatever other gore coated the cell. Still, at least, this one didn't smell as foul as the prison I had enjoyed before being dragged here; disease and death reeked through the mouldy bars.

"Well, in that case," I replied, my voice echoing off the stone walls, "I hope I don't disappoint."

My head was reeling as memories of the last few weeks trickled in slowly, making my heart pound. The magic of the spell left a bitter taste on my tongue like crabbed apples. Fae magic was unfamiliar and, as it faded, the remnants of the foreign and invasive spell added to the nausea rising in me.

The attack on the city had been ruthless; it had wiped out our forces, destroyed the ward towers, and burned so many buildings the sky had turned black. The remaining citizens had fled the Capital and kept running. If they were wise, that is.

"You must stay in here, Your Highness," my most trusted maid, Hackley, had said moments after the first strike had fallen in the lower districts, smoke rising like an omen from the South. "You'll be safe."

Her words wobbled horribly as the rest of my ladies exchanged looks. I could see the lie in her smile that didn't reach her eyes. Nowhere was safe. We all knew it.

The flashes of light flooded through my windows and lit up their terrified faces. I tried to leave my room with them, but no part of me could get through. My protests had fallen on deaf ears as I was magically sealed inside as per my father's orders: no one in and, more importantly, no one out. I couldn't even use magic.

My last order to my maids was for them to get to safety. Hackley and May tried to object, but I demanded it from them. Hackley's white face was lined with worry and May had to wipe her cheeks with her sleeve.

I remembered closing the door behind them and a heavy weight lodged itself in my chest and throat. But to my relief, I finally heard the noise of their slippers disappear from the hall. If I was about to die, I was not going to condemn my beloved maids to that fate too.

When I felt the magic dissipate around me, I knew my father was

2

dead. Sorrel too, most likely – he'd been fighting on the front lines. Abel was gone too; after the battle broke out, he was quick to disappear.

It was treason to disagree with my father, but perhaps if he had listened, many – including him – wouldn't be dead. No one had expected the Demons to align with the Fae. After that, there had been no hope for us. Yet my father would not hear of it. The possibility of losing was utterly incomprehensible – the great Riachian Empire could not lose!

Everything seemed to flash by. Figures in onyx-black armour quickly overran the palace and my quarters were swarmed before I could act. I fought back with a poker stick from the fireplace, but one of them threw me against the wall and knocked me unconscious. When I came around, the smell of acrid burning and blood overwhelmed me.

I couldn't decide if it was kindness or cruelty that had led them to enchant me during my incarceration. My head was throbbing painfully now, but then it seemed like reality had no foothold for me. The cries of my people sounded like birdsong; the last battles were like an orchestra tuning their instruments; death turned to music.

I recalled the steel shackles biting into my wrists, the sliver of moonlight through the grimy iron bars onto the dank floor. I remembered the smell of death and ash and the taste of salt on my cheeks. Had I been lucid, I would've burned them all down; myself too if it had helped. I guess I was lucky the enchantment hadn't driven me mad. Or perhaps it had.

The cells surrounding me were empty – the Fynix Fae took no prisoners. And even in my state, I hadn't understood why I still lived. I knew they would not grant mercy or kill me quickly. These Fae were savage in battle, that they made a sport out of death. From my cell, I had seen my father's corpse beheaded, and the head raised high on a spike by the Horned King.

I think I remember my last moments in Kya. A scroll was passed between two guards, speaking in low tones. My sentence was wax-sealed by the King himself. As for me, well, I hadn't expected a trial. With my father dead and my brothers missing, they assumed I was what was left of the Royal family – the last Wryfirth. Their sentence fell to me.

For war crimes against the Fynix Fae, you are hereby sentenced to death by Tower.

Death for crimes against the Fynix people and the Horned King – it would work well as a warning against whoever stood against Riach's usurpers. And once again, I was paying for the decisions of my father and my brother. Even from beyond the grave, they were messing with my life.

The Tower was so tall you could see it from the coast, commissioned by my great grandfather as a cage for an ancient evil. A monster unlike any other: immortal, destructive, and bloodthirsty – the Wraith of the Wastes. Rumours spiralled around what happened to those sentenced here. Only one thing was for certain: no one had lived to tell the tale.

Now that fate awaited me.

What unnerved me the most about the tower was the lack of noise. No cries of despair; no fire magic; no winged beasts pillaging the city: there was nothing. There was only the sound of my heart thundering in my ears as it all came back to me. My plan? My plan was very simple: live.

The creature slid forward, its eyes both hungry and haunted. I forced myself not to turn away, even though my skin itched to be away from it. Its body seemed to be a mass of ink floating in mid-air and unending smoke.

The monster was legendary. The stuff of nightmares. A murderer. The Wraith of the Wastes. Even my illustrious, battle-worn brother would have fled from it. Entire villages had been laid to waste, endless families devoured, and ancient clans annihilated until the head of my family had captured and imprisoned it here three generations ago.

"Curious," the voice said again, its tone completely neutral. "Most of them would've been begging right about now. Spare me. Help me. *Save me.*" Its head tilted to the side. "They'd faint at the mere sight of their blood at first."

"You can tell they weren't women," I replied in as light a voice as

4

I could manage. The creature said nothing, but its eyes creased at the corners. I shuffled back onto my heels and leaned against the wall to get onto my feet.

As I stood up straight, I watched the creature pull itself to my full height. Immediately, the black mass dropped away to reveal a skinny figure in a torn, filthy nightgown. I blinked – a shapeshifter. It had turned into a mirror image of me. My blonde hair was dirty with sweat and grime; blue eyes, dark; my cheeks, hollow from lack of food; my skin too was now pasty white rather than the golden tone I had inherited from my mother.

My stomach clenched, and I suddenly wanted to heave. I watched as its mouth – my mouth - formed a sickly smile, but instead of my teeth, sharp canines filled its maw. Each rotting and jagged tooth dripped with red.

"Are you afraid?" the monster asked, leaning in close. I could smell its rancid breath and my stomach lurched.

I clenched my fists, seeing myself in the darkness of its eyes. It knew the answer already, of course. It could hear my heart thudding in my chest.

"More like uneasy," I said, crossing my arms and rubbing my elbows. "But I wouldn't dwell on it if I were you. I don't scare easily."

The creature kept the form and moved back. It ran its eyes up and down my figure as I fought to keep myself from shaking from cold or fear, I wasn't sure.

"I'll decide that," the creature said, as it waited for my next move.

"What should I call you?" My knees wobbled terribly, so I resigned myself to sitting back on the floor. The wraith watched with curiosity. Sitting on the floor wouldn't be a good move in a battle – but this place had no weapons, no objects for me to defend with. Standing up wouldn't make me any less dead.

The move made the corner of the grisly-faced creature's mouth twitch a little.

"No one has asked my name in over a hundred years," the creature said. I gestured to the space in front of me and, to my surprise, it shifted its form again. An oily black snake curled in front of me and hissed. "I have been called many things. Perhaps, you should assign me a name from this era," the creature said amusedly, shifting form again to a huge spider the size of a cauldron with long and furry legs. "Make it good."

I saw my face reflected in its numerous bulbous eyes before the spider grew smaller, jumped onto my leg, and climbed up my arm. I resisted the urge to swat it hard – spiders were no stranger to me in the catacombs I loved under the castle. Yet the creature's needles traipsing up my arm made my skin crawl. I ground my teeth together: this was a test. It would kill me before I lifted a finger.

"I am honoured," I replied. The furry feet of the spider made me shudder, and I was glad when the wraith climbed off. "But I have only named the songbirds my father let me keep," I watched as the shifter became a fat rat with a thick tail like a long and knobbly finger. "Do you fancy Tweet-Tweet or Flappy-Do?"

"Do *you* fancy dying?" the wraith responded, and I couldn't help but smile. None of the soldiers spoke to me during my imprisonment – not that I was able to form many words then either.

"Hold on, I can do it," I said. The wraith suddenly shifted into a giant brown bear in front of me, its maw dripping with blood. It consumed half the space in the room, blocking out the glow of the moon. "Fluffy?"

"*No*," the wraith responded. This time I heard it echo through my head and I jumped. That time the wraith actually chuckled in response – a rasping noise that sounded like gravel. Psychic magic was forbidden – not like that would mean anything to something like it.

"Impressive," I said. "Now I am intrigued as to why you didn't just kill me as I slept. It would've been easy with those psychic abilities."

I would never have come round - it would've stopped my lungs from feeding me air. Cut my brain off. Paralysed me while I was prone. The reasons for the magic's outlaw were countless.

"Where's the fun in that?"

The monster turned back into the form of the snake.

"And, like I said," it replied. "I can't recall the last woman who was fortunate enough to be sent here. *I was curious.*"

The last words echoed in my mind, and I shivered.

"How about something floral?"

The wraith sidled up to me and curved around my arm, its skin cold against mine, black scales shining in the light.

"Do I strike you as much of a Daisy? Or a Rose?"

"You'd make a lovely Daisy."

"*No*," the creature said with finality. "Honour your last moments with a good name, young one."

I aimed to stretch out those last moments as long as possible. The snake slid down, pooling its slippery body into a ring, its eyes glowing with moonlight.

"How about Brenn?" I proposed, the snake dissolved back into the smoke-form I had first met. "Once, I had a steed called that."

"Was he a good horse?"

"No, he was a total arse," I responded flatly. "Threw me into a hedge on more than one occasion." To which the wraith actually laughed – a strange, strangled noise that echoed around me.

"Brenn, it is," the creature said before changing form once more. This time, it took the shape of a young girl. No grisly features or terrifying mouth. Just a dark-haired girl; innocent apart from those soulless eyes staring out.

My heart stammered. This was far more unsettling than the other creatures he had just formed.

"Nice to meet you, Brenn." I extended an arm to the girl. Its eyebrows lifted in surprise before it took it. It clutched my forearm in our traditional greeting - it felt cold and clammy against me. Despite all the years it had been trapped here – the ancient mark of respect hadn't changed.

"A mark of respect for a monster," Brenn said with a smile too wide for the girl's face, but I pressed my teeth together to keep my polite smile still. "Who are you, Name-Giver?"

"Bryony," I replied, crossing my hands in my lap. "But surely you knew that."

The girl crossed her arms.

"Indeed, *Princess*," she said with a sarcastic smile. Those empty eyes seemed to be growing wider, like a whirlpool, fathomless and deadly. Her tone was nonchalant as she continued. "Such a sad little story of woe – surprising for one so sunny." The girl popped her lips.

"Forgive me if I do not share much empathy – it was your ancestors who placed me here after all."

"And now, here I sit too," I replied. "What irony." Brenn shrugged, no longer changing forms, clearly content with the unease this shape gave me. "I see you gave up on trying to figure it out."

Brenn glared at me.

"A smart Princess - how strange. Humour me – what do *you* fear?"

When I was a child, my greatest fear was being left alone in the nursery. The sounds of silence would stretch on for hours. But now I was older, only one figure came forward in my mind. The angry sneer stained on his face.

"He's dead now," I replied. I thought of the head on the spike and my stomach curled. I knew Brenn must've seen it in my thoughts – this was all about making me squirm. The wraith grinned with triumph.

"Your father. The King," Brenn replied. It tilted its head. I felt a pressure in my temples like fingers were pressed in deep. Suddenly, the memory of my father's anger after I'd been caught in the market again rose to the surface in my mind, the roar of my father's wrath filling the halls of my chamber. He rarely used his fists: that was Sorrel's job. But at least I could hit him back. The memory faded and the wraith looked complacent. How much had it just seen? Pulling memories from me with expert ease was an impressive feat indeed.

"You don't *seem* much alike."

"Thank you," I replied, I couldn't help but feel relieved. "I can't think of anything worse."

My Father had never known how to be more than King or a soldier. Worst of all, he'd forbidden my study of magic. The boys would learn the useful magics like conjuring, manipulating and all manner of school-based spells, but only highly talented girls would be permitted to study healing magic or performative magic for dances, music, and the like. To my father, a woman was an ornament. I was to be a present to a nobleman of our court – a gift to appease – to gain some advantage in battle, politics, or social standing.

"He had very traditional ideas of who I should be."

My father grimaced at the idea of independent women, and we

fought viciously over my education. Instead, I had to steal library books about any magic I wished to learn, and was caught only once, after Abel had sold me out. I had been back since, of course: I knew that palace's secret coves better than anyone.

I recalled my punishment being the murder of two of my birds. He yanked them from their perches and snapped their necks before I could rescue them. After he threw them at my feet, I felt my blood rage and overcome me. Before considering it, I summoned a strike of lightning. Too surprised I knew such illegal magic to deflect it, I blasted him back into the hallway. The look of shock on his face was worth the entrapment in my wing for the remaining quart of the year. I was forced to watch the world tick by outside my window.

"And he was an arrogant fool."

I was lucky when I found the catacombs. It was my realm. And the only people there were the souls of the dead and the rats. Neither of which I minded or seemed to mind me.

"*You are fiery,*" Brenn said. I knew it had been in my head watching, too. Its smile suddenly widened. "No wonder you are not wed." It transformed into a handsome man in front of me – I recognised him instantly, my chest tightened, and I froze. "Your heart was stolen."

I leaned back against the wall – feeling the scratchy stone on my skin through the thin cotton of my nightdress. Randall's face didn't fit here; it was too good, too full of hope to be in a place like this. The familiar floppy brown hair, the smattering of freckles across his lean face, and those full lips I loved so much. His head tilted to the left – and the forked tongue of a demon swept his lower lip. Bile rose in my throat, but I clenched my jaw: he wasn't here – this wasn't real. The grimace on my face made the wraith snicker and I waved a hand as nonchalantly as I could despite the tugging in my chest.

Randall deserved so much better than to be a memory of mine.

"Go back to being the bear. I have no intention of "wedding" anyone," I finally said – looking the shadow form of Randall in those familiar brown eyes. Those eyes made me think of home, of lying in a dimly lit barn with his arms holding me close. Annoyingly, Brenn seemed to be reluctant to change forms, and Randall's features twisted into a dark smile. My heart clenched. "I think I have bigger

9

concerns facing me, don't you?"

"Headstrong women are the fear of all men," Brenn said, then, thankfully, its face changed again. Me again, but younger, my eyes glowing in demonic swirls of black and red. Blood dripped from my eyes against the ghostly pallor of my cheeks.

"Headstrong is a good word for me," I said before using all my remaining energy to get up off the floor. "Now are we getting out of here or would you rather reminisce on every element of my tale of woe?"

The wraith didn't react as I brushed the dust off my hands on my dress.

"Clearly, stupid is another word," Brenn said, its voice deadpan. It changed back into its snake form once more and whipped its long oily tail across the ground. I was careful to step over it.

"You sound like my brother," I replied. I wandered across the cell to the window. It was small, but I could easily climb through it. I reached out and felt the magic waiting there for me. An ancient holding hex – I could feel the breeze coming through, though solid air met me, stopping my fingers from going further. "Sorrel stole all of our family's stupid before I was even born."

Brenn slithered up to me and shook its serpentine head.

"I am afraid there is no use in that, Your *Majesty*," it said, sounding increasingly bored. "Hundreds of more powerful, dangerous villains with earth-shattering power have tried and failed to escape here." I frowned at the snake, who looked rather happy about my predicament – as far as snakes go to looking happy, that is.

"They weren't me though," I replied drawing my hand back in and rolling my sleeves up, "so there's hope." I pulled the knot from the drawstring of the nightdress and tied up my massive length of hair into something like a bun; it was hard when you didn't have a mirror to work from. "Also, don't call me, Your Majesty. Majesty is for the king or queen. It makes me think of my father. Your Highness is more correct."

"Anything you say, Your Majesty."

I gave it a withering look, "What if I called you Wraith? How would you feel then?"

The snake form instantly vanished, and the original smoke figure returned.

"Then you would be correct, and I would feel nothing."

"Yeah, yeah," I replied. "Don't worry, I'll still call you Brenn."

"Thank you, Your Majesty."

I ignored it, closed my eyes, and took a deep breath in.

"Ah yes, praying will definitely help you," Brenn said in a sarcastic voice. "It helped your predecessors too."

I listened for the magic and stretched out my arcane senses to search for any weaknesses. My arcane senses were my first mastery – I could learn much from a room from the magic left behind; when I focused on a person their aura would spread from them like ink in a well of water. My father's was a deep plum colour, Sorrel's was all red, and Abel's magic – when it was strong enough to appear – was a pale blue. Deep rich colours represented power and then changes in those could reveal emotions or even traits. It was the ultimate truth-teller – unlike people, magic didn't lie.

I felt the repressed dark magic coming from my companion. Lurking in the darkness, I heard screams and cries. I could smell the metallic tang of blood against the wisps of dust that came and went with the wind. But the ringing emanating from the window was ancient, familiar magic – which meant I knew exactly how to break it.

Swiftly, I ran my hands around the stones of the window. They were coarse but not enough to do more than graze me. I groaned inwardly. Suddenly, a kind of pressure appeared in my head, and I turned to Brenn with a scowl. The wraith looked at me innocently.

"I would appreciate it if you didn't rifle through my mind like a stack of parchment."

Brenn blinked.

"If you wish to bleed you need only ask," the creature said, a clawed paw reaching from the shadows before withdrawing.

The next part of my plan was the crucial one. I ran over the steps in my head again.

"I have a proposition for you." I turned to Brenn. The Wraith of the Wastes seemed to acknowledge this as their shadow form grew to match my height. "A pact I wish to draw."

"Your Majesty, whatever pact you have in mind I can guarantee it will not delay your death. There is no escaping this place."

I crossed my arms.

"What if I said I knew a way?"

"I would say you were bluffing – if there was a way it would've been found by someone stronger than you."

I sighed and shrugged. "Then I shall go without you."

Brenn laughed then, "Go where? To the doom outside the window? I saw your mind. You can't fly – you know *lightning* spells – basic self-defence at best." The wraith chortled, "And *they* couldn't even save you before."

I bit my lip to stop myself from smiling.

"I would be out of another cage I have found myself in," I replied. Most of my life had been cloistered in a tower just like this; hidden behind gossamer, lace, and satin. Sorrel was the lion; Abel, the cub; and I, the lamb. That's what everyone assumed.

Everyone was *wrong*.

"You're bluffing," Brenn said, coming so close I could smell their rancid breath.

"I swear on the Mother of Light - *Celine*." I declared. Brenn bared its teeth at me as I crossed my arms. "What do you have to lose?"

Brenn took a humanoid form of skin, no nose, and a black slash of a mouth. The eyes were the same soulless pits. My skin prickled on the back of my neck.

"Your Gods mean nothing to me, Your Majesty," it said brusquely. "But you, you intrigue me. What are the terms?"

I clenched my fists tightly by my sides.

Hold your nerve.

"When we get out, you will be my guard, guide, and companion to protect me and keep me safe until I release you from our contract."

"I thought keeping slaves went out of fashion," Brenn remarked in a dour drawl. No slaves had been kept in Nos in generations – that was one of the things my father had been clear on reinforcing.

"Not a slave, a *guard*," I replied. "I will pay you if that would sweeten the deal. Once I have funds that is - if money was your issue. Forgive me, but I never thought a wraith would want for money." Brenn narrowed its eyes. "I am a Princess."

"Correction – you *were* a Princess before you were invaded. Now you are no one." It quipped. "Besides, I don't want money. I want to *eat.*"

My stomach flipped over as I stared into its deep pits of darkness.

"You will eat whenever I say you can," I replied. Brenn scoffed. "You won't kill unnecessarily – but I daresay, I have many enemies who want my head. I'm sure you would never go hungry."

The grim reminder of the Fynix's Horned King, his army, and my death sentence came back into my mind and filled my stomach with a gnawing unease.

This made Brenn grin and it rubbed its grey hands together greedily. What was it thinking? I resisted the urge to find out.

"Your conditions, then?" it said finally after a minute.

"I saw my brother do this when he bound his guard to him," I explained, drawing my hand up to my lips. I bit into the flesh until my eyes stung. Blood dripped from my thumb.

The wraith extended a sharp pointed finger and drew a deep welt through their palm. Their grin was frenzied; when had its last meal had been? The thought made me nauseous.

Quicker than my eye could see the Wraith had my hand and drew the welt across my palm too. The blood spilt out across my hand, and the cut smarted against the cool air. I hissed and yanked my arm back. Brenn gave me a look of dubious innocence.

"If we want to honour tradition, we need more blood. Your brother must have been a wimp."

The Wraith licked their finger clean of my blood and its grisly stained teeth were revealed. I tried not to look too disgusted.

"I don't like to waste anything."

"I don't have any paper so the floor will have to do," I said, getting onto my knees and letting the blood drip from my hand.

As I wrote the passage in the dust on the floor my fingers blackened with dirt. Brenn inspected it and nodded. I felt a swell of pride and fear in my chest as its cold, dead hand embraced mine, our blood mingling between our palms.

Our words glowed a deep scarlet as I recited them, and they echoed through the room.

13

"Thou shalt act as my hand,
Thou shalt honour my command.
Thou shalt trust in my soul,
Thou shalt always bear the toll.
Thou shalt fight my cause too,
Thou shalt never be untrue.
With these terms now you are mine,
Until the day, at last, I die."

With the last utterance, the spell burned red-hot for a moment before the words turned to ash and the remnants of them covered the floor.

"Well, then, Your Majesty," Brenn said crossing its arms. "I do long to see this plan of yours." It looked around the room as if they expected a herd of unicorns to materialise. My hand was hot. The newly formed scar resembled two long, thin, black marks as if I'd been struck with a poker twice. The 'x' felt raw and warm, but relief surged through me. There was still blood dripping from my thumb – perfect.

"And you shall, my new companion," I said. I lowered my mental shields and used my magic to breach the gap between us, diving into its mind. It was cold, slippery, and defenceless. *"I do long for some cheesy bread."*

Their head snapped up. I pulled out of its mind before it could retaliate and threw my mental shields back up again. I had learned from my mistakes in the past; secrets were precious things indeed.

"You wield psychic magic too, Your Majesty?"

"Apologies for the trickery, Brenn. But I rather like living."

I pushed my hand into the holding hex on the outside; the magic writhed against my palm.

Time to put my theory into practice. Hopefully, for once, my family would be of use to me, since it *was* my great-grandfather who set the snare. I smeared the blood up my hand with my fingers before stretching it out.

Building psychic walls was one of the first feats I had accomplished successfully in my study of the forbidden magic. I could hide my memories in case any monsters proficient in the art ever attempted to traverse my thoughts. Like a castle, the mind was

14

large and, could only be explored in parts. Secret rooms and catacombs needed more exploration to be found.

As powerful as the Wraith was, they hadn't noticed beyond the rooms I had shown them. The floors the creature had traversed had been operated by me. Sometimes it paid off to be paranoid; after all, the magic was illegal in Riach but that didn't mean it wasn't studied in secret. In the Fynix Kingdom, they were part of the retained forces; used in unsavoury activities, no doubt.

I drew the symbol of Destruction, a diamond split down the centre, on the wall of air in a red smudge of blood. "*Break*," I whispered imbuing it with my magic. The zip of magic crackled through me as I felt the hex snap and break as wind flew into the cell. Relief surged through me as fresh air filled my lungs.

"Blood magic!" Brenn exclaimed over the howl of the wind. "Against the law and deeply forbidden, Your Majesty." Its face was a picture of glee.

"Apologies, Brenn. I am a royal rule-breaker."

In my defence, it had never been my intention to break the law, but the only magic books down in the catacombs were those whose magic was banned. Blood magic and lightning were not the only two strings to my bow, but they were the most reliable.

I stretched up into the air and stuck my head out of the window. I saw the breadth of the island; the trees, the boat house, and then nothing but the endless sea. I imagined the lights of Riach in the distance calling me home as the darkness of the horizon met my gaze.

I clenched my jaw as my resolve steeled inside me. This lonely isle would not be the place I died. Not today.

"Time to test that pact out then," I yelled to Brenn over the wind. I climbed up onto the frame. "I command you to catch me!" I yelled, watching their eyes go yellow as the magic of the command washed through them.

"What are you —"

I leapt through into the open air, shrieking in delight, feeling the wind on my bare legs. Behind me, I saw the wraith jolt through the window in a mass of wings and smoke.

Freedom at last.

Two

I only fell for a second before the steely claws of Brenn clutched my shoulders tightly; the great talons didn't pierce me, but my heart spiked all the same.

"You are insane, Your Majesty," the wraith said, now in the form of a Riach Eagle but with a shadow plumage and pitch eyes. "Do you make a habit out of tricking monsters into your command and follow it up with defenestration?"

With a few mighty flaps, we descended the length of the tower, and the tiny window shrunk to a dot above us. I whooped as we dropped – air rushing past my face. The Wraith's eyes glowed.

"How long has it been since you were out of the tower?" I asked as the ground grew closer to us.

"Your Grandfathers wouldn't have been born for years to come," it remarked. "It was the third of your line that imprisoned me here." With that, it looked far across the raging sea as if they could see onto the shores of Riach itself.

"I would say I was sorry about that, but I read about your, um, *adventures,* and one might argue that you brought it on yourself."

Brenn chuckled as my feet touched the grass and a thrill ran through me.

"They were the *height* of fun," it replied before its eagle form disappeared completely and they turned back into smoke.

I couldn't knock the smile off my face as I ran across the green, leaving Brenn behind me. The magic here was thin, but the air was filled with the salty smell of the sea. Despite the cold wind blowing over from the icy realms of Draig, I wasn't cold. I was too excited for that. I took my hair down and let the wind hold me in its breeze for a moment.

To the West lay the outline of the icy plateau; it broke off in shards where it met the water's edge and made the coast look as if it were consuming the sea. To the East, a mist loomed where I assumed the Wastes dwelled in murky obscurity. I squinted but could see no sign of the shore at all. The Tower was too far from civilisation to see anything clearly, but the longing to see it all burned in my chest like a fire that kept me smiling despite what lay ahead.

I flopped down onto the grass and felt the cool tips tickle the backs of my legs and my neck. The stars shone above me as my breath bloomed against the night. Maybe the Gods were up there too. Celine, the Goddess of the Sun, and the Goddess of the Moon, Serena, watching over the horizon with serene expressions. I waved an arm their way – just in case.

Just watch me.

I wondered what lingered beyond the clouds. Then I turned and saw that Brenn had taken to the skies and was flying higher and higher, growing larger and larger, their roar sounding across the isle. I held my breath: it took a dragon's form.

Giant black wings, like sheets of smoked iron, and a long, sharp tail descended upon the Tower. Its eyes burned a hot ember orange as its maw bloomed smoke. Its next blood-curdling roar revealed long jagged canines ready to devour. My heart raced. The tales didn't speak truthfully of the power of the Wraith; Brenn exuded dark magic with every heave of its almighty chest. Had he been free to do whatever he wanted, I had no doubt I would've been devoured as so many had been before.

The creature turned its attention to the tower, batting it once with its tail. Then they flapped their wings and struck the tower again. And again. The foundations of the tower began to crack, and the rumble echoed around our desolate isle.

An idea came to me. I stepped back and inhaled deeply to stir my magic. I focused on the energy I had become accustomed to and extended both of my hands. I imagined the magic flowing through my arms and felt every one of my cells charge.

I pointed forward and yelled, "*Ignite!*"

The bolt charged forth from my fingertips and struck the roof of the tower with a mighty blow. Brenn roared once more, summoning its own fiery breath alongside it.

The Tower went up like a beacon, spouting smoke that pummelled the clouds high in the sky. I hadn't meant to send a message – however, it seemed only decent to provide a warning.

There was no enchantment on me now. I was coming for my crown. And this time I wouldn't lose.

The tower started to topple, and as the roof caved in, I realised that maybe I shouldn't be so close. Turning on my heel, I sprinted through the forest to escape the rocks and the dust cloud that would surely follow. The cacophony of the tower crashing to the ground behind me was followed by a wyvern screech – somehow it sounded joyous.

I reached the edge of the island in a matter of minutes. I turned and saw the spot where the Tower now lay destroyed. Brenn was up in the air, the beat of its wings causing the dust to spill outward to the sea. I covered my eyes until it passed.

I had made it to the shore; there was an old boathouse and a small shack, the windows black with age. I peered into the boathouse and saw the ashes of a recent fire near the water's edge.

Landing with a thud, Brenn appeared still in their dragon form, but a moment later it changed shape once more, the smoke shrinking and forming the familiar snake. It then slithered up and around my leg before ending up on my shoulder. I shivered as its tail curled under my right arm like a snakeskin sleeve. As Brenn spoke, his tongue flicked against my neck.

"That was the most fun. The lightning was most helpful, Your Majesty. If not a little uncontrolled," Brenn sounded amused. "You need more practice if you aim to make Warlock in that field."

I scoffed as I pushed the mouldy door open to reveal a simple living space.

"Lightning is difficult to control and I am a novice," I reminded him, investigating the space.

"You chose the worst elemental magic to begin with," Brenn tutted from my ear before resting his head on my shoulders as if the flying had worn it out.

Around the room was a moth-eaten bed and an old set of worn cooking pots. The remnants of an old army uniform were shoved in one of the drawers: a ragged old brown cloak, some stiff cord black trousers and a grey shirt. I picked it up, feeling the tough fabric under my fingers. It would have to do.

Brenn slid across my shoulders to my other ear.

"Should I assume you kept other magical abilities under wraps in order to get me into your service?" Brenn added. I placed the shirt back down. Naturally, Brenn knowing my psychic powers would've put a halt in my plan. If the wraith had known to look for barriers, he could've escaped without my pact. My blood would act as a key. My magical abilities, limited as they were, were simply on a need-to-know basis.

"Sorry for the trickery. But you were going to eat me."

Brenn sighed dramatically and looked as sorrowful as a snake could.

"And yet I remain denied."

"I am sure we will find some food once we get to the mainland."

"A small village should do."

I ignored him as a quiet wind whistled through the creaky doorframe. The hair on the back of my neck stood up.

"I wonder who lived here?" This place had clearly been gutted many times before; there were marks from many boots trod into the wood.

"The groundskeeper," Brenn said in an upbeat voice. "Nice boy."

"What happened to him?" I asked. Brenn said nothing to respond, and I rolled my eyes. "Of course."

"I am a creature of habit," Brenn retorted.

"Yeah, well, no eating others unless I expressly say so." Brenn stuck their forked tongue out at me. I looked at my gown and accepted the grotty alternatives. "I guess this is what it shall have to be."

I placed my arm on the bed and Brenn slid off immediately.

"Would you rather a gown, Your Majesty?" it replied, cocking their head.

"No, I would rather not," I answered, throwing off the remains of my nightdress. I still had cotton briefs on for which there was no alternative, so I kept them, hoping I didn't smell too much. "I believe it is safer to travel as a man in Nos," I confessed. "Women get too much unwanted attention in Riach. I assume it is like that everywhere."

Brenn said nothing, watching me closely as I hiked my new attire on and shivered at the cold cord against my skin. The rough scratchy fabric was a far cry from the gowns from home.

19

"I don't suppose Your Majesty knows any glamouring spells? Not many men have chests like yours or hair as long as that."

I grimaced. Glamouring was an art, one I had not mastered in the catacombs below the castle. You needed light and a delicate refined power – Glamour Mages were highly sought after for quick fixes from ladies at court and gentlemen looking to make a good impression. It was an incredibly desirable gift. Once, my brother, Abel, bribed one to make him look more like Sorrel; square-jawed, handsome, with a rugged complexion one could only gain from battle and hard-toil. Yet, it did little to improve his chances with any of the ladies at court, Abel's innate arrogance and lack of self-awareness shooting him in the foot. Sorrel had more hope there – he was handsome enough to woo anyone – but his first love was himself.

"No, I am afraid not," I replied. My breasts were going to be a problem. "It is on my list for what I wish to study – but there were no books on that in the catacombs." Brenn had relaxed and was resting its head on its body, much like a dog would when curled up next to a fire. "Do you know any shapeshifting tricks that could help me?"

"My shapeshifting talents come from me being a wraith – they do not extend outwardly, Your Majesty." It sounded bored and sleepy. "Maybe you should've focused less on illegal magic and more on useful ones."

I began tearing off strips of my nightgown for makeshift binding.

"Blood magic only became illegal when murderers started using it to control their victims," I said with a sigh. "Imbuing a liquid with magic and having it perform to your will is no different than water spells."

Brenn tutted. "You're missing the part that blood magic is ultimately more powerful than water magic though."

"I like a challenge," I replied. I wrapped the strips around my breasts and pulled them tightly around my back before doubling back and pressing them against myself. Somehow, I had given myself yet another corset. I grimaced before putting the ragged shirt back over myself. It was considerably flatter than it had been before even though it was uncomfortable.

"Much better," I declared, to which the wraith said nothing, so I assumed I'd done a good job. "Now, I'm already pretty dirty so the

20

face should be fine. But the hair…"

I searched the space for something sharp and found a pair of rusted shears. I pulled my hair free and ignored the gnawing in my gut as I pulled it into one hand.

Brenn opened one eye. "Are you sure you want to do that? It doesn't look like you've ever cut it."

My hair stretched down past my behind. It was one of the things that reminded my father of my late mother – her hair had allegedly grown to the floor, so I wasn't allowed to cut mine. It wasn't dead or dry either – long, flowing and healthy, even though it was unwieldy and difficult to contain.

"There is only one thing for it," I declared before taking a deep breath in. "I could use a mirror," I said it without any magic, and despite their reluctance, Brenn changed into a flat mirror which was propped up on the wall. "That's a neat trick," I said, gripping my hair firmly.

"*You have no idea,*" chimed Brenn in my head, though the mirror didn't falter at all. Despite the panes of my cheeks being caked in dirt, I saw my mother's rounded face with my father's sharp jaw and nose. The eyes were hers though, soft and blue like the lakes of Arelle. I held my locks tightly at the scalp and chopped through the grimy layers of hair as they slipped through my fingers to the floor.

I tried to ignore the twang of sadness in my heart – it would grow back. This was only temporary. "Fear not, Your Majesty," came the wraith's response. "You'll make a fetching boy."

I grimaced in the mirror as I chopped the back and sides as short as I could go without cleaving the top. It looked as though I had a mop on my head. The hair stuck out at all angles – the air felt absurdly close to my skull and my head felt light. I wiggled my head from side to side and my neck felt bare. Running my hand up it – a prickly feeling passed through me and made me shiver. I pushed the hair back, so I had a little side parting to the right of my forehead. My appearance surprised me – I didn't realise how much I would look like a skinnier, blue-eyed version of Abel. I frowned – the blonde would have to go.

"I don't suppose you can conjure up some hair dye, can you?" I asked as the mirror changed back into a snake.

21

"Unfortunately, I have not eaten in three decades and have used a great deal of my remaining energy today," Brenn said in a clipped tone. "Cut off an arm of yours, I'll fly to Riach, and make you a pot myself."

"How long can you go without eating?" I asked. "Just so I know when to marinate my liver and such."

"A few decades, at least. But the less I eat — the less..." It searched for a word through serpentine lips. "*Amiable*, I become."

Hmm, amiable indeed.

"Noted."

I looked in the fire pit and spotted some ancient-looking coal and thought that would work for now. After I leaned across the floor and picked up a few lumps, I rubbed the powder into my palms until every line in my hands was black. I wasted no time running my hands through the bristly, short locks still on my head. Then I worked the stone across the back of my skull and behind my ears. "How do I look?"

"*Ridiculously male.*"

The darkened hair offset my skin and made my eyes shine. Then I used the coal to line my jaw as much as I could to make it look a little like I had a shadow of facial hair, at least temporarily, until I could sort some make-up, or maybe a glamour out. I lined my temples too — changing my face to a narrower, gaunt look. I drew back — thankfully looking suitably less like Abel but more of a homeless street rat than I ever had before.

"Good," I replied. "That's exactly what I was going for."

I got to my feet and brushed the floor dust from my trousers. The shirt felt airy around my back and clearly was made for someone wider than me. The trousers I could adjust with the drawstring at their waist — even though they were still baggy. "I will have to acquire a new outfit the moment we come to a town."

Brenn changed back into a snake. "Do you have a plan?"

"Of course," I scoffed. I did not, but I had a vague idea of where I wanted to be — the rest I would figure out on the way. "We are to travel to Wist — my aunt lives there."

"That's on the other side of the world," came the disgruntled reply. "That will take *months* on foot."

"We better get moving then," I said, picking up Brenn so they could wrap around my shoulder again. Brenn groaned.

The boathouse had one lone vessel waiting sadly in the outhouse. A rusted rowboat with a circle hook on the front, as if it were going to be pulled along by a larger boat.

"Come on then, Brenn," I declared, pulling the boat away from the wall with effort. It took me a few pulls to inch it closer and closer to the water. Brenn watched me and said nothing. I heaved with my whole body and eventually, it slid from the walkway, plopping onto the water, where it landed with an almighty slap. "I hope you're good at rowing."

"I don't have any arms."

"You could get some," I reminded it as I pulled the two weather-beaten oars away from the wall. Brenn didn't reply after that — perhaps all the chat was covering up the fact that really it was exhausted. "Only kidding — I've got arms for the both of us," I declared, throwing the oars into the boat before climbing in.

I placed my hand on the seat in front of me, and Brenn slithered down and swayed as the boat bobbed. The unending beat of the waves had us rise and fall with every sigh of the water.

The wobbly feeling under my feet reminded me of boating on the lake by the castle a few summers ago with once with Randall. He had rowed us somewhere quiet where lilies danced on the water and the lake's pixies came up to sing. The sun warmed my face, and he joked about making poetry for me. Randall had made even the worst days seem bright. My heart grew tight in my chest.

I placed the oars in the divots on the boat's edges, turning the cool wood over in my palms so the paddles were submerged in the water. They were heavy, but at least we had them.

"You don't propose to row to Wist, do you?" Brenn's onyx eyes narrowed. "I do not fancy being Kelpie chow." I didn't admit it, but that had been a previous idea of mine. But without any food and water, there is no way we would survive. Well, Brenn probably would after feasting on my corpse, and then they would be free to devour whomever they felt like. Let loose on the land like a terrifying, unstoppable scourge.

23

That outcome was less desirable.

"No. I propose to row to the lovely land of Draig – then we will travel south via boat and then end up in Wist."

"You don't mean to say you plan to go *through* Fynix?" I unhooked the boat and pushed the vessel gently away from its bearings. It emerged from the boathouse slowly, carried along by the tugs of the waves; the wind seemed to be holding its breath as the endless blue unfurled in front of us. "The people that your family were at war with – who murdered your father and your brothers?"

"Not if it's avoidable. We'll head down through the Shifter-lands. I have friends in the South," I said. It gawped at me. "If we went the east-ward way, we'd be travelling completely blind to the Shadow Lands. I don't wish to cross the Divide if we don't need to."

"I don't think you understand how insane you sound," Brenn said as I began to row. With a snake and I as the only passengers, I did it with more ease than I had anticipated. "They will roast you in Mount Dia if they catch you."

"Let's hope they don't then," I said as I pushed us further into the waves. The sea was dark under the cool night sky. I turned and saw the fire had ebbed away, leaving nothing of the Tower but blooms of smoke joining the clouds above us. It was a strange relief seeing it gone - now the isle was empty once more. "And if they do, then you can enjoy a roast dinner."

The wraith swished its tale.

"An unexpected but welcome development. I no longer doubt this plan. Go right ahead."

Damned, wraith. It stretched out its long neck and watched as the island drifted into the distance with every stroke. It had been imprisoned for many years, long before I was born. I wondered how the world would look now – through their eyes.

Brenn hissed slowly.

"You need to learn motion magic. Then your weak little arms won't hurt, and you can have a nap instead."

It was right: my arms had started to burn.

"I don't suppose you know how to do that?"

But the wraith had gone to sleep.

Three

I rowed until my arms ached and then kept rowing. Hours had surely passed as the wraith slept on the bench opposite me. How much energy did Brenn have reserved? Perhaps I had been naïve to assume that such a being would be immortal and unstoppable. It was exhausted.

My next issue pressed into my thoughts: how was I to feed it? I couldn't just let it eat anyone. Yet I had no money on me to buy anything fresh. Theft was my next option. Or grave-robbing, as unsavoury as that was. Still, once the soul was gone, the body was left to feed the earth, and I was sure Celine could spare a few.

By now, the coast of Draig had snuck into view, a smudgy black line on the horizon. The next problem was how not to freeze to death in the cold air. As the boat edged closer, any sweat I'd mustered from rowing started to evaporate, leaving me with a chill down my spine. I clamped my teeth together and rowed until I found a short, rocky cove to mount the boat.

"Wake up, Brenn," I called as the nose of the vessel crunched against the stones. I jumped out onto the shore as the damp, cold sand sunk into my toes. Then I heaved the boat further onto the sand and groaned loudly as it took the rest of the energy in my arms. I wished the old guard hut had spared me footwear of some kind: the night air was frigid, and I worried my feet wouldn't survive the cold. If it had not been the summer season here, I knew I would've died already.

The snake opened one eye and then lifted its serpentine head to inspect the area. Its eyes fell on me and then it curled back up.

"We are not yet in Wist," it said sarcastically. "I can remain asleep."

It closed its eyes once more.

"My toes will fall off at this rate," I replied, but it didn't move. I placed my arm next to it. The Wraith of the Wates lifted its head and gave me a curious look. "Up you come." It slowly slithered over and wound its way up my arm, continuing until it lay along my shoulders with its head resting on my right collarbone.

"Onward steed," it said, tapping its tail twice on my upper arm. "Dick."

Before leaving, I looked at where I had left the boat. I had contemplated kicking it away, but it could be handy for a quick escape if this all went sour. I cast a look at my weary companion. I knew if I stopped for a rest the exhaustion would hit me too, so I gritted my teeth and started to walk, ignoring my burning limbs.

Wist was our ultimate goal: Aunt Gloria was family and she liked me. She said I had spirit, like her sister, my mother. All we had to do was survive. That couldn't be so hard now, could it?

I trekked up the short beach and climbed the rocky cliff face up and over onto a frosty-grassy hump. Turning my head around, I could see the island in the distance. The smoke had subsided, and now it was only an obscure little island once more. Brenn raised its head a moment, and I heard it exhale slowly before it closed its eyes. The frigid air whipped all around me as snow, light as dust, whirled around on the breeze. If Brenn was cold, he was being quiet about it – a sarcastic comment had not passed his serpentine lips in a while.

I crossed my arms across myself to keep some warmth but my throat started to burn. My calves were streaking with pain and my joints creaked as we kept walking.

Turning back to my path, I could see the snow-topped mountains and hills of Draig. If I headed south, I should avoid the clans of the North. And their dragons.

I knew they had not met with my father or come to our aid as Kya was marched upon. The people of Draig kept to themselves apart from trade. You rarely saw a Rider away from their homeland. Much to my dismay, dragons were not allowed in Riach. Though our forests were full of animals with just as much rarity and, in some cases, dangerous habits – my father was keen on keeping that Old Law in particular active.

Thus far, besides Brenn's shadow form that I had seen earlier, I had seen only one real dragon. It was when the delegation from Draig had arrived for the Summer Solstice celebrations.

I had snuck away from my governesses and seen the leaders arriving in all their leather-clad glory. I was nine when I saw it. A giant silver-scaled beast with wings like huge leathery sheets and a head larger than a carriage. My transgressions earned me a departure the following year. I was sent away to the north of Kya with a horde of governesses. My brothers, on the other hand, were allowed to attend all the celebrations and discussions.

I picked up a piece of frosted grass and let the wind take it north, so we knew which way to avoid. It was a couple of hours before the outline of something resembling a town teetered on the edge of my vision, but as we neared it, it turned out to be a collection of trees. Disappointment burned in my stomach. My knees ached and my breath had become laboured and raw in my throat. My feet had frozen past numbness and Brenn had done nothing apart from being sarcastic and small.

"Maybe, your Majesty should consider going to the capital of Draig for aid?" Brenn mumbled from my shoulder. "I'd prefer Gortia any day over freezing to death."

I laughed at that, though my teeth were already chattering from the ridiculous drop in temperature. Just when would it be morning? I was determined to not be killed by sarcasm alone.

"They would turn us in, Brenn," I said. The grass underfoot was uncomfortably crunchy and sharp against my soles. "Speaking of turning – I don't suppose you could turn into a pair of boots for me," I asked. Brenn hissed a laugh.

"I could turn into *a* boot," it sighed, "if only I had a body to feast on." The Wraith's quick wit made me smile – despite the cold that had sunken into my bones.

"If you see a bird you can hunt, I give you permission to do so," I said as I stomped forward.

"How attached to you are you to your fingers?" it mused, raising its head eagerly. I cast a look down at my hands; dirty nails, and skinny bones.

"Very," I said. It flopped its head back down. "Sorry, Brenn."

"You don't need all of them," it grumbled. Then it raised its head, eyes wide. "Stop!" it hissed, suddenly awake. I stopped instantly.

I held my breath and heard a rustle in the air. Brenn's head was suddenly poised like an arrow on my shoulder. As the seconds ticked by my heart started to pound before they spoke again.

"Wings."

27

I cursed loudly and started to sprint back to the trees for shelter, but immediately my vision became blurry. Heat seemed to stretch to my head from my neck, and I couldn't move my feet. I fought the exhaustion, but my body refused. I stalled.

Stars started to slip across my vision, blurring into a million eyes watching us both. The white plume of my breath burned my throat. Numbness spread up my legs.

"Highness?" Brenn hissed into silence.

I felt my hands fall to my knees. My eyes began to blot over as a jarring heat spread over my chest. My lips tingled.

"I'm out," I said, before my knees gave up and I fell back into the snow. Brenn slithered up onto my chest.

"Well, it was...interesting knowing you. Brief as it was," Brenn said, its beady little face hovering above me. "I look forward to eating you once we are captured, and you are slain."

I opened my mouth to respond but then darkness seeped into my vision. It couldn't let me die if there was a way he could save me - surely, the pact would save me? At my silence, Brenn flittered next to me. I saw a flame of black magic as Brenn changed form one more time – black eyes glowing with power. It had clearly been lying about the magic it had left.

"You suck."

My eyes shut. Darkness claimed me.

Four

Truthfully, I didn't dream of anything at all. But I did feel light. Like I was being carried upon the wind. And then I was warm. Toasty warm. Like I was being bathed in the warm glow of an open fire.

Suddenly, I heard a noise like something metal being dropped, followed by a bunch of colourful curses. The voice was male – young and bright – and it was headed this way.

"Wakey wakey, Mister," he said gently. I slowly opened my eyes. I must've slept for a long time, as it was difficult to let the light in once more. Immediately, warm golden eyes met mine. "There you are!" he said, grinning widely.

I felt soft grey cotton pyjamas on my arms and legs. My skin prickled in apprehension – was I revealed? Was I facing my death any moment now?

The boy had dark ebony skin and long, braided hair that lay across his shoulders and down his chest next to braces that hooked into his trousers. Perhaps sensing my discomfort, the boy softened and patted my arm.

"All is well, Mister. You are safe here," he added.

The sleeves of his grey shirt had been rolled up to the elbow and the cross-fastening at the top was undone. I recognised the pocket-filled leather belt around his waist and knew he was a healer. I had no doubt that inside were a multitude of liquids, powders, and solutions suitable for healing magic. Even his trousers had extra built-in compartments and pockets around his hips and knees.

"When we picked the pair of you up from the border, we were all so surprised that you survived. A pleasant surprise but a surprise nonetheless," he sped on. "Your lips were blue and everything." I opened my mouth but before I could speak the boy held a glass there.

Calling him a boy didn't seem right anymore. His mannerisms were that of someone much older. He was so tall, stockily built, and I assumed he was close to my own nineteen years.

"Time to get some water in you, friend," he said as he tipped the glass. I quickly drank the entire thing – suddenly desperate for water.

"Excellent work, Mister."

From looking at the room, it was easy to deduce this was a healer's quarters. The walls were full of jars, each one brimming with flowers, herbs, and plants – some of which I didn't recognise at all. A stone-laden fireplace crackled with heat in the corner; beside it, the wood stock was stacked with logs of all shapes and sizes.

An arched window sat opposite, with curtains held behind two brass hooks. Outside, lay a white courtyard bordered by snow-topped trees. The sky was pale, and it was snowing gently.

"I'm Hector, by the way," he added. "Your brother said your name was Aaron but I can call you Mr Noyin, if you prefer," he said in an upbeat voice. Aaron Noyin. A Noyin. Of course.

Calling itself my brother was surely another facet to which the shapeshifter could torment me. A fellow sailor would've suited us better: I needed no more reminders of my family.

"Yes, that is me," I dropped my voice as low as I could, suddenly all too aware of the lack of masculinity in my voice. I thought of how Sorrel spoke and tried my best to channel him. "Thank you, Hector, but where am I?"

Hector nodded slowly and his eyes turned to concern.

"Mr Brenn did say you had a head injury that made it hard for you to recall things." He felt my forehead for my temperature. "I did inspect your skull but thankfully I didn't feel anything untoward." He frowned, the lines between his eyebrows deepening, but after catching my eye, he softened. "You're in Clawton, a big ol' town in Gortia."

I blinked at him. My innate sense of direction had led us exactly to the place I didn't want to be. I needed to invest in a compass - maybe I could make Brenn turn into one. Hector watched me carefully. "Your ship went down off of Rynd after a fire aboard. You two are the only survivors."

I nodded slowly. It did not surprise me that Brenn was good at lying. I thanked the pact that I had made - surely Brenn was compelled to keep me alive after all. My spell-casting had worked.

"Where's Brenn?" I asked, rubbing my eyes with the back of my hand. My fingers were still stiff. I tried to push myself up but Hector flailed his hands about.

"You must rest, Mister," he said placing his hands on my

shoulders. "You decided to walk to Gortia – despite the freezing cold. You have been attacked by the frost badly, especially on your feet and the weather can affect the joints too. We had to submerge you slowly in a warm bath upon your arrival but—"

"You've lost a toe, *brother*."

I propped myself up on the bed just as a tall, lean figure turned the corner. The stranger wore a white shirt, a tan jacket with a fleecy lining, and a pair of those trousers with lots of pockets that Hector had been wearing. They were cuffed at the bottom and showed off his laced leather boots.

"Ah, there you are, Brenn," Hector said brightly. "Appetite quelled, I hope?"

His lips quirked. He had a little stubble around his squared jaw and I would've considered him handsome if that familiar smug countenance didn't spoil it. And, of course, if I didn't know exactly who he really was. Yet perhaps what was most unnerving, was that he looked a little like me. Ignoring the thick brown hair braided back by his temples, it was like looking in a distorted mirror. Our faces were similar in their jaw structure though his was sharper; I saw my eyes on his face, but his seemed to be an icier blue. I was sure he would pass for my brother, though he was too broad for Abel's lean form and too short for Sorrel's stature.

"I am sated," he said with his usual airiness.

"I'm glad to hear it." Hector turned back to me. "The good news is that the rest of your feet seem fine. You might be a little wobbly for a few months, but once you get used to it, I'm sure you'll be fine."

Hector went on to explain that the effects of the cold in Draig had stolen many toes and fingers – especially of travellers just passing through. He went over and pulled a copper kettle off the fire. It was whistling steam and a small cloud of it went up as Hector prepared us tea.

"We dragon-kin have the fire in our blood that sustains us," he said as he handed me a terracotta mug. The smell of lemon and chamomile filled my senses and I sipped. "But at least it isn't winter currently – you would've likely frozen through within the hour you arrived."

I thought of being submerged and assumed Brenn had

31

glamoured me himself. There were no questions about my gender. But Hector's golden eyes were still filled with concern.

"Take this morning slowly. You will regain full strength soon enough, but make sure to keep warm and keep drinking too." Hector cast a look at Brenn. "Let me get you some food too. If you did want to get up there are some spare clothes in the chest of drawers opposite you. Your clothes are not suitable for this corner of Nos, I'm afraid."

"If you need anything ring the bell," he added finally before nodding and heading out of the room.

I waited until Hector was out of earshot before properly facing a smug Brenn.

"Good morning, Your Majesty," he chimed with a mocking, flamboyant bow. "How is my favourite toeless idiot, Aaran Noyin?"

I narrowed my eyes as a ball of shadows manifested on my lap and then dispersed quickly, revealing a pile of folded clothes and a bundle of bandages that fell on me at once.

"I see someone is enjoying their freedom," I replied, trying not to grit my teeth at his insufferable expression.

"I did warn Your Majesty about the concerns of the weather, but she did not take heed," he added for good measure.

"I didn't see you brimming with ideas either, Brenn," I sighed in a hushed voice. I resisted the urge to pull back the blanket and see what damage had been done. I couldn't feel any difference but perhaps that was due to the tea Hector had given me. It was singing with sweet magic that surely had painkilling properties. I kept my eyes on the door.

Brenn pulled up a chair next to me, resting his hands on his knees as he sat next to me.

"Fret not, Majesty. No one can get past my expert hearing – even those proficient in stealth magic." Brenn's eyes glittered. "How do you think I got away with being such a keen assassin?" I rolled my eyes.

I investigated the pile and saw some Draigian clothes similar to his.

"Are you not going to compliment my new appearance?" Brenn said, wiggling his eyebrows.

32

"Oh, I have no doubt it will haunt my dreams," I replied. He grinned further still, and a long serpentine tongue swept out of his mouth as his teeth elongated like some undead ghoul from the realms beyond. I grimaced as I inspected the outfit.

"I don't care how neat your form is: you're still a slimeball," I told him. "How did you pay for this?"

Brenn shrugged. "Just fabricated an illusion when we were rescued and stole some for you when we got here." I glared at him. "I'm a Wraith – I don't have pockets."

"You do now." The loose trousers with all the compartments seemed something of a Northern fashion that I hadn't encountered before. "Does everyone wear those?"

"Anyone with a dragon does," he said, looking bored. "Hector stinks of dragons."

I lowered my voice. "Does he know I'm not a man?"

Brenn leaned in and whispered back, "If I say yes, then can I eat him?"

"Still no." Brenn pulled a disgruntled face.

"I glamoured you when they were reviving you – you're all man in their eyes," he grumbled.

I narrowed my eyes at him.

"So, you can glamour," I scowled. He must have been laughing away to himself when I was covering myself in the soot from the fire to appear less like myself. The hair would've had to go either way – it was too much of a burden to maintain.

Brenn shrugged his shoulders.

"I am thousands of years old, your Majesty," he said uninterestedly. "My speciality is shape-shifting but I have had the time to at least practice other magics. And you never asked."

I flopped back down on the pillow.

"Ever helpful, aren't you, Brenn?"

"Undoubtedly so, Princess."

I felt the fabric in my hands. A soft cotton shirt and a sturdier leather jacket felt soft between my fingers. Brenn's eyes were ever-watchful.

"Does her Majesty find everything to her liking?"

"She does," I replied. Slowly drawing my legs over to the edge of

33

the bed. I pushed back the thick duvet to my knees. "Does my brother feel adequately *restored?*"

He raised an eyebrow.

"Indeed, the breakfast they provided returned my energy to me," he caught my eye and chuckled. "No corpses, just bacon, ham, and these delightful lamb sausages." He waved a hand at me. "I should be sustained for a time." He reached into one of the pockets on his legs and pulled out a short cork-stopped bottle.

I picked it up. The label was peeling, but on the front were a few notes of application to do with wet hair written in draconic. "Hair dye?"

Brenn shrugged.

"Your scent is marred in my presence. But I have imbued this dye to restore your masculine features even when I am not present, should the occasion arise. It should last a few weeks."

"I would like to learn this myself. Glamouring always seems like it could come in handy," I muttered, stretching my legs for the floor. My right foot had been bandaged up. Suddenly, the sensation of imbalance made me stop and breathe. I waited until my vision cleared before moving again. The crawling sensation in my stomach filled me with apprehension. "Remind me to buy a book when I am home."

I stood up now and was surprised to be met with silence. I turned to see Brenn's masculine face lit by the sun. His lips pressed together in a prim sort of smile – as if he'd been caught doing something he shouldn't. Another moment passed.

"Out with whatever you know, Brenn," I said, resting one of my hands on the wooden bedframe. My worries resurfaced as he smiled.

"Only that 'home' for her Majesty will be rather a long wait," he said in a morose voice. "Hector was talking about it this morning. Kya will be the new Fynix colony; the old town has been totally razed. Most people have fled to the East or the West. The Wryfirth line has ended, and Celine's people have been scattered across the world to take refuge."

The new colony was not a surprise. After all, it was the Fynix people wanting to take over the Northern Isles had added kindling to the feud between our countries. And yet, it still stung in my heart. The world that had thrived outside my window; the schools, the temples with their domed roofs, and the palace standing over it all. Now every part of it would be re-shaped into Fynix's image – nothing of my country's heart would survive. My skin prickled, and I clenched my fists.

"And news of me and you?"

Brenn folded his arms.

"You're not going to like it."

"Nothing new then."

Behind him, the snow had started falling thick and fast. When it snowed in Kya the people filled the streets with ice magic; magnificent sculptures and snow scenes appeared across the city. Competitions were held in the artists quarter and the spectacle was truly worth the sneaking out I had to do to join in. My heart ached terribly all of a sudden but it was quashed by the smug grin of the Wraith.

"News has reached here of how the Wraith of the Wastes devoured Princess Bryony Wryfirth and defeated the tower once and for all. Now it's stalking through the land planning its next move." The gleefulness in his voice was grating. "All of Nos is up in arms. I am still the endlessly powerful being of mortal peril, and you are as dead as the rest of your family."

My temper flared. Of course, that was the solution they had come up with. Rage burned in my veins as I met Brenn's joyous eyes. I could not forget he was still the Wraith of the Wastes – still a creature of bloodshed and misery. I had forced his hand. The moment I died, he would leech upon me, devour all I had ever been, and the world would remain at his mercy. Had we not been rescued I would be a corpse now, perhaps the magic was not as strong as I thought. Brenn could have helped but didn't. Had the dragons not shown up, I would've been his breakfast.

My insides had twisted themselves in knots. It was imperative that I remember who it was I was dealing with. I may have been no stranger to being trapped, but Brenn had existed years before my parents' parents were born. That kind of captivity must eat away at the soul – if he even had one.

I shrugged my shoulders and gathered up the clothes and hair dye.

"Great. Well, if I'm Wraith food no-one will be looking for me," I said. "So, if we keep a low profile, we should be able to get to Wist without any unnecessary damage."

"That would be possible if we manage to evade the onslaught of forces that the Horned King, the Demon King, the Hydrean and Dean Fae forces, and even the Council of Shifters have sent North to hunt me."

I groaned.

"Wonderful," I seethed. "Your reputation clearly precedes you. Meanwhile, I am enjoying a peaceful afterlife." Where had Hector said the washroom was? I cast a look down the wall to where an oaken door was.

"Well, the rumours say that you gave me the strength," he added.

"A cow could've done that," I replied.

Brenn grinned with a mouth full of surprisingly normal teeth.

"We both have reputations." He added. "Yours is just awful."

I gave him a deadpan smile. "Says the murderer."

Annoyingly, Brenn didn't look ruffled at all.

"That might fix our money problem?" he proposed in a hopeful tone. "The problem being we don't have any."

I narrowed my eyes. My inheritance had surely gone to the Fynix people. Yet I thought of the catacombs and knew my treasures would be secure if too far away to be of help to any of us.

"Don't you have any left from when you went shopping?"

Brenn shook his head with feigned sadness. "Things used to be a lot cheaper." He popped his lips. "Let me retrieve a mid-day snack and then our problem will be solved."

"Is murder your answer to everything?"

"Only most things." He rolled his eyes. "Can you sing? Or dance?" Brenn said, watching me closely as I wobbled to my feet. "I daresay a young gentleman would've paid more for you to take off your clothes had you not looked like a prepubescent teenager."

"A tempting suggestion," I waddled slowly in the direction of the showers that Hector had mentioned. "Can *you* sing?"

"Only the sweet melody of death," he told me. "I've never had any complaints."

I turned back once more.

"See whoever has the worst mind and take what they won't miss," I said.

"On it, your Majesty." He feigned a salute.

"Don't get into any trouble," I warned, but as I turned, he'd already disappeared in a puff of black smoke.

It took me a moment to understand how to get the water running. Back in the palace, I had bathed in a deep copper tub that was filled with warm water and spices. I used long creamy bars of floral soap, smoothing bath oils, and lay among flower petals. After rubbing the suds to foam between my fingers, I would take my time washing my hair and languish in silence where no one could disturb me.

The bathroom was nothing like that here. Water ran out of a wooden pipe over my head when I pulled a hooked wooden handle. I wasn't sure how to adjust the temperature, so I left it as it was as I washed out the grime that had accumulated on my skin, taking care to rake my nails through my hair and cleanse my scalp from the coal that had stained it.

I traced the lines of the tiles before me with a finger. Now the dirt was gone from my nail beds my hands looked more like mine again. I followed the smooth squares up until I reached the wooden pipe – it seemed to be leading in from outside.

How did the mechanism work to provide that never-ending stream? This part of Gortia must've been full of wealth to have hot water running so freely. I applied the dark dye over my head, the smell made my eyes water. I added a smudge of it on my eyebrows too; blonde eyebrows would look strange.

My body looked bony and haggard when I looked down at my thighs and chest. I mean, I was never slight like the ladies at court. I would never be a delicate Fae or a sharp Elf whose lean bodies were built like the stalks of flowers. But now, unlike their elegant forms, I was gangly - my curves lesser. I guessed it was a good thing for my disguise, but my body felt strange. I eyed the trousers and white shirt that Brenn had stolen – it was the only part of my plan that hadn't been accounted for. We would need funds – if only I had access to my savings at the palace. There, I had my own secret stash in the forbidden catacombs. No one knew about the tunnels apart from

Randall, and even he couldn't navigate them without me.

I wondered if Brenn could portal like Mages could. Maybe he could teach me? I remember when Sorrell had mastered using a portal, the knob. He rubbed it in my face as much as he could. He used a wand – our family's heirloom – when casting big spells like that. Abel had no interest in learning, but Sorrel wouldn't teach me it despite me all but begging.

I found myself gritting my teeth. I looked down at my bandaged foot. The white linen had darkened with the water. I sucked in a breath before leaning to unwrap it. My hands shook a little as I revealed the warm pink skin of my foot. There were a few knicks along my sole, but my smallest toe had been reduced to a stub. I sighed and wiggled my other toes. My stomach squirmed and I felt a strange sorrow pass through me for the lost toe but I forced myself to look. It looked like it had been stitched up neatly and then a healing spell had been gently applied.

You're still alive. Toe or not. I reminded myself as I spotted the pink scar that had curved around the remaining stub. My balance had been affected which I felt through the wobble in my knees. I wondered if I stood still long enough if I would eventually veer off to the left.

Still, it was only one toe. A foot would've been way worse.

I bound my chest with the bandages and felt the familiar pressure around my ribs. The coat Brenn had stolen was miles too big, cut like his, though the leather was a darker tone and the lining light grey, like wearing a bear hug over my shoulders. I found a pair of worn leather gloves in the pocket too and felt a twinge of sadness for the person Brenn had stolen this from.

I looked in the mirror as the steam had subsided. My hair was not as dark as I thought it would be. Had I left it on long enough? I looked closer and rubbed it dry a little more.

The brown had come up in a mousier colour that matched Brenn's current form. The colour made me look faded, a far cry from my usually radiant complexion, and the dark, heavy-handed eyebrows made my forehead stick out.

Then I dried and put the clothes on. The strange cotton fabric felt scratchy and new against my skin. The weight from the jacket too was different to the dresses I wore daily before the war. I imagined my father's aghast expression at this outfit, his frown so deep it could carve a river into the earth. I couldn't help the grin spreading across my face. There was no way that I would've stepped foot out of my chambers – yet here I was on the other side of the world.

My gaze shifted downward to my hand. The cross remained embedded in my palm, leaving a muted red scar behind. I wondered if Hector had tried to heal it when I was brought in.

When I returned, I found that Brenn had also stolen me a pair of thick-soled leather boots with tight laces going up the front.

"I guessed the size," he said. He glanced at my right foot. "You'll have even more space now."

I sat on my bed as I worked the first boot on. The taut leather was far from the dainty slippers I wore during my lessons in the Palace. Yet I found myself liking the firm feeling underfoot, it would help steady my newfound lack of toe.

"When *did* I lose my toe?" I asked. Brenn was slouched in his chair, picking at imaginary lint on his jacket. He didn't look up.

"A few hours in," he said. "The sun was coming up, and you were prattling on about something boring, but still it seemed rude to interrupt you."

Then my heart clenched.

"Did you-?"

Brenn just smiled and I felt a wave of revulsion. Clearly, there were loopholes in my pact – I hadn't thought to plan for the possibility of a toe falling off.

"You're going to want to see Gortia, Your Majesty," Brenn said as I finished lacing the second boot. "Dragons everywhere."

A thrill raced through me, but I steadied myself.

"We can't stay now they know you left the island," I replied as Brenn looked pleased with himself. "Feel free to fill me in on everything I missed while I slept."

Brenn pursed his lips.

"We were rescued by three riders looking for the survivors of a ship going down off Dion. I heard their thoughts as they got closer, and they believed my talented portrayal of an unfortunate human."

He crossed his arms as if to say, '*so there*'. I frowned – that seemed too easy.

39

"Unless you ate the real riders who saved us and you're using your psychic powers to possess everyone," I suggested instead. I'd read the stories about Brenn – his atrocities had haunted my people. Yet, to think that the same being from all those tales was currently rolling his eyes at me seemed beyond my comprehension.

"History seems to have been pretty kind to my reputation," he crossed his arms. "After destroying the Tower and travelling with you, my power was pretty limited to some close-range psychic powers and shape-shifting," he explained, a smile playing across his lips. "Besides the toe, if I had eaten, say, a decade earlier, everything you said would be possible. And, providing you were unconscious, and they were a threat, I would've eaten them, eaten their dragons, turned into one, and then flew us to Wist."

I heard Hector's feet growing closer and I shot Brenn a look and he stuck out his tongue, a forked black thing. I pulled a face before the bright eyes of Hector fell on us.

"Goodness, Mr Noyin," he said his bright eyes landing on my hair. "I could've sworn you were blond."

It took me a beat to remember that was me. I could tell him about the dye but now wasn't the time to arouse suspicion – perhaps the glamour was working a little too well.

"Please, just call me Aaron. Yes, in certain lights I do appear rather bright," I said. Hector's smile wasn't mean – just surprised. "But it's our family's colour," I explained.

Hector nodded and surprised me by taking my face in his hands, as his soft fingers felt around my jaw, and I blinked as he pressed a warm hand against my forehead. "How are you feeling? Drowsiness? Nausea? Temperature-related illnesses can drive a person to see hallucinations, become confused, sweat profusely, overheat, under heat, grow dizzy, or make a person feel like they are dying." He stopped running his eyes over my head. "Any of those apply to you?"

Beside Hector, Brenn smirked.

"Nope, just a bit tired," I said politely. He tapped my cheeks gently before he removed his hands and nodded, a pleased look on his face.

"You're very lucky, Aaron. Very few people have braved the cold plains, utterly unprepared, and lived to speak about it afterwards." He looked a combination of bemused and impressed. "Your devotion to living is very commendable."

"My brother wouldn't die under such circumstances," Brenn said. "Not when he has *so* much to live for."

I bit back my grimace at that sarky smile of Brenn's and turned to Hector, who hadn't appeared to notice Brenn's tone. Then I remembered the story that Brenn had relayed about the ship going down. "Did you find any of the others?" I asked. Hector shook his head sadly.

"We can only hope they made it to the other border of Dion," he said. "I am sorry for your loss." Brenn nodded, his face the dubious picture of mournfulness. I gave him a respectful nod. "May they find peace," Hector added reflectively.

Brenn clapped loudly which made Hector and I jump.

"Right well, we must be off – family, commitment, duties, activities, etcetera –" Brenn said, getting to his feet and turning to suss out where the door was. "If you wouldn't mind showing us the way to your nearest port, we would be most grateful."

Hector seemed abashed for a moment and was immediately apologetic.

"Yes, yes. You did say you were keen to get home, of course." Hector grabbed a coat draped over a chair that looked a similar style to my own, but it was longer and had flaring corners at the bottom. "But first, at least let me show you around a little. Since the Council pays healers there are a multitude of us, and I never have any new people to converse with."

I looked towards Brenn with a smile of my own – he narrowed his eyes.

"You see, the heart of the city is full of Summer Solstice celebrations – you don't want to miss it!"

Of course, moving on was of the utmost importance, but I couldn't seem to bring myself to refuse Hector's unbeatable smile.

"And who better to show us than a local!" I chimed in. Brenn stared at me and Hector threw his coat over his shoulders.

"That's the spirit! Come on, Noyins," he said gesturing us to follow. "I'll show you around our slice of Gortia's glory."

41

Five

Before I was allowed to leave, Hector further swaddled me with a huge green knitted scarf alongside a white and brown furry hat that was far too big for me. Brenn, having somehow acquired a black hat and scarf of his own, kept pulling mine down over my eyes when Hector wasn't looking. Yet, however ridiculous I looked, I was glad for them when we embraced the cold and my lips stung against the morning air. My words froze on my tongue as I took in the ice-covered world that surrounded us.

The healing quarters that Hector kept were in a grand house made from wood and stone with slanting curved roofs that wrapped around the reverse of the house. It was full of large arched windows and ancient masonry that was well-kept despite clearly having been around for a long time. However, the most breathtaking of all was the snow; it waited on every surface in perfect white blooms and my fingers itched to pick up some and lob it at Brenn when he wasn't looking.

As we left the front porch, I noticed a family crest I didn't recognise carved in smooth grey rock. I knew the crest of the ruling clan of Draig – the DuVale clan – was a dragon perched on a crescent moon. But that was the only one I could remember. This one was a Dragon in a ring of fire. Besides the name Athanas there was Draconic written under the plaque – *Heal, Help, Home*. I assumed that was the family's motto. It described our new healer companion well.

Hector led us up a path that had been newly cleared. The grey stones led off onto a forest path from the clearing that the house lay in. Thick sage green trees coated in snow thrived among the blistering cold as sunlight peeked through the falling flakes.

Part of me was desperately sad to leave Draig before seeing nothing more than the front door, but it would be best for us to go before the arrival of whatever horrid reinforcements were sent north to capture Brenn. I thought of the Fynix assailants that had attacked me in my room; recalling their onyx armour glinting in the witchlight sent a chilling sensation down my spine. But that wasn't even the worst of it: Dean Fae assassins were infamous, and shifters were some

42

of the most skilled when it came to any works of espionage. Yet, the Demon King's forces were a horror all by themselves: the Reapers; the Clandestine; and the worst of all – Bonekeepers.

They were immortals. Demons who lived past any measure of time and whose sole purpose was enacting the orders of the Royal family. Their work took place in the shadows, but the legends of gore and horror haunted all of their actions. Of course, none of these tales ever compared to the terrifying Wraith of the Wastes. My chest tightened at the thought. The sooner we were out of Draig the better.

For everyone involved.

The grand house seemed hidden by a forest, so we carefully followed Hector for the right route. Snow crunched under my boots, and I pressed my hands into the pockets. Part of me wanted to ask him about life here, but I worried it would raise suspicion. The idea of climbing into his mind and learning more about him drifted through my head but I pushed it aside. I shouldn't just rifle without meaning.

Looking at Hector's honed frame, I wondered if he had any dragons himself. Earlier Brenn said he stank of them, but the healer hadn't mentioned anything. If he was a dragon-kin individual, why wasn't he covered in scales? Perhaps that was just a myth after all. I knew that dragons had to pick their riders. You couldn't just select one – just the reverse. You either rode or you did not.

"You know, I do not have the prepositions about the privacy of the mind that you do," Brenn said in a lowered voice so Hector wouldn't hear. "I spent nearly all my time in Hector's mind before you awoke." He declared, his dark hair shining in the sun. "It's an egregiously sunny place to be for the most part."

I shot Brenn a warning look and the corner of his lip quirked as his dark eyes focused on the road ahead of us. Hector was telling us how the wildlife here survived living in such a cold environment, I nodded along but simultaneously opened our mental link.

"What did you find out?" I whispered.

"Why are you whispering? You're in my mind," Brenn replied, his eyes glowing.

"You're incorrigible," I rolled my eyes. *"He seems nice. Even more than nice really – he took us in without a second thought."* Brenn's lip twitched at the corner. *"Anything I should know?"*

"Can't say. If I did, that would be a massive invasion of privacy." Brenn tilted his head and glanced at our sunny companion. I scowled – like that mattered to him; he was just determined to be unhelpful. *"We could just ask him?"* he added. I lurched out to grab him, but my fingers closed on cold air as he zipped on. I tried to speed up, but the snow was soft under my feet.

"So, Hector," Brenn said, watching Hector turn. His golden eyes were bright in the sunlight streaming through the trees. "Did you always want to be a healer? Draig is rather famous for its extreme dragon-based sports – that never interested you?"

Brenn smiled like he was a human too; it sent a chill of uncanny down my spine. But if Hector was put off, he didn't let it show.

"Oh, always. My parents taught me," he told us. He slowed his pace so I could walk alongside him too. "They're the best healers in Gortia, without a doubt."

"They pretty much raised my brother and I to be healers too," he added softly, his braids swinging as he walked. "However, my brother had other plans. Mainly, involving him being a jackass." He kicked some snow on the way. "Every family has their quirks."

"My brothers are jackasses too," I said before I could stop myself. My stomach dropped as Brenn sent me a wary look. Hector gives us both a soft smile.

"You have other brothers?" he asked. The resemblance between Brenn's façade and my face made me nervous. Thankfully, Hector hadn't questioned it. He didn't seem the type who would intrude.

"Two, actually," I said. "Both jackasses in their own ways." A twinge of something bitter curled in my gut. It was most likely that the pair of them were dead. Sorrel probably went down looking suitably heroic, and Abel probably fainted and then passed on when his heart couldn't take it. My throat suddenly felt tight. I didn't want to think about it.

"My grandma always says that families are your greatest strength and your worst weakness at the same time," he added, his voice trailing off at the end. "She also loves to tell me I'm missing out as I'm not married yet, but that's just her way of showing affection."

I wanted to tell him I understood that particular pressure; had my father got what he wanted, I would have been married off to a boring

Duke living in Eilaf years ago.

"Why would you marry a Duke when you're a Princess?" Brenn commented, his voice sliding through my thoughts. *"Surely, he would be below you?"*

I pulled a face.

"It wasn't a status thing," I replied. *"My father would've sold me to anyone who would have me at the end. But I wanted to make the decision myself."*

Besides, until the end of spring, I had Randall; no one really stood a chance against a stable boy with the best laugh.

"Radical," Brenn replied deadpan.

Through the path, we passed many stubborn flowers poking their heads above the snow. I knew the crocuses, but I was unfamiliar with the bright leaves and curling stems of the other blossoms growing. Patterns of animal tracks dotted the landscape, and I spotted a burrow dug deep into the earth – the small nose of a white rabbit-like creature emerged briefly. Black-set eyes with perked-up ears, a hare perhaps, but it seemed a great deal bigger than the normal burnished-brown hares I saw roaming the gardens in the mornings.

"The Snow-Hares are everywhere," Hector said, following my gaze. The creature disappeared back down beneath the earth. If I looked for the humps of soil, I could see the rest of the warren. "Some people think of them as pests, but they feed the wild ones fine."

"Wild ones?"

Hector looked up and I followed his gaze.

The trees above us were full. I spotted birds high up in the canopy – their morning song bright and cheerful. Long stretching shadows filled the woodland path, and I squinted past the sun breaking through. I heard a quiet rumbling over the chitter. I gazed further up still and saw the silhouettes of bigger creatures. The trees seemed to span into the clouds and every once in a while, a tail or wing would emerge from what looked to be a nest raised high. My heart stuttered: *dragons.* I tried to focus on seeing them, but they were just too high.

"But they're so close? Why have they not attacked us?"

Hector laughed. "Have you done something to upset them?" He shook his head. "You Southerners know so little about dragons," he sighed, but there wasn't any sense of malice in his voice. "No, unless you've maddened them, you're pretty safe. Wilder dragons who live in the mountains where food is scarce may attack, if they consider you a worthy meal, that is." Hector gazed up thoughtfully. "Usually these are pretty friendly, I would've thought they would've come down and said 'Hello', but they seem a little shy today." He added. "It's most unusual for this particular clan."

I glanced towards Brenn who met my gaze with his hands in the pockets of his jacket. He gave me an innocent smile and shrugged his shoulders. Clearly, the dragons sensed the danger that walked among us better than Hector did.

"That's a shame," I said.

We emerged from the forest path and the snow evened out to reveal a new, well-worn stone track. Our route flourished as flowers and ancient stones lined the path, and it became increasingly busy with people heading into the city; merchants, travellers, locals, you name it.

Men and women bundled up in thick coats like ours walked alongside us as traders pulling their stands on wheels made their way into the centre. The kids, in packs, followed our route with eager steps – keen not to waste the day. I noticed that dragon-kin varied wildly in skin and hair colour – neither Brenn nor I stood out among the crowd. We looked rather plain compared to some of the more colourful residents. People wove their hair with braids, beads, talons, and feathers in ways that I had never seen before. Even the men wore long braided styles under thick hoods. And, of course, Hector knew everyone we encountered.

Soon enough, homes started to pop up alongside the road. Many curved roofs gave way to short, rounded houses with thick stone walls. Shops too – selling everything from bushels of hay to iron ore. Painted signs hung above doorways: *Seamstress, Healer Brandon, Butcher, Yarn*. I did my best to keep my face neutral, but I couldn't ignore how amazing everything was.

Looking up, I realised that part of the forest had simply grown along with the rest of the Gortia. Trees filled the sidewalks with homes and cabins built around them. Life was busy and bright under the summer sun despite the snow. Vendors served travellers as they passed by, and locals conversed from their windowpanes with hot drinks steaming from mugs. Interspersed between posts and trees hung bright banners with all manner of patterns printed on them.

"For the Summer Solstice?" I asked, remembering what Hector had said earlier as we walked through the moss and snow-covered entrance archway. The healer shrugged his shoulders.

"Yes, but not just for the solstice," Hector said. "People like to decorate the streets with the colours of the clans to show their support and allegiance. It brightens up the place when you have so much snow."

Folks wrapped in thick cloaks of all colours with fur-lined boots milled about in the street as we walked by. My heart jumped into my throat as we neared people. I couldn't remember the last time I had walked out in Kya's city centre. But I tried to look as unfazed as I could as Hector led us through the crowd. The smell of freshly baked bread wafted by with the opening of a door. My stomach grumbled and Brenn snickered at me.

Draigians sold fur-lined wares; leather cuffs; wooden tools; ceramics; and pottery in small shops or outside under large, coloured awnings. Many places sold food hot and piping too, so many unfamiliar savoury and sweet scents drifted by as our feet joined the footfall. Huge fires kept in clay pits gave the streets a warmer air. There were wood stacks near every few buildings to keep the fires lit.

A roar behind me sent my skin tingling, and I ducked as a dragon flew overhead. It was a burnt umber colour with colossal wings. Another flew by a beat later, green scales glittering against the sun, the air vibrating with every flap of wings.

Even Brenn's eyes were wide as we watched them soar off into the distance. Our faces must've spoken for us as Hector laughed and patted me on the shoulder.

"You'll get used to them," he said with a grin. "Everyone here has one."

"Do you?" I asked. Hector's face didn't change, but his shoulders gained a stiffness.

"I did once," he said. "He died a few years ago now. He was very unwell."

The sad tone of his voice sounded foreign coming from him. I offered my condolences but before he could reply my companion piped up.

"That's ironic," Brenn said. "As you are a healer too. Very unfortunate." I shot him daggers, but Hector didn't bite. Instead, he sent Brenn a tired look of wariness.

"It is, isn't it?" Hector replied, tucking his hands into the pocket of his worn brown leather jacket. "It's why you must always cherish life – you never know how fleeting it may be."

Life in the city seemed to revolve around communal firepits; people roasted meat, gathered for warmth, and even dried clothes around the pits. The houses too curved around them, like the hearth of a home. The smiling faces and easy laughs of the people here made me feel both warm and cold inside at the same time. I couldn't stop thinking of Kya and comparing the two capitals. One full of life: the other obliterated. I tried to clear my head and focus on this new corner of the world. I couldn't change what was already done, but I could change my people's future.

After a while of ambling through the busy streets, Hector led us through to an open area. There was a plateau space that was empty apart from children using the area to play. It seemed like somewhat of an auditorium space with seats carved in stone, making up the banks around the sides and back. Around the edge, massive mangers of water were built; presumably for the dragons to drink from.

"This is the Core of Gortia," Hector explained. "It's where capital issues are brought before the people to discuss. And we also hold plays here, concerts, and dances."

We walked through the area, arriving in front of an extensive circular building with a curved roof.

"Welcome to the Clan Headquarters – the Summit," Hector said, gesturing wide. If I craned my head back far enough, then I could see long sweeping scaled dragon tails hanging from a balcony at the top. "They use the building for Clan-related matters like law-making. They're all meeting soon to discuss the borders with representatives from Fynix."

My heart jumped in my chest at the name of the Fynix Fae but I reminded myself we would be long gone before any of them set foot

48

here. Brenn, however, jumped at the opportunity.

"That sounds interesting," Brenn said, with way too much enthusiasm. He looked at me as if I was going to immediately agree to him eating my enemy. "Can we go?"

I shot him a frown. We needed to stay on task, however much my curiosity itched the back of my mind.

Our guide shrugged. "I don't see why not." Hector paused a moment. "Let's pop in on my mother. Perhaps she can put us in touch with one of her contacts to get you back to Dion sooner."

"Does she work here?" I asked as we headed forward.

"As the Healing Council's Chair, she has an office for state business."

Hector led us through a wide porch filled with people in fur-lined leathers and dragon-riding boots. Cloaks of all colours and types swept the stone floor that was filled with flakes of snow and mud trekked in from outside. Eventually, we passed a pair of doors that were flung open wide. Inside was a taller version of Gortia's core. The circle space had no roof, but I was certain there was an enchantment that stopped the snow from falling in. At the centre, a giant bonfire was kept in a pit lined by copper stones. Magic radiated here like the embers of the fire - I assumed it was to enhance the warmth given off from it.

There were lines of seats for the first few rows before boxes bordered the sides — much like how a theatre stacked its patrons. People clustered on the balconies, either watching the debates take place or hollering over the bars to the people below. The seats went the whole way round the stage, whilst overhead dragons lay in wait for their riders, their enormous heads lolling through iron bars at the top, tails swishing impatiently. I had to tear my eyes from them, so I didn't lose Hector.

As we followed Hector upstairs, I noticed more individuals go by with draconic features. Scales grew across their cheeks or nose, even claws extending from one or both hands. I tried my best not to stare as we weaved to the upper floor of the building. So many people from all different walks of life all in one place. Brenn and I garnered a few curious looks — it was a good thing we would be leaving soon.

"When do I get to eat?" Brenn suddenly chimed like a bell in my

49

head, the bond between us making my head throb. *"If you want a dragon, I could eat the rider, and we could fly off to Wist in time for afternoon tea."*

"How about you just turn into a dragon and fly us there yourself?" I fired back. *"Also, you don't suppose any of these dragon-kin can tell I'm not really a man? Aren't they hypersensitive to smells and such?"*

Hector drew up at a large oak door and knocked.

"Some of the older clan families will surely have those traits but not all. Anyway, the hair dye is a strong glamour and the jacket you're wearing smells a lot more like Hector than you. So, yes. You smell like a man." I gave Brenn a withering look. *"Besides, I haven't had enough human flesh for that kind of shapeshifting."*

Before I could say anything, the door was flung open. A woman slightly taller than me with a warm expression smiled widely in greeting. She wore a thick grey leather jacket too that had been fastened tightly down one side of her chest with black woollen leggings and fur-lined boots up to her knees. Like Hector, she had beautiful golden eyes, and long, dark hair plaited across her head on down her left side. All of a sudden, I found myself missing my long tresses and the back of my neck seemed to prickle.

"Hector!" she exclaimed, clapping her hands together. Her gaze fell on us. "And your guests! I am so happy to see you both in tip-top shape."

"Ma," Hector said, embracing her. "This is Aaron and Brenn Noyin. Guys, this is my Ma, Daphne." She gave us a cheerful wave. "How is Headquarters faring without me?"

"Well, only three brawls have started today and two of them were over mead," she announced, putting her hands on her hips. "So that sounds like a win to me!" I could see where Hector had got his sunny disposition from.

"And the dragons?"

"Nothing to report thus far," Daphne rubbed her leather-gloved hands together. "Your father is with them now if you want to go up."

"Thoughts on stealing a dragon and flying to Wist?" Brenn said into my mind.

"That doesn't sound discreet or easy," I replied, though I had to admit, I was thinking the same thing.

50

Hector gestured to us.

"I need to get these two home," he said with a smile. "As lovely as Draig is I am sure they would love to be home with their own family. Can you set us up with anyone you know at the docks?"

"We can wait a moment if you have an errand to run," I offered, secretly hoping to see more dragons up close. Who knew if I would ever be in Draig again? My curiosity was eating away at me. My thoughts were full of Brenn's laughter at my less-than-steel resolve.

Daphne and Hector looked delighted.

"If you're sure," Hector said. "And then I will show you to the port. Brenn was telling me earlier how much he missed home."

"Ah yes, always been a homebody," I added.

"Oh yes," Brenn said enthusiastically. "No place like home." Hector's mother looked delighted.

"Dion, yes?" she asked. "Well, then we'll get you an escort through the Dio pass."

Brenn grinned, nodding ecstatically, but my stomach dropped. The sooner the pair of us were off by ourselves again the better.

"How did you know?" he added with feigned incredulity. My smile was stiff, but Daphne didn't seem to notice.

"Oh, most of our trade comes through Dion and Fynix," Daphne explained. "The chances were obvious. Though you both have more of a refined Riach accent."

"Being at sea for a while does things to your head," I said cheerfully with a laugh for authenticity. I gritted my teeth – worrying that I sounded too much like a woman. That damned Wraith hadn't thought to tell me of the blasted glamour, so I didn't know how well it hide things like my voice.

"*It turns Princesses into men for one thing,*" Brenn added in my mind.

"*Be inconspicuous please,*" I fired back.

"I can imagine it does," Daphne said happily. She cleared some papers off her desk and pulled a furry hat over her head. "After thirty years here, you think I would be accustomed to the cold." She headed out of her office, gesturing us to follow, and then locked it behind her. She winked at me. "Just so people don't mistake my office for a bathroom." Her voice said it all.

We headed back through to the curving central corridor. The

noise of the main chamber was loud enough to be heard from here. Dragon-kin were yelling loudly and occasionally, something or someone roared. Or maybe that was a dragon? I couldn't decide if the havoc sounded like chaos or more like fun.

"Where are you from, Daphne?" I asked. She smiled happily, tightening the straps of her furry hat under her chin.

"I'm dragon-kin but I was raised in Fynix," Daphne explained, leading the way for us. "I've got dragon-sight to prove it." I had a feeling that if we weren't there, she would've skipped. My heart thudded: dragon-sight must've been why her and her son's eyes were the tone of gold they were.

"Is that why your eyes are that colour?" I said, as we passed a herd of young men and women in riding leathers. I recognised some of the clan sigils on their clothing and my mouth suddenly went dry. Hector waved as we passed and called greetings to those he recognised. Each time, people were delighted to see him and then their eyes fell on us. I tried my best to embody a confident air but the smile on Brenn's face filled me with unease.

"Yes, but they're also great for detail when it comes to injury and brilliant when it comes to flying – I can see for miles when I'm in full power, as in when I'm not tired. Also, I can see through any illusions and any low-level glamours too."

I sent Brenn a glare and he frowned at me.

"You honestly think **I'm** *a low-level spellcaster?"* He raised an eyebrow. *"I am offended."*

"She might be being modest," I retorted.

"Wow, that's fascinating," I replied. "And they're so pretty too."

"Thank you, Aaron!" Daphne said happily as we ascended what felt like the millionth set of stairs. "We've all got them in our family," she said, clapping her hands together merrily.

Suddenly, we passed through a wooden-framed door that opened up into a massive circular space with a giant hole at the centre filled with dragons of all shapes and sizes. A thrill ran through me as I took in the number and sheer size of them, and I couldn't stop the grin taking over my whole face. Brenn remained stoically passive, but I guess you've seen it all if you're ancient.

A massive red one lingered close to us, lying like a cat, sprawled out by the door. We had to be careful stepping over its long tail and then its claws. It had a saddle of some kind strapped to its back; long leather-like bands stretched under its stomach to secure it there.

"Afternoon, Ryser," Daphne called to his head. He opened one amber-coloured eye, huffed a sigh, and then closed it again. "Lazy dragons," she added, but her voice was softer.

"I've found, Dad," Hector said. I followed his eyeline and saw a man with dark skin standing next to a curled-up green dragon. His hair was plaited just once down the back of his head, and he had eyes that were soft and green like shoots of grass coming through the snow. Next to him was a slimmer version of Hector with golden eyes and a grimace on his face – he had his hair shorn short, unlike the rest of his family. His face fell. "And Inigo." He turned to his mother with a suspicious expression. She shrugged her shoulders.

"Oh, what a pleasant surprise," she said, unsurprised. "Maybe you two can talk to each other like brothers and not like people about to go to war."

I watched Hector's face become rigid. His demeanour changed and he stalked over to the rest of his family. We dodged the other lounging beasts on the way. Most ignored Brenn, though a few of the dragons with weathered scales or those who wore marks of warfare seemed to regard him strangely. Nostrils flaring, low rumbling growls, and tentative hisses filled the air.

"Ah, there is my handsome husband," Daphne hollered as we got closer. The husband in question raised his head and grinned as she came over. Inigo's expression didn't change as we approached but after he glanced at his brother, his face darkened. Hector clenched his jaw.

Daphne planted a kiss on her husband's cheek and then did the same on Inigo.

"Afternoon all," Hector's dad said. "I'm Ajax Athanas." He extended a hand to me, and I took it and then he took Brenn's too. "How are you both feeling?"

"Splendid, thank you," Brenn said in an uppity voice that made my skin crawl. It reminded me of the snobs at court who were trying to get on my father's or Sorrel's good side.

"Turns out I may survive after all," I added. "All thanks to the perfect Healer."

Ajax's face became proud, but his green eyes sparkled with mischief.

"Ah, like father, like son," he proclaimed jokingly. Daphne nudged him on the shoulder. "I'm glad you are feeling well enough to come and see the city when we are celebrating."

The beautiful buildings, the snow-capped landscapes, the communal fires, the colourful banners, and the even more vivid locals of the Clan-orientated city filled my head.

"Clawton is beautiful," I said. "I had no idea how big your capital is. Thankfully Hector is a font of knowledge when it comes to your lovely corner of the world otherwise, we'd be lost trying to find the port." I added truthfully. It seemed to sprawl out in every direction, like the many points of a snowflake.

Hector's shoulders eased a little when I said that. He sent me a small smile that warmed my heart.

"Be careful," Brenn said into my mind. *"That boy isn't into women."*

Brenn was being finicky – I was just being nice.

"You're only allowed to go into the heads of those who might be an enemy, Brenn," I warned him.

"So...everyone?"

The brother spoke then, his tone filled with dismay as he looked at Hector.

"I didn't think we'd see you until the *Winter* Solstice. Maybe you aren't such a wet mop after all."

The healer crossed his arms as a new expression crossed his face: icy displeasure.

"Nice to see you standing upright. I didn't realise you could anymore," Hector responded coolly. "Between spending so much time on your back in the stables with whatever that will have you and drinking away your pay at any tavern you're not banned at - I thought it beyond your current capabilities."

My eyes widened and I thanked Celine that Brenn didn't change his composure.

Daphne and Ajax exchanged a wary look of familiarity as Inigo's cheeks tinged pink. His gaze fell on me, and his expression turned furious.

"Why did you bring them here?" he said, gesturing to us. "They could be spies."

"We'd be pretty poor spies if you thought we could be spies," Brenn responded flippantly. Hector's face flushed.

"And they almost *died*," he added. "Aaron lost a toe!"

I nodded. "It was my favourite."

Brenn snorted as Inigo's face steeled further.

"Have you investigated it? Why did we find no other survivors?"

I didn't want to dwell on the correctness of his concern. We were not who we said we were, but we were no spies, and it wouldn't matter as soon we would be out of the capital. On our way to the next part of our adventure.

"We're obviously spies," Brenn said in a bored tone as my stomach dropped. "Why else would we walk in the snow for hours just to reach you?" Brenn shrugged. "I knew we should've just died." He sighed dramatically. "Save us all from this confusion."

Hector let out an exasperated groan.

"Ignore my brother, he's a fool. You are welcome here," Hector said firmly. Whirling on his brother, his words had a bite to them. "Do me a favour and go back to the races – drink away your winnings and sleep in a ditch somewhere."

As his nostrils flared and Inigo clenched his fists, I gave in and peered into his mind. He didn't have any defences in his thoughts and the feeling of bitter sadness made my tongue taste salty. A wave of anger flooded his head and suddenly I saw my skinny figure through his eyes. Then a memory stirred, and I saw a fight flash in his mind. A dragon lay on the forest floor, lifeless. Inigo had a knife in his hand, and it was bloodied. There was such an array of sadness and anger in his heart that I retreated from his mind immediately.

Inigo muttered a curse as he stormed off past Brenn and I. The family exchanged looks of disappointment and embarrassment. Hector clenched his jaw.

For a moment, the only noise that passed between us were the lazy purrs and growls from the dragons. Then Brenn clapped his hands together.

"Well, he was spirited," Brenn added before I elbowed him in the gut.

"Put a sock in it," I hissed at him.

Hector raised his hands.

"I'm sorry, guys," he said. "Inigo is a piece of work." Ajax and Daphne exchanged a sad look. "The boys want to get back to Dion," Hector added quickly to his parents. "Do you know of any traders heading that way? I was thinking of Marsha, but I think she's still having time off with the baby."

Ajax frowned. "Hector, the port is closed until the delegations have come and gone. Even dragon flights must be kept in-land."

"But that is days away," Hector replied.

Daphne shook her head. "Not anymore. The delegations will be here in the morning. It seems they are anxious to get started."

"They're portalling as close to they can to the border – it seems they've hired some of the best mages around to accomplish it," Ajax added. "We're expecting more delegations later this week too. The Dean and Hydraen Fae – even the Werewolves of Syree."

Hector raised his eyebrows. "Goodness, plans have changed."

"I assume it's for public safety concerns," Daphne said. "Demons are not exactly known for their predictability and with the Wraith somewhere in Nos – well, the Clan Council are trying to quell public fears." Beside her Ajax nodded.

My stomach swirled as Hector gave me a sympathetic look. I tried my best to not let my disappointment appear on my face. My concerns were offset by Brenn's attempt at concern.

"Oh dear, that is most unfortunate," he shook his head and put his hands on his hips. "What are we to do now, brother?"

"You are more than welcome to stay at our home," Daphne said. "These are dangerous times and I want to make sure you are safe."

Her eyes glowed with genuine concern, and she looked so much like Hector. The family resemblance was truly uncanny.

"As long as you don't mind," I found myself saying.

Brenn's expression turned to surprise, but it quickly returned to boredom. No doubt he would say something sarcastic momentarily. But what could we do? Leaving when it was prohibited would easily get us into trouble quicker than if we snuck out with everyone else.

"In that case, I guess you'll be staying a little longer with us," Hector said, upbeat. "At least I'll be able to keep an eye on your recovery."

"As long as that is okay with all of you?" I asked. Daphne and Ajax nodded eagerly.

"Of course," Ajax said. "Cold sickness can have symptoms that last weeks and we don't want to hinder your recovery by making you do too much too soon."

Daphne smiled at me and despite the concern in my chest, I gave her an optimistic smile.

"Have there been any new rumours about what happened?" I asked. "We knew Riach had fallen a couple of weeks ago, but news is scarce when you're at sea, fishing."

Brenn's lip twitched.

"Well, after the Wraith of the Wastes somehow escaped the Tower of the Last Isle," Ajax said grimly, "rumours are that it went West so must be somewhere on Draig."

"How terrible." Brenn said, feigning apprehension.

"Quite," I added, sending an admonishing look to Brenn which didn't deter him in the slightest.

"So, do the Fynix plan to kill it?" Brenn said, crossing his arms like a concerned citizen.

"Nothing that old and evil can be killed," Daphne said with a sad smile. "They plan to imprison it. Or at least, that's what I think they should do."

"Do they know how it got out?" I asked.

"No idea," Ajax said. "Apparently, the Fynix king sent the Princess of Riach there, and after devouring her the beast managed to escape."

"That sounds plausible." Brenn said with a nod and a sympathetic smile in my direction. It was always sobering to know that if my plan had gone pear-shaped, I would only go down in history as being breakfast for a monster.

Hector's lip curled.

"That's barbaric," he said, shaking his head.

"The Fynix King holds grudges," Ajax said solemnly. Daphne's eyes flicked up to his – a sombre look in her eyes.

I nodded, and a stone sunk in my stomach. Our people had paid enough for this foolish war that could have been solved if my father had swallowed his pride and tried to stop the divide between our people and the Fae. Yet generations later it had finally come to a head – and the archives of our world would note the tragedy of our people's defeat.

My sinking feeling was offset by my theatrical companion.

Brenn sighed, "I hope they catch it. Something like that could cause so much *damage*."

Everyone nodded in agreement. I caught the glint of pleasure in his eyes as they met mine and had to resist a grimace.

Stupid damned Wraith.

Six

Since we were tied to Gortia a little longer, Hector dedicated himself to showing us more of his city. I caught his concerned glances from time to time - checking we were enjoying ourselves, no doubt. His caring nature made him easy to listen to and, like with everything I'm sure, he threw himself into the role of tour guide.

It was refreshing to be spoken to just as someone normal; like I had a normal family, normal job and normal problems. Most people didn't need to deal with war-loving fathers in charge of a nation of people. If I had been born less driven, I could've easily settled for that life; a life where there was beauty in the everyday. But I made a pledge to my people; I would not concede now - not when peace has not been restored and my people returned home. Seeing all these houses here in Draig, though wonderfully different from home, only made me long for it more.

From the headquarters, he showed us the realms of small shops and businesses that seemed to curve around its never-ending streets. I was surprised to see horses pulling carriages among the swishing tales of smaller dragons. Children made snow sculptures under windows and in potted gardens by the street. Men and women collected herbs and traded with each other to fill jars with different leaves.

The colours of the Dragon-kin were as vibrant as dragon fire itself. Many sported patterns on their clothes to represent their clans, wore paint, donned piercings under their noses and ears, and wove their hair into plaited styles much like Hector's. When my hair grew back, I made a promise to myself to try a few of them.

Thankfully, Hector didn't seem to mind my endless questions, and Brenn said very little.

"Don't get comfy," his warning rumbled in my head. *"You said it yourself – staying here would be a bad call. The sooner we get to Wist the sooner we are safe."*

"Yeah, yeah, I heard you. But what can we do?"

"Sneak out?"

"That would arouse even more suspicion if we just disappeared."

Of course, we couldn't stay forever, I knew that. But something about the communal fire pits warming the streets kept me toasty inside as well on my cheeks.

On our travels, I met countless dragons and found them the most fascinating creatures. Sure, they were terrifying beasts when they didn't like you – they'd growl deeply, flash their giant teeth, and thrash their tails, which were lean and sharp like a whip. Yet many were calm and complacent like overgrown house cats; too aloof to care about mere mortals like us. A few head pats later though and you could win them over easily – even more so if you could rub their tummies.

They seemed happy to see me, but most were wary of the wraith in the human guise. A dragon with white scales and black-tipped toes snarled at him fiercely, thumping its tail and snickering a warning. Fortunately, a few strokes on their muzzle from Hector easily mollified them.

"So, how old are you when you are given your dragons?" I asked, as Hector led the way to the next stop on his list. His mother had been insistent about us going to see the younglings now that we had more time on our hands. Hector had been delighted by the request and I agreed straight away. Brenn, of course, followed us around like a bored shadow.

"It's a big ol' ceremony," Hector explained. "When you're deemed responsible by your parents, guardians, or teachers you're allowed to participate." We had come out of the main throng of Clawton, and the houses grew in distance between each other. We took off up a long stone path sheltered by a tunnel of fir trees. "You're taken to the Silvest Mountains where the newborns will have come of age themselves. The higher the mountain, the better chance of a dragon taking roost there for the season. If all goes well, one will choose you and you begin your journey together as dragon and Rider."

A curved brick building appeared from between the green, its top extended to a point like a straw hat, emitting smoke like steam from the spout of a kettle. The worn stone path had been recently swept and lanterns glowing with witchlight led to the structure.

"Can only Draigians acquire dragons?" I asked. The temptation of acquiring one for myself lingered on my mind. If I could handle a

Wraith, I was sure I could handle a dragon.

At that precise moment Brenn gave me a sideways look: *don't you dare*. I sent him back a challenging look.

"Well, our people know all the ways of the dragon," Hector explained. "Plus, from what I've seen, the rest of the world isn't exactly dragon-prepared, so Draig is a great place to raise them." He shrugged as we reached an oak set of double doors. "But, ultimately, it's up to who a dragon chooses."

He pushed the doors wide, and the space immediately opened into a circle room. A cacophony of crackles, tiny roars, and gnashing noises met us. The pad of eager feet had me searching for the source. Nests of straw laid around the room and at the centre was a fire pit kept carefully behind a domed cage.

My heart melted: these dragons were no bigger than kittens. There were many sprawled out by the fire, napping in the hay, and coming over to greet us. A grey one, close by with pale eyes mewled softly after it realised who had opened the door. The green one who had been playing with a dragon with yellow scales quickly abandoned his companion to trot over.

"Excellent," Brenn said warily while looking about the room. A few curious younglings began to amble forward, "Dragon babies." His shoulders stiffened as they came closer. Hector crouched to the floor and sat cross-legged as the spindly creatures came over.

I couldn't help my wide smile and immediately joined him on the floor. Over wobbled three different tiny beings; their eyes shone like jewels and their harmless claws were small enough to hold in my hand. They nuzzled up against my shins and a red one rubbed his head against my hand until I scratched under his chin. If I wasn't on a mission myself, I could've easily stayed here forever.

"They seem to like you, Brenn," Hector said, holding a small black-scaled beast in his hands. I turned to see Brenn overcome with pocket-sized dragons. After seeming surprised by his presence, they seemed to have bonded with him and a collection of them gathered in his lap, their pointed heads resting on his knees and thighs; one had even climbed up and nestled in the crook of his arm. He smiled for Hector, and this time, the smile in his eyes seemed genuine.

"Are these the new dragons for the riders?" I asked as an ember-coloured one chomped into my hand playfully. It didn't have any teeth yet, so it didn't hurt but I bopped its nose to release me. Its red eyes were wide and innocent, but its nose had a cut across it, the scales absent around a slender auburn now-healed gash.

"No, these are all orphans, Aaron," Hector said sadly. I felt my face fall. "Dragons can be bloodthirsty creatures, even with each other. Wild ones who have no riders frequently battle for land across the mountains." His eyes fell to the babies in my lap and then he glanced about the room. "We couldn't just leave them there."

There must have been upwards of twenty little bodies here. My heart squeezed in my chest – they looked so helpless.

"Do you release them back into the wild when they are old enough?" Brenn asked, his interest seemingly genuine. I was proud of him for having feelings. He met my eye and glared at me – thankfully, Hector was distracted by the dragons in his lap.

"Most of them, yes," he explained. "Some, however, become too domesticated and linger here. We have about six who continually fly here and mind the keep for us." He shook his shoulders. "We call them the Guardians of the Keep, and they get paid in food, so it's not a bad life."

As we had played with the dragons, Hector set about doing his routine: refilling their water troughs, tidying out their nests, cleaning any of the messier ones, and then nursing the smallest babes. As he worked, I hand-fed them square chunks of what looked like beef from a wooden bowl he'd filled up. Thankfully, I had never been squeamish which was handy as some of the food was rather bloody. However, the hatchlings didn't seem to mind. Some licked my fingers after my bowl had been emptied. Their minute pink mouths chewed with tremendous effort and the nubs of some teeth that had already come through flashed every once in a while.

After eating their fill, many rolled over onto their backs and started to nap. A few took up positions around my legs, enjoying my warmth. Once again, I found myself calling into question the importance of my mission. If I didn't reclaim my throne and didn't die in the process – I could raise some baby dragons. Retreating into the wilderness and living off the land seemed like a dreamy way to spend your life.

However, Brenn took my distraction as an opportunity. As I looked up from the crimson babe newly nestled on my lap, I found Brenn devouring some of the dragon's food – the raw flesh must have been a temptation he could no longer resist. I watched in horror as he ate what appeared to be a lamb leg whole. His mouth distorted through his shadowy magic, stretching uncomfortably wide, and the lips thinned out and those jagged teeth emerged. At once, he pushed the whole thing into his mouth, bone and all. My stomach churned as he munched away smugly.

This reminded me of the loophole in our pact. I specified he couldn't kill anyone to eat without my permission. If he didn't kill – he could eat whatever came his way. Such as the lamb leg, breakfast meat, or even a frost-bitten toe. That latter still made the skin on the back of my neck crawl. I watched as Brenn smacked his lips together in satisfaction.

Having witnessed Brenn's greed, a black dragon growled angrily in his direction. Brenn turned to it and gave it a bloody smile. The dragon growled even louder. My stomach fell to my knees as Hector began to turn too but instead, I gasped dramatically and pointed to the water manger.

"He's drowning!" The blue-scaled dragon in question appeared to be blowing bubbles underwater. Obviously, he was completely fine, but Hector immediately bolted over and scooped the swimming babe in question up into his arms, giving my bloodthirsty companion enough time to wipe the red from his lips.

"You are incorrigible." I sent to Brenn's mind.

"My terrible owner doesn't feed me enough," he snapped back.

"You need to be more careful, Hernell," Hector said, pressing a fingertip to the head of the little dragon. After checking him over, Hector set Hernell back on the straw-covered floor. The babe waddled off with a surprised expression.

With the babies, time seemed to fly and soon the sky had darkened, the main source of light came from the witchlights hanging around the room. Hector readied himself for outside and at the gesture, the baby dragons climbed off me and went to see him, as if they could convince him to stay.

"Time to go and see who is lingering about," Hector said,

brushing his trousers free of the hay. I got up to follow him, turning to check on Brenn.

I wondered if they could sense what he was. If they did, they didn't seem to fear him at all. Having since devoured one of their snacks, a few of the younglings regarded Brenn with intrigue or kept their distance, but most seemed to think of him as just another human. I left Brenn contently sitting on the floor with the dragons. It was a strange sight – to see someone like him be peaceful among the hay.

Hector led me out a side door into something of a storage room, full of wooden drawers and cupboards with food, toys, hay, and kitchen space. There was a worn table, and I spotted a small hatch that I assumed would lead to a pantry below. After opening the connecting oak door, we went out into the crisp air once more. My skin prickled with the frigid breath of wind across my cheeks, which sent me hiding in the warmth of my fur-skinned jacket.

The glade was empty besides a few trees standing firm under the weight of the snow. I noticed massive paw pads in the snow. My feet barely constituted a toe in comparison.

"Oh," Hector said, his brows furrowing. "It seems someone is shirking their duties." He crossed his arms. He whistled twice in a high pitch. Silence. "Odd."

Suddenly a nicker over my shoulder made me jump. A green face, longer and more vast than my whole body, stared at me curiously, its eyes deep and green like the depths of a lake. A brush of cold later and I saw Brenn zoom out of the door. He must've felt my shock, and I watched his eyebrows raise as he took in the extent of the dragon. It was one of the biggest ones I'd seen since being here.

"There you are, Astyanax," Hector exclaimed as he wrapped his arms around his giant muzzle. He didn't seem in the least scared and the dragon even lifted his head, hauling Hector off his feet too. He laughed happily as Astyanax put him down. "This was one of my first-ever babies," Hector said, laughing. "After Idaeus, my dragon, died, I retreated up here to sort myself out." He spoke sadly, and the round mossy eyes seemed to watch us carefully. The sheer size of him was beyond impressive. "Astyanax was the first one I found."

The dragon, too, seemed pleased to see him, lowering his head so

Hector could scratch between his ears. Of course, Hector was telling the dragon who we were and why we were accompanying him. If he understood, I had no idea, but Astyanax seemed very patient and still so perhaps he did. I caught a few wary glances towards Brenn though that Hector chalked up to curiosity.

While I listened to our healer talk animatedly about Inigo and his stupidity. I couldn't help but think: Hector was so kind and helpful: surely, someone as open and sweet as him would be on my side? I don't know - maybe it wouldn't be such a bad plan trying to recruit him as an ally. He was a healer after all. Those kinds of skills would be invaluable if everything came down to a fight.

"Oh yeah, I think that's a great idea," Brenn drawled in my mind. *"You'll be either handed over to Fynix to die or will be eaten by a dragon. And once you're gone, I will rampage through this town and eat everyone I can."*

I watched Hector and tried my best to ignore the sadness in my chest.

"Maybe not then."

"Very wise, your Majesty."

"How come he's so much bigger than the others we've seen about town?" I asked, taking in Astyanax's long, scaled body; his tail alone was as long as one of the trees around the younglings' keep and as it swished back and forth, it made a pattern in the snow and whisked the flour-soft dust back into the air.

"I can only assume his parents were also massive," Hector replied. He ran a hand down the flank of the marvellous creature. The dragon snickered and nuzzled at his shoulder.

"Earlier, you said dragons chose their riders…".

The dragon was clearly very fond of Hector as he had not moved. Not even when Hector hoisted one of the dragon's wings over his head as he looked for signs of damage. He seemed to be checking him all over for anything unusual. Always the healer at heart.

"When you rear one the traditional way you develop a bond," he explained. "They live, eat and breathe with you. It goes beyond physical ties: it's old magic." He added with a smile. "You can feel them – more than a pet or a companion – they become *part* of you. They never want to leave your side."

If Hector was so close with his first dragon it was no wonder he was beside himself when he died. Though I'd never had a dragon, I knew what loss felt like. It seemed my life up until I had met Brenn had just been a never-ending cycle of me losing. My mother, my freedom, Randall. My heart tightened in my chest.

No, we couldn't tell Hector. This was too important.

Now it was my choice how I went forward, and I had no plans of losing anything again.

As Hector finished his duties at the keep, Astyanax kept poking his head inside the keep to check on the younglings: I now understood the size of the door.

After we laid some more straw down and gave the younglings one last cuddle, Hector led us out of the keep. We left Astyanax taking his role as Guardian very seriously, as he lay in front of the door, his huge body curving around the building. As he breathed through his nose, steam rose as white plumes into the night. I patted his muzzle as we passed by, and he whickered softly.

"That's approval," Hector told me proudly. I grinned as we headed back down the path.

"That's made my day," I said, truthfully.

Brenn said nothing. He didn't pat Astynax but instead nodded his way. The dragon watched him as we walked deeper into the woods. Even though I was looking ahead I knew that those deep green eyes were on Brenn's back.

The dark sky was alight with stars, with not a cloud in sight. The moon was full, but Clawton was far from quiet. Bonfires filled the streets and families gathered outside with their dinners. Riotous laughter flooded the paths between residents and neighbours who shared barrels of mead or bottles of wine on hay bales left in the street.

"Are parties a regular occurrence in Draig?" I asked as I watched a group of young men carry a half-naked gent shining with what appeared to be some kind of syrup to a chicken coop. Drunken laughter came our way, alongside with the annoyed clucking of the birds.

Hector shrugged, "People always tend to get a bit boisterous during the Summer Solstice celebrations." He explained. "However, the Council tends to lay on celebrations for state guests too." He trailed off as his eye was caught by a swaying elderly dragon-kin man dancing dangerously close to one of the street fire pits. "He better be careful if he doesn't want to burn his clothes right off his body."

As we headed through the capital, the auditorium that had been empty earlier was full of people laughing and chatting alongside tapped barrels of beer and mead set up on long wooden tables. Music was beating at a lively pace from a string quartet sitting on the steps. They filled the space with cheery melodies that had men, women, and everyone in between, enjoying a dance together.

Someone passed around a dark, rounded bottle of some clear liquid with a fierce cinnamon smell. Hector took a gulp and then passed it to me and I read the label: Dragon's Breath. The sweet fiery kick filled my tongue and I swallowed. Heat scorched up my throat and I coughed which made Hector laugh. Overall, the sensation was pleasant but perhaps next time I would half the drink with some bubbles or juice.

"You're brave, Aaron," Hector said amusedly as I passed the bottle back to him. "Most foreigners would never take so much on their first go."

"Don't imagine bravery from foolhardiness," Brenn said, airily.

"Ever the critic, Brenn," I replied as the instruments began their next piece. The band had struck up a merry tune I recognised, and a quadrille took place on the beaten snow. I found myself nodding along with the beat and a giddy feeling overtook me.

Of course, dancing was one of the few things my father had allowed me to do. Women of noble birth were expected to keep feminine skills, after all. Your dancing skills spoke volumes about a woman's education – in the eyes of my father that is.

Truthfully, I loved to dance but expressing myself in a ballroom was not the purpose of my education at all. Those lessons were to help find me a husband: to show the court the kind of prize I could be. I quickly learned the attention I garnered dancing was not worth the consequences of attempted suitorship and courting offers.

Thus, I danced with every father, soldier, and woman I could, my aim being that my partners had no interest in me whatsoever. It was worth my father's ire. Many dukes, marquises, and lords had been snubbed at my hand in exchange for a dancer with no impressive title or expectations. Most of them would try anyway, if they pleased me and we engaged in courtship they had better chances with my father. It gave me immense joy to politely cast their offers aside and settle for partners who did not see me as a means to impress the King. Of course, word would eventually return to my Father and I would be escorted from the ballroom and sent to bed.

But he was not here, and I was no longer a Princess.

I whirled on Hector.

"Fancy a dance?" I asked, my excitement made my voice light. Hector looked at me in delight. Brenn did not look impressed.

"Of course," Hector agreed animatedly. We both looked to Brenn.

Brenn's expression didn't change.

"I don't *dance*," he said simply. "But don't let me stop you."

He didn't need to say anything more. I grabbed Hector's hand and led him to the dance floor. The first tune was a raucous number involving lots of jumping about and kicking. As the night drew on, I found I didn't know many of the other dances as they must've originated in Draig. However, Hector was a patient teacher and helped me keep up.

From the sidelines, people were clapping, conversing, or singing along with the tunes. However, when I cast a look back at Brenn, I saw him glowering in the silence on one of the benches. As the lone figure between multiple couples engaged in love-lorn activities, he scowled from his seat beside the tangles of limbs. His lips were pressed together in a thin line.

"Having fun?" I asked him between dances as I tried to get my breath back. The cold temperature made my throat burn, or perhaps that was the mead.

"You look ridiculous."

"Like that is anything new," I called back to him.

Brenn didn't reply but when I turned round I saw that even more couples had joined the bench. Brenn's face had never been stonier.

And yet he refused to move.

Before another song could spring into action, Hector and I stumbled from the dance floor as fresh snow began to fall like confetti from the sky. Despite the time, the night didn't seem to be dying out and the weather did nothing to extinguish the activities.

I wiped my forehead and noticed flakes already building up on my gloves. Hector took my hand and led me back over to where a, now frosted, Brenn was lying on a bench on his own. The couples had somehow migrated to the floor.

He must've heard us coming as he sat up immediately, pulling a face at how sweaty and exhausted the both of us were. I crashed next to him, Hector following me – my face ached from smiling, but I couldn't seem to stop.

"Do you guys do this every year?" I asked, still getting my breath back. "I must make a note to come to your Solstice Celebrations on an annual basis."

"It's the Dragon-kin way," Hector said with a shrug.

Just as he said this another cheer went up among the people as a couple of women – one with short shorn hair and the other with skin as dark as the sky started energetically kissing in the snow. The applause caused the pair to spring apart, but it was too late, and the next song began alongside the laughter.

I watched the couple abandon the dancefloor for, no doubt, a quieter, more private space. Their silhouettes moved into the dark corridor between some of the houses before disappearing from sight. Despite myself, I felt my cheeks flush – Randall skipped into my mind once more. Those times we'd spent in the dark hayloft above the stable rows made my chest tighten. I wondered if I would ever feel such intimacy again. It didn't seem possible now that he was as still as the tombs of the catacombs I loved so much.

Brenn brushed the snow off his shoulders.

"The party is to celebrate the arrival of the Fynix delegation," Brenn said in an upbeat tone. The happiness in my heart was quickly doused with a bucket of iced water. His eyes met mine and there was nothing joyous in there.

Hector's eyebrows shot up.

"They're early," Hector said, a grim expression held his features. "I suppose they were keen to discuss terms while they begin their search."

"Terms?" I asked.

69

"I guess this could be considered them beginning to sweet-talk us," Hector explained. "The Fynix are planning on dividing the country between themselves and the demon forces. Extending the territory of the shadow realms beyond the barrier of the East and the West."

My heart turned to lead in my chest as Brenn spoke for me.

"Why would they do that?"

Hector grimaced before he spoke in a strained voice.

"Dragian forces helped take Eilaf," he explained. His eyes met mine and I would've sworn those eyes were forlorn. "Our family didn't agree with it, but our leading Clan and the majority voted for it."

Eilaf was one of the larger cities on the edge of Riach, and we never thought it would fall: until it did. There had been rumours that dragons had been involved but the survivors had fled South to Wist or to the Shadow Realms so information was scarce and untenable at best.

My heart thudded in my chest. I looked about at all these happy faces and felt my stomach clench. These people had all been involved in the fall of my kingdom. How had I not known about this? I felt Brenn glance my way and my skin felt cold.

"What about the Wryfirths?" I asked, perhaps there was bite in my voice as Hector gave me a strange look.

"The king is gone and the heir too. The youngest boy fled, and we know what happened to the Princess already."

Suddenly, I didn't want to sit on this bench anymore. Suddenly, I wasn't sure I could be here right now. I was too hot and too cold – everything felt tight. Maybe I was drunk? Or maybe I was just sad?

I knew that war was inevitable between Fynix and ourselves because of years of tension and battles. But the days of the Riachian Empire were long gone. For Draig to get involved, alongside the demons of Raize, what had changed within world that made this come to pass? What had Fynix promised them?

"I'm going to get mead," I said before quickly jetting in the direction of the table closest. Hector said something but I was too focused on the table to focus on anything else. I couldn't seem to shake the tightness in my throat.

Unfortunately, all that was left in the barrel was a dribble of dregs that filled my tankard with a sad gulp of foam. The bearded dragon-kin whose job it was to restock it claimed he was too drunk to do his job and from his beery smell alone, I was willing to believe him. With a bleary look in his eyes and a slur in his voice, he directed me to the next alley and told me to roll a new one over. Thus, I set off in the direction of the barrels and found them stored behind a rickety looking tavern and opposite a set of stables.

I went to pick the closest one up and immediately discerned my arms were unable to lift it at all. My fingers gripped the smooth panels of the wood to no avail. I hugged it tightly and heaved with all my might, but I could barely shuffle it. To make matters worse, I didn't see anyone around and there was no movement inside the tavern. If Brenn could feel my anger – he was ignoring it. Resolved to edge it forward, I shoved it inch by inch, cursing with every damned shove.

I tried twice more to haul it with my arms, but it was no use. I managed to kick it over into the snow, but couldn't push it despite all my effort. I wished I had motion magic to roll it for me or some other kind of propulsion method instead.

I tried using a foot to kick it on when suddenly I heard something like a *chuckle*. My foot slipped over the top and now I was straddling it with no balance. I slipped back into the snow, my legs falling over my head. Great - now even the horses were laughing at me.

I groaned as I rolled over. My fall hadn't been hard because of the cushion of fresh snow, but the cold leaked down my neck uncomfortably. Looking up at the stars, I wondered if my father was laughing at me too. At the stupid girl I was. He'd never had anything nice to say to me – only notes on my improvement.

But, maybe now he was up there with my mother, he would be the soft soul he once was. That's what Nanny Willow had said. After Mother passed, he had hardened into a crystal with unbreakable skin. One with an ancient grudge on his shoulders. The only father I had ever known, anyway.

I shook my head. Perhaps I was more drunk than I had thought.

There was another whicker from the stables, and I lifted my head.

A dark horse nudged between the sandy mare and the white stallion. I sat up and climbed to my feet. Its mane was black and tipped with white but what really made me stare were its eyes: a scarlet red.

"You're a Shadow-feld, aren't you?" I said, abandoning the barrel for now and heading over to the horse. His dark ears flicked forward as if he was surprised at the attention. I lifted a hand and slowly lowered it to the velvet, soft muzzle of the steed. He whinnied softly and I rubbed his nose. Those eyes – deep red – were full of nothing but love. "What's your name, handsome?"

"Coesau," a deep, gruff voice spoke behind me, making me jump and turn round. Coesau sniffed in the direction of the voice: standing in the street was a towering man wearing a long dark cloak. My arcane senses responded to the magic radiating from him –strangely, something about his magic felt warm. The magic of my people was something that felt fresh, like wind through the rushes on a lake or the first gale of spring. Obviously, this differed from person to person: but this…. this was new. It felt like standing next to an open fireplace.

"Is that your name, Coesau?" I said to the horse and rubbed his nose once more. "He's lovely," I said to the man. He drew closer and I could see that he looked different to any other dragon-kin I had seen, with tanned skin and eyes that were a deep scarlet too. He had a strong nose and a prominent chin; his jaw was stubbled with dark hair though the rest of his face was hidden in darkness and the high collar covering his neck.

"He doesn't usually get attention," the man added quietly. "Shadow-felds scare people this north of the Divide."

I shook my head and gave Coesau one last nuzzle with my knuckle.

"Nah, not this softie! You couldn't frighten a mouse – could you, Coesau?" I smiled at him one last time and then looked back at the man who hadn't moved, just tilted his head slightly as my eyes met his. He brought the smell of the forest with him as oak and pine filled my senses – clearly, he'd been travelling. Besides that, I couldn't tell much about him but he did cast an intimidating shape with his broad form. "I don't suppose you're feeling strong, are you?" I gestured to the barrel. "Turns out all my muscles are for show," I joked. He didn't respond, only looked over to the barrel and whispered something. Then he waved a gloved hand, and I felt a wave of magic brush past me – red smoke circled the barrel which, to my amusement, began to float.

I walked to it, my feet crunching in the snow. Now free of all weight I was able to push it. I grinned as I was able to give it a tiny shove and it floated off in the direction of the auditorium.

"Thanks, Mister," I said, pushing it on. The man inclined his head, stroking the head of the horse. I wheedled the barrel all the way up the road before I heard him speak again.

"You're welcome, Miss."

My blood iced over, but the barrel didn't drop. The magic thrummed through my fingertips, and I felt my heartbeat in my ears. The way he said it was so indifferent, I would've missed it if the road wasn't quiet. I slowly turned back to him; to retort; to laugh it off, I would do that. But he was gone - only a print in the snow remained. I stretched my senses and felt the fleeting presence of old magic, but nothing else.

I walked back up the road the snow falling faster now. But it didn't seem to dampen the mood of the partiers as I pushed the barrel over. The barrel still floated; the enchantment was strong enough to last all the way to the table where it landed with a thump. It woke the dragon-kin who had sent me, he was impressed I was able to carry it. I didn't correct him as he quickly tapped it, refilled his own and then poured me a tankard and then a second as a thanks.

I spotted Hector chatting animatedly to a snow-speckled Brenn as I headed back to the stables. There was still no hooded gentleman.

I stroked the nose of his horse and placed the tankard in the snow in front of him.

I wrote 'Thank You' in the snow before I headed back to the boys, drinking as I went.

Well after midnight, we decided to turn in and retreated back to Hector's house, Brenn and I taking beds in the healing quarters once more. But I couldn't sleep; what Hector had said turned around and around my mind. He spoke about it so casually; perhaps, being this

North of Riach meant that everything felt like it was happening so far away it was no concern of yours.

The betrayal of the dragon-kin stung, though I wasn't sure I should've been surprised. The dividing of the country was a wound I had expected, but the Demons and Fynix sharing a space seemed like a terrible idea. That was why the barrier between the East and West was first established. It was an alignment of peace that allowed both cultures to exist simultaneously. Without it, surely there would be chaos.

"You are thinking too loudly for me to sleep," Brenn called out from the bed next to me.

I scowled into the darkness.

"Wraiths don't need sleep," I replied. I kept my voice quiet in case we woke Hector up.

"That's not very nice," Brenn replied. "I don't sleep but I do meditate. Keep the mind clear and," he took an exaggerated breath in, "*positive.*"

"And I didn't think you liked Hector," I replied crossing my arms.

Brenn sighed. "I don't like anyone, your Majesty," he said simply. "But I don't hate him."

I gawped at him.

"High praise there."

"Shut up."

I grinned in the silence.

"We leave when the borders reopen," I told myself. If we left now it would be suspicious. This way we could leave in among the masses. "This won't be so bad."

Brenn popped his lips together.

"I guess so. Not that we have any money or edible support."

I ignored him.

"We go through Dion and then through the Dean lands to the South to get to Wist."

Brenn hummed.

"Seems less suicidal than the first plan, but still reeks of naïve idiocy."

I was satisfied with that response. My aunt surely had forces we could use and monopolise. From there we could surely gather some kind of response force. Wist was full of refugees – I could help them by calling for peace. And then…well we could figure out that bit when we got there.

"I wish I had your outlook," Brenn added in the silence.

"So, you think it'll work?" I asked.

Brenn shook his head. I heard him pop his lips.

"Hell no, but it'll be fun to watch."

Seven

The next morning, we found Hector in the kitchen making breakfast. It was a decent-sized room made of light-coloured wood with brass handles. Colourful plates were stacked on a wash tray and a collection of flowers grew on the windowsill in a copper pot. Warmed by the fire, Hector wore a pair of those brown trousers with all the pockets and a beige top with the sleeves rolled up and a lace-up collar.

Brenn was set on us sneaking away the moment the borders reopened, but my heart sank as I thought about betraying Hector. The healer was living proof that the goddess Celine had favourites: how else could he always be so happy? Brenn, hater of all things, said he found it irritating but, to me, the fathomless optimism was exactly what I needed.

"Do they not dance much in Dion?" Hector said, handing us two plates of sunny yellow eggs, bacon, toast, and sausages. I blinked. "Only you jumped at the chance last night. Even though you knew very few."

Brenn grabbed his fork and began devouring the meal, sating his appetite so he didn't eat Hector instead. Hector couldn't hide the sad look in his eyes as he did so. I knew he must think we come from poverty and that made me feel worse about the lies.

"No, they dance," I responded between bites, so I had time to forge my response. "But only on special occasions – like Yuletide, the Winter Solstice, Summer Solstice etcetera." I shrugged my shoulders. "Most of that time we were away at sea."

Hector nodded understandingly.

"Well, the people of Draig love a party," he said with a smile. "It's an unspoken rule that if a party doesn't have at least three fights then it is a bad party."

"And there had been six," I added. "So clearly it was one for the scholars."

I was resolved to come back here when things were better. Despite their role in my people's war, it seemed this part of the world was untouched by all of the horrors that came with it. Everything here seemed as fresh and as innocent as the snow on the ground. The riotous dragon-kin way was a belly full of laughs and I don't know - if I had not been as driven as I was, I could see myself being happy somewhere like here.

I wondered what Randall would have thought about it. He had never been anywhere close to here. It rarely snowed in Riach and the last time it did – he wasn't there. I wished I could have said goodbye, but his body was never returned to the castle. Of course, my father would have never allowed it.

I brushed the thoughts of Randall aside before the lead settled in my stomach. Hector joked about a party that was so riotous it went on for three weeks before the clan leaders themselves had to come and disperse it because nothing was getting done. As I looked into Hector's face, my heart ached. He'd only been good to us. He was a good person. He didn't deserve the drama we would bring him. It was kinder to run. That way we'd just become a weird story shared over eggs.

After breakfast I went back to the healing quarters to prepare for the outdoors, I shrugged on my jacket and did up the laces on the boots. The fire still crackled on and the flowers by the beds had been topped up. Hector's organised mess was still something to behold.

"I'm going to miss you when you both move on," Hector said as he came into the room. His golden eyes glowed as he came forward. He'd pulled on his jacket and adjusted his plaits again.

"And I'll miss you." Hector's soft half-grin was a knife in my heart. I ground my teeth together for being so sensitive. Brenn had it easy – the only emotion he seemed to have was hunger. I wasn't sure if sarcasm counted as a feeling.

Hector came and sat on the bed opposite me.

"You know," he started slowly, crossing an ankle over his knee. "Our family eyes are pretty good at spotting strange things."

My heart was in my throat, but I tried my best to keep a calm complexion.

"Oh, really? That's impressive."

He tilted his head to the side.

"I can tell when someone is lying," he said softly. "*Aaron.*"

Our eyes met and I knew there was no point in denying it. My chest went tight and I dug my hands into the mattress. I opened my mouth to reply but found I had to shut it again.

The jest was up. We had barely even left the starting line and we were already finished. My gaze dropped.

"Whatever it is," Hector started. "Whatever happened to the pair of you, I'm sure I can help."

I shook my head, gauging how much he knew. He hadn't mentioned Brenn, which was a good sign.

"This is just going to get more complicated, Hector."

He crossed his arms.

"I'm sure we can handle it together," he said. "The moment I brought you in I knew something was wrong – your glamour is too good. Most people with eyes like mine wouldn't have noticed it, but you don't look the way a male human is supposed to."

Words evaded me as he pressed on.

"I know when someone is lying because they almost always show it," he explained. "You don't even realise you are doing it."

I shook my head.

"I'm sorry, Hector." His golden eyes made my chest hurt.

"I can help," he offered, something desperate leaked into his voice. I shook my head again, but I took his hand and grasped it.

"I promise I'll tell you," I said, feeling his calloused palms in my hand. "But not now."

Hector nodded and gave my hand a squeeze. His smile was filled with warmth, but I couldn't ignore the flickers of sadness in his eyes.

"I'll be waiting," he added before he got up. "We leave for the Summit in twenty."

"I'll be ready," I called out and he gave me a happier look before he disappeared behind the door.

I sat there a little while longer. Part of me wanted to run back to Hector, but those feelings paled against the worry and heartache that grabbed my throat tightly and wouldn't let go. No, it wouldn't do. Now Hector knew it was only a matter of time before someone less kind discovered us too. Suspicious or not – we needed to leave now.

"*Brenn?*" I yelled through our mind-link.

"*I did hear, your Majesty,*" he said, coming round the corner. He lounged on the door frame, dark hair tied back in one long plait like how Ajax wore his.

"It's time to go."

He nodded. I set him to work gathering a pack of essentials for the road to Dion. They could catch us easily on horseback but by foot, we could evade by hiding.

My fingers were shaking as my heart started to thrum in my chest. A muddle of feelings overcame me that ranged from regret to fear. My stomach churned uncomfortably as I pulled my jacket on over my shoulders – the weight of it so much heavier now. I noticed there was a spare snippet of parchment left on the side of the table close to the door frame. I checked Brenn was not close by and wrote Hector a letter. I told him everything. Who I was, who Brenn was, and our mission. I apologised for the deception. And I promised I would make it up to him.

Finally, I signed it as Bryony Wryfirth and folded the paper over. I scrawled *Hector Athanas* across the front and left it on my bed where he could find it. Brenn was going to kill me, but I could deal with that. I'd rather have Hector find out from me – we owed him that much.

The Summit was riotously noisy and flooded with people. Besides the groups waiting in the hall for others to join their parties, citizens were swarming through the door to get to the pit below the platform or traversing the huge stone staircases on either side to reach their seats. I recognised the crests of family different families embroidered on the back of weathered cloaks or sewn on the pockets of jackets. Callas. Galanis. Zika. Vlahos. I remembered seeing their histories printed in books among the relics of the catacombs. As a symbol of their conquests, it seemed my ancestors took history when they couldn't find objects they deemed valuable. I had no doubt these people would want them back if they still knew about them.

Draig, like Riach, had many ancient families with colourful histories but unlike Riach they hadn't expanded their borders. Draig seemed big enough which was true, it dominated the north of any map. But that hadn't stopped my ancestors from trying. The Draigian artefacts in our treasury were a testament to that. My people's attempts at colonies anywhere this north of Riach failed miserably.

My stomach churned – perhaps that's why they got involved in the war after all. They were owed their revenge. I doubted my father's dedication to ancient feuds landed him any allies and maybe that had finally sealed his fate. I pushed those thoughts away as Hector led us through – focusing instead on staying out of anyone's way and planning our escape route.

I noticed a few Draigians shared similar features, like facial piercings that looked like the work of metal mages in the South of Riach; one had a bar through their nose and the other had the tip of their ear welded with a point. They seemed to like to adorn themselves with piercings in their lips or ears. I had my ears pierced when I was a child but to see so many of them stacked on the ears of the dragon-kin made me consider getting more.

Standing off to one side stood a group of people with long hair down their backs but the sides of their heads were shaved or plaited. The spaces where hair could grow had been filled with tattoos of flowers or black clan marks woven into patterns. Tattoos usually made my skin crawl – they were part of demon culture and had been a symbol of barbarity to the likes of my father. However, these designs spoke of art and control – far from the demon ink I had previously imagined. Among them, I spotted a girl who looked younger than me standing by the side of a man with the same style of white hair. They both had eyes that were glowing purple and violet scales on the slants of their high cheekbones. The group were not as noisy as the rest and seemed to have kept to themselves in the corner.

"Hector! Hector!" I suddenly heard Daphne holler over the noise. I spotted Hector's parents and a scowling Inigo in the doorframe between this room and the next. Then a short sharp horn sounded three times – making me jump and Brenn chuckle.

The congregations of people started making their way through the foyer and we pressed our backs against the wall to not get caught in the wave of people suddenly making their way to their seats. Eventually, we navigated through the crowd to Daphne and Ajax. Inigo had already disappeared.

"I'm so glad you made it!" Daphne said, embracing her son and then turning to us delightedly. "The DuVales are here too. They are our leaders – they were in Fynix until they flew back a few weeks ago."

My stomach grew tight: perhaps they weren't temporary allies at all. I still wondered how Fynix had convinced Draig to get involved after all this time. Hector's brows furrowed.

"It seemed the Horned King has bought Aegius after all," Hector crossed his arms.

"I guess we're about to find out," Daphne cast a look behind us. The stragglers were sneaking in to find their seats. "There should be some places to stand left in the pit next to the stage," she said, "go get a good spot." Then she turned to her husband and Hector. "Ajax, you're on dragon duty with the boys – I'm sure Inigo is skulking in a corner somewhere. Keep an eye out will you? Before you go, Hector, I need to borrow you." Ajax gave us a wave before heading up the stairs with Daphne lingering behind. Her face had misplaced its usual joy and seemed somewhat pensive. However, Hector either hadn't noticed or didn't want to mention it. His friendly smile made my chest ache all over again.

"See you in a moment, lads," Hector said. I returned the smile.

"In a bit," I said. When Hector was out of sight, Brenn turned to me with a feigned look of empathy.

"Feelings are such a burden," he started, "I could always eat your heart."

I gave him a deadpan look.

"Thanks, but I need that."

The foyer was empty: no one would notice us sneaking out now. Yes, we'd be gone before anything more happened. But looking at the door I could hear the thrum of voices and feel the apprehension in the air – whatever that was about to happen here was going to be big. I could feel it – my arcane magic senses noticed something of what was about to come. Tensions were at a boiling point, emotions ranged from curiosity to fear: change was in the air like an impending storm.

Perhaps it was just anxiety clawing at my thoughts or just my unruly curiosity, but I found myself unable to move. The people partly responsible for the destruction of Kya were behind that door, plotting their next step. I turned to Brenn; my face must've said it before I voiced it because he was shaking his head rapidly.

81

"Let's go watch whatever news there is and then leave," I said.

"That's a terrible idea."

"Look, they won't even notice us."

Brenn stuck me with a glare.

"There are many powerful presences in there if it goes sideways," he gritted his teeth. "It could be a bother."

"It's not going to go sideways," I said assuredly. "Besides, if it does, then you might get to eat something."

With those words, Brenn's jaw slammed shut. The temptation was too strong and a muscle in his forehead appeared to twinge.

"You are awful at sticking to plans," Brenn seethed. He crossed his arms, and I couldn't help but smile. He worried too much.

"All we need to do is listen," I said, steeling myself for the onyx armour of the Fynix forces. "If we do that then we couldn't possibly get into trouble."

Brenn raised one eyebrow.

I took his elbow and dragged him inside.

The noise that surrounded us as we stepped into the sphere was deafening. Where Brenn and I stood in the pits we were pressed right against the back; if the plinth at the centre of the Summit hadn't been on a raised platform, I wouldn't have seen a thing. I mean, I wasn't small, but some of these people were giants or at least had giant blood in them. All the people around us seemed to have pints of mead or other drinks in their hands. It seemed this meeting was just as important as it was a social gathering – well, Hector *had* said they had come from all over.

A short but stocky young woman with a flame pixie crop of red hair stamped her foot twice in the centre of the stage. Instantly, people ceased their conversations. She pressed her jaw shut tightly but there was something of a smile in her eyes and at the corner of her lips.

"Welcome, one and all," she called out. A resounding cheer went out as people stamped their feet on the floor, banging the railings of their balconies. The woman looked on approvingly; upon a closer look, I could see one of her eyes was a shade of green whereas the other was brown. She wore knee-high boots, laced to just under the knee. Her coat was short at the front and long at the back, in a tan hide with a cream fur lining. The family crest – a dragon perched on a crescent moon – had been engraved on the shoulders of the sleeves. She wore bronze gauntlets that matched a bronze torque at her neck. Then the woman raised her hand as the place fell silent.

I couldn't imagine anything political being decided in a place like this. My experience (albeit limited as it was) was that everything was decided behind closed doors in my father's study. Important matters were never discussed in such an open way.

"*Different cultures have very different ways of keeping the peace, your Majesty*," Brenn said, smugly.

"*I know that.*" I retorted quietly in his thoughts. "*It is just surprising to see them in practice.*"

"Our leader, my father, Aegius DuVale, has some announcements he would like to share with us," the young woman said, gesturing behind her.

A giant man with a long red beard and the same mixed eyes stepped up onto the stage. The moment his foot touched the floorboards of the platform, the audience lit up with cheers and yells. All around us, the people raised their hands and roared in greeting. They banged on the wooden bannisters in front of them or raised their drink or fists in acknowledgement.

The leader cast his hands wide, a wide smile on his face. I noticed two elongated teeth at the bottom of his jaw. So, this was their king, a towering male with a black cloak lined with wolf fur. Two buckles fastened across his chest and under that was a jacket of tanned leather, the same bronze gauntlets as his daughter, and dark breeches with those riding boots that dragon riders wore.

"My people!" he called out, as the noises finally ceased and the whole area listened in attentively. "We have prospered these many years alone, trade has boomed, our borders remain secure: the North belongs to the Dragons!" That was met with more cheers. Behind the man, his daughter stood in the shadows, nodding at every word. "As the world has festered in turmoil, we remain steadfast, like the Mountains of Sivia: unbreakable."

The noise made my ears ring.

"We have witnessed the great house of Wryfirth fall into

83

oblivion, the Tyrant beheaded, and its people scattered. The ways of the magic folk of Riach are no more."

I was glad at that moment for the wall behind me. My father's empty eyes stared at me, and nausea overtook me. Back here, no one could see my face. The Dragon-kin's leader changed his tone.

"But there are calls for us to rejoin the world," the man said. "Much has changed in recent weeks," he began. "And with the ineffable threat of the Wraith of the Wastes set to wreak havoc on society once more, we need support from beyond our borders."

Next to me, Brenn was suddenly looking more engaged than ever. But I couldn't stop the sinking feeling in my bones as a darkly clad group edged towards the stage.

Aegius gestured to them, and breaking the silence that had now descended, I could hear the familiar *chinks* and *clicks* of their metallic armour as they braced the stage. They received no applause when they stepped onto the platform: instead, almost a shiver seemed to pass through the crowd. I recognised the pointed ears of the Fae and the onyx armour hidden by a fancy cloak tied across one shoulder. One, the leader I assumed, had a sword with a dark blade hitched at his waist. On his head were the jagged horns of the Fynix people. The symbol of the Horned King's forces.

I saw five other soldiers with similar attire now standing next to the young DuVale and her eyes were wide. The rest trailed in and stood in behind the stage.

I could feel the nerves creeping into my gut – their presence sent chills right through me. A full platoon of Fynix soldiers was here in the North; it seemed the reach of the Horned King had only continued to grow after the fall of my country.

Murmurs broke out among the people around us.

"What is Aegius going on about?"

"Draig is better alone."

"The Fynix are a bloodthirsty people – look what they did to Riach."

He raised a hand once more.

"Which is why Draig is to be forged anew," Aegius declared. "As official allies with the Horned King's Fynix and their endeavours."

The response around the room was palpable, and behind Aegius, his daughter's face fell.

My heart tightened. I watched as people turned, plainly conflicted. Some in the crowd outwardly voiced their worries, whilst others cheered, banged on the railings, or threw their drinks at his feet. Or his head. This went on for a few minutes before Aegius could get control of the crowd.

Next to me, Brenn lay back on the wall with his arms crossed. I hadn't looked at him directly, but he leaned in close.

"Well, Fynix did win the war," Brenn said quietly to me. "Of course, Aegius is very frightened of me. But I'm sure he's more afraid of them." He sighed dramatically and rolled his eyes. "Oh dear, that's a few more enemies for you then, isn't it?"

"Oh, shut up," I said, focusing back on the scene in front of me. If I saw a grin on his face, I would have to punch him. This pushed my hope of forming allies with the dragon-kin swiftly into the Dark Sea. My people had seen enough war, but my hopes for a peaceful diplomatic solution were fading fast.

But for the people of Draig? I think we just witnessed their invasion: quiet and unassuming as it was. If the platoon standing on the stage were any indication, the door had been opened for them. Brenn's power was legendary, but I wasn't sure Aegius could pin this extreme political move entirely on the Wraith.

Suddenly, the door closest to the raised platform open. A tall figure entered, and my heart jumped into my throat. I instantly recognised him from last night's festivities but in daylight he looked irrevocably different. The magical power radiating from him was immense – he was a different person entirely. Sharp edges, shadows, and death.

His hood was still drawn up, but his tanned skin looked gaunter in daylight compared to his dark cloak which was drawing shadows across his long face and sharp jawline. However, this time I noticed the savage-looking twin swords hanging at his waist. Across his chest were dual bandoliers filled with what I imagined were knives, mottled steel pauldrons sat on his shoulders, and across his wrists, he sported grey silver gauntlets. He was a warrior of standing – everyone could feel it, including me. Even some of the Fynix soldiers behind the generals exchanged looks and shuffled nervously. Now, in daylight, I knew he was no dragon-kin: he was a demon.

Silence swept through the headquarters as people craned to get a look, but everyone moved away from him. Next to me, Brenn raised his eyebrows.

"This just got considerably worse," he murmured into my thoughts. *"A Bonekeeper."*

The man stood taller than even the clan leader – nearly seven feet. Nothing about this man was the same as last night. His eyes, red as fresh blood, caused my skin to go cold. His expression reminded me somewhat of Brenn when I had first met him – a jaded look of disinterest. But even from where we stood, I could feel the presence of his magic – though this time it was grim, dark, foreboding, and white hot. I glanced to Brenn and saw that he had gone completely still.

My blood iced over. Even with his hood up, I could see the shape of his face – a long nose, heavy eyebrows and defined cheekbones. I knew that high demons or noble ones had two forms rather than just one – this must've been its mortal form.

"My friends," Aegius continued. His face had become pale. "We are honoured to have General Titae of the Demon King's Bonekeepers here with us. He is here ahead of his squadron, to search for the Wraith of the Wastes. As I am sure you are all aware, our world is mobilising against this creature, and we have heard reports of other units being sent from all over the world to help end and to prevent-"

"Look at the fuss you caused," Brenn tutted in my mind, pulling me from Aegius' ill-received explanation. Neither were helping the nerves filling my chest.

"Sorry, next time, just eat me, will you?"

I glanced towards the door – to leave, we would need to do some serious weaving. I turned back to the front; the Bonekeeper said nothing as he surveyed the room. My chest pounded painfully.

"I accidentally did something last night," I said to Brenn in his mind, allowing him to access the memory of my interaction with Coesau, including the part where he saw through the glamour.

Brenn's jaw dropped.

"You made friends with his horse?" he hissed at me in a low

voice. I couldn't take my eyes off the general. My stomach went tight —

"I thought he was just a traveller!" I retorted quietly. "And Coesau was lovely."

"The floor is now open for discussion," Aegius announced, and the hollers came from above. People yelled questions out, but I couldn't hear them as the crowd swelled with pent-up fury. I pressed myself as back as I could go.

"How drunk were you?" Brenn snapped. The Fynix unit on the stage looked at the broiling crowd with concern – a few of their hands fell onto the handles of their short swords. The archers moved into defensive positions too, nocking arrows to the string of their bows. "We need to go now," Brenn's voice was low as he started to move along the wall, weaving between the dragon-kin with me in pursuit.

Strangely, the Bonekeeper didn't move at all. Apart from his eyes – they remained wary and alert. But as those red eyes fell on our area of the room: he stopped. Despite the shadows, the crowd, the noise, and our position, I felt his focus.

Those eyes met mine and the General stilled. His gaze slipped to Brenn and then back to me. My blood iced over as the hair stood up on the back of my neck. My heart missed a beat.

He tilted his head.

Whatever Aegius had said next caused outrage which I caught the tail end of as Brenn wrapped his hand around my arm as he yanked me from the wall.

"We're fucked," he said as we fought through the crowd, I didn't look to see but I could still feel the chill on the back of my neck. Away, away – we had to get away. "We're so unbelievably fucked." Brenn's voice was tight.

We finally reached the door and thankfully, someone was pushing it open from the other side. I caught it and pulled it forward.

"Thank you." Behind us, the crowd seemed to be rapidly moving away from the entryway. I felt my stomach drop instantly as my blood seemed to have gone still. The dark hood emerged first, along with the rest of his imposing figure.

"You're welcome." The Bonekeeper said, letting the door shut behind him. Brenn froze behind me. I was tall but he was a tower. The ease I felt at the stables was long gone as I found that I couldn't move.

Of course, he could portal. He reeked of the kind of powerful magic needed for it. Jumping from one spot to another – it symbolised a mastery of the sorcery of space.

Around us, the crowd seemed to have moved aside to form a path from us to the platform at the centre. The voices died down and an uneasy silence replaced it as everyone stared. The Bonekeeper brandished a dagger – a curved, wicked blade with a leather-bound handle in his right hand.

Neither of us moved. The crowd around us had fallen silent.

"What is the meaning of this?" Aegius demanded from the centre. "General, explain yourself."

The Bonekeeper didn't lift his head to acknowledge him. Those red irises seemed to glow as they took Brenn and I in fully. Questions filled his eyes. I swallowed the heart in my throat and gave him a smile.

"Good morning," I said in an upbeat tone. "Sleep well?"

The Bonekeeper said nothing as he moved closer to me. I kept our distance and Brenn moved like my shadow beside me.

The Clan leader did not take kindly to being ignored.

"Leave my people alone, General," he bellowed from the stand. "You stand gravely outnumbered if you try anything here."

His eyes narrowed and only then did the general's expression turn icy.

"They're not *your* people," he said bitingly, in that low voice of his. "You've been harbouring the Wraith, Aegius."

Gasps of horror sounded through the headquarters, and fear broke the stillness. People pulled away from us, when I saw the Fynix Fae's troops edging forward I knew we had no choice.

"Brenn, I give you permission to protect us," I said quickly, feeling the magic surge through me as if it could sense the danger, "by any means."

I heard the arrow loose before I saw it. It flew with a whooshing sound towards my shoulder, but Brenn caught it easily. I saw his eyes change to a dark gold and my stomach clenched. The movements happened so fast they seemed to become slow.

"You take them – I can handle myself," I said to him.

Brenn narrowed his eyes. "If you say so."

The wraith's form faded to the shadow monster he was at his core; a storm of gnashing teeth and growls filled the air as the headquarters were plunged into darkness. A long tail whipped around as he lunged for the archer, and I moved back to draw away from the Bonekeeper. Then the rest of the Fynix platoon lunged for Brenn, and his giant form disappeared behind me.

The thunder of panicked feet and voices sounded all around as people ran for the exits or readied to fight. Some had magicked the witchlights to blast the space with bright rays but against Brenn's magic, their beams waned like the moon behind clouds. The din too was muted behind his deafening roars which made the hair stand up on my neck.

I didn't take my eyes off my foe for a moment as the screams of the Fynix filled the air. The grisly sound of bones snapping under pressure and the overwhelming smell of blood were enough to convince me Brenn had everything exactly where he wanted it.

The Bonekeeper kept Brenn in his sights, but he seemed to know I had the Wraith under my power. I wondered if he had seen my hand yesterday during the exchange with his horse. Either way, he drew one of his swords too as I readied my magic. I pulled the lightning from my fingers like thread, and as he lunged, I leashed one of them. The lightning flashed between us as he dodged it and swung a sword to my right. He was so fast his blade cut my jacket before I could move; tearing a gash across the shoulder before I had time to leash another bolt. If he was fazed by the forbidden magic, he didn't let it show as he swung a second time that I had to duck for. I felt the burn of the lightning as it left my fingers: my options for offence were limited but I was by no means powerless.

"There I was thinking you were nice," I said as I scrambled over the platform. I had no idea where the clan leader was or anyone else for that matter. All I needed to focus on was staying alive. Brenn wouldn't let me die – he couldn't. The pact would compel him to support me. But that didn't mean I couldn't get hurt, and that didn't mean Brenn couldn't be distracted.

More Draigians had emerged with weapons to attack Brenn who beat them easily in his giant form. Brenn swiped at the demon with his tail, but he dodged it, the Wraith's attention divided between the Bonekeeper and the onslaught of new attackers.

"You're aiding the Wraith of the Wastes," he said, jumping easily up on the platform.

"Technically he's aiding me," I said, pulling to my feet only to have a hand come up behind me and get me by the neck. I felt a curved blade against my throat. I pulled up against it and felt the bite of it against my palm and cut into his. Blood flowed down my hand as I was pressed against his solid form.

"What do you mean, Witch?" His voice was a growl now.

I threw my hand up in the air. He could see the mark among the blood and all the red gave me an idea.

"Any questions?"

I shook my bloodied hand and splattered us with it. Using the motion to call a bolt of lightning, I threw it back into the demon's face, burning my hand but making him lose his grip as the stun sent him stumbling backwards.

I escaped his grasp and infused my blood with magic. I drew the symbol of control on my arm, the diamond crossed twice, and reached out as my blood took hold of his body. Brenn's savagery was all I could hear but I focused on my spell with the precious few seconds I had before the Bonekeeper was on me again.

Blood magic felt different compared to the lightning, it made my bones ache. I watched as the tan skin covered in my blood blotted and leeched out like bites from invisible creatures - marring his face and drawing the colour. He froze and I knew I had him. I saw him try to summon a portal, so I tightened the muscles in his fingers and gritted my teeth. He gasped as the power took over and his eyes darted back and forth as I struggled to hold him.

I hadn't done this on such a big body before, but I stretched my blood magic out through his veins, holding his form as tightly as I could. I felt his power inflame my own; now I was in his system it was going to be difficult for him to release himself.

I could feel his fury throttling like a flame under my fingers. It travelled up my neck and coursed through my heart with unnatural heat. Those red eyes scorched into mine and I knew should I fail, I would die.

I pulled the blood from his knees and made him drop before holding him there.

"Impressive, your Majesty," Brenn said as he reached the stage. The darkness was fading and the area around us was disturbingly empty of Fynix soldiers.

"Oh, this is nothing," I hissed through my teeth as the general fought hard against me. His crimson eyes stared daggers. I could feel his power in my veins, hot like coals; he wouldn't be caught off-guard again. Luck had been on my side for this battle, but I would need to train seriously to hold my ground properly. I overpowered him with Brenn, and my lightning was intense - but he had years of experience. Not that it would ever stop me from fighting.

"I could've taken him," Brenn said, as if to himself. Then the wraith dissolved into a mass of smoke and morphed into a new beast, a great lizard with a sweeping tongue. It took me a moment to realise he was a dragon – or at least his interpretation of one.

"You were very helpful," I ground out. Brenn's expression didn't change.

"It seems like you had it under control here though," he said, gawking at the general. Brenn opened his mouth wide and kept it open as if I was going to grab the General and haul him in like a sugar cube for a horse.

"Leave him alive," I said, the strain of the struggling was waning. "If we anger the Demon King, there'll be no hope of reconciliation."

"We didn't show the Fynix such mercy," Brenn shot back.

"I think we might be past reconciliation."

I glanced around at the empty auditorium. The sounds of groaning Draigians filled the air, and I felt a deep shame crawl through me. A low voice growled out in the darkness.

"Princess?"

I turned to him, the Bonekeeper had halted his struggling.

"The one and only," I said as his expression changed. I took this moment of stillness to lower his blood pressure. His eyes flashed once at me before darkening and he dropped onto his back. He was unconscious and with any more blood loss, soon I would be too. The demon's blade had scored deep between my fingers. I would need to bandage myself up soon but that would have to come next.

"Get us out of here," I said as I crawled onto Brenn's back.

"With pleasure," he said before reaching up high into the sky. A few flaps and we were in the air. The dragons that remained above watched on in curiosity as we passed. Hector's face was crestfallen among them.

He soon shrunk in the distance, but I could still feel his sad eyes following us as we made our way out of Clawton. The sun was out, and I squinted against the brightness as Brenn glided over the city. The buildings below sprawled out in curved shapes among the trees. My throat felt tight, and I decided to look ahead instead. The endless white space stretched on for what seemed like aeons. The higher we went up, the cooler the air became; I wrapped the coat tighter around myself.

"I didn't kill any Draigians – only disabled those who wanted to harm you."

I inspected my burned hand – the blood had conducted my lightning and brought the veins to the surface in tangled red strikes.

"I admire your restraint," I replied, raising my voice over the wind. "That explains why there were so many Fynix left behind."

"My hunger has no bounds," Brenn said as we drifted along past the rural houses. I couldn't resist and glanced back. No one was following us – everyone had dragons and yet no one was willing to attack Brenn. His reputation proceeded him before this - what had transpired would surely only grow his infamy.

"You flatter me with your thoughts. But it is just psychic magic, your Majesty," Brenn added. "They cannot follow, they must flee; it's a simple command and once they hear it. It's a very effective deterrent."

It hadn't worked on everyone though; the dragons wouldn't leave without their riders. I remembered Hector's face and my stomach twisted. I shook my head, thinking instead of the general and how close he had come to victory. My magic only had an advantage over those who were caught off-guard and next time he would be prepared.

"I barely won against him," I said. "I need to train. And so do you." Brenn sniffed at that. "You can't eat all your problems."

"I definitely can."

"Where now? The Fynix will be on high alert."

"Dion is closest."

"Dion it is."

Eight

The wind growled louder as we edged towards Dion's borders. The snow persisted and fell in powdery flurries; the towns created islands among the endless white that whipped by as we passed them. My fingers had numbed with the cold, and it seemed my heart had too.

I couldn't stop thinking about that general. The quickness of his movements, his lethal ability with those blades, and his magical power made my heart pound. I would surely be dead now if it hadn't been for my blood magic disabling him. I could still feel his muscles constricting under my fingers, his heart struggling against me as I tightened the surrounding blood; the pain shooting through his nerves like dagger strikes. How easily I could've killed him then - but he wasn't another rat from the catacombs.

Those red eyes had pierced mine, filling my veins with ice. I could feel the power that radiated from him as I forced him to yield to me. It was like a raw flame fighting with an icy wind to stay aglow. It was enough to make anyone tremble: but I refused to fear him. I had endured enough brutal soldiers in my life thus far to concede to one now I was free. Especially not a demon.

I knew if I peered into his head, I would see nothing but darkness. Had I let him, I would be dead now – nursing my ambitions alongside my father in the afterlife. I found myself grinding my teeth together. The Fynix Fae were one foe but the demons of Raize were another feat entirely; our exchange rattled around in my head.

How drunk was I to not notice he wasn't a dragon-born? Perhaps the alcohol had thrown him off too – if he could portal, the chances are that he could see right through the glamour. I cringed at the thought. I guess I had the Dragon's Breath to thank for that.

I hadn't met many demons before – only envoys from Raize who had come to talk trade at the solstice events or public holidays. And most of them passed as Riachians. I knew some could sport horns, serpent tongues, claws, or even fangs – perhaps without the hood the General would look different too.

I wished I had studied more on the demon people then, but the

94

Divide between the East and the West had meant that cultures were utterly estranged. The Shadow Lands: Qicog, Raize, Faytonia, Smotia, Silvia, and of course the Wastes, lived such radical lives in comparison to us as they lived without the sun. I shuddered at the thought – days without light seemed such a miserable way of existence.

Of course, Riachian priests and templars would claim it was due to the unholiness of the people: Celine refused to shed her light upon them. It was the Great Balance that had been upset by citizens turning from her. The Great Balance, of course, was a theory depending on peace – a historically ignored doctrine from even my own people.

My father had always spoken of the Demon people in disgust. But he would happily take their money if he knew he could benefit from it. Half of our trade in the city came beyond the Divide, not that it mattered to my father; his prejudices ruled his mind.

I wasn't my father, but I felt a gnawing sense of guilt in me from the deaths of those Fynix and what I had done to the General. It crept into my veins – perhaps my mercurial nature came from him? I grimaced at the thought.

"They were trying to kill you," Brenn snapped suddenly. "They would have too. And I have to eat." The noise of the wind whistling past filled the silence.

"I don't want their blood on my hands," I said.

"I devoured, not you," Brenn snapped. "You think very loudly, you know that?

"Sorry, I just don't want to turn out like him."

"I should hope not, he's dead." I rolled my eyes. Brenn groaned then before speaking again. "Are you willing to do whatever is necessary for your people?"

"Of course," I said firmly.

"Then you will have to be comfortable doing far worse, your Majesty," Brenn replied.

I didn't reply after that, instead turning over our exploits in Draig in my head. Hector's horrified face was etched into my mind. I tried to push him out of my thoughts, but then I recalled the letter I had put in his bedroom – well, soon enough, he'd know the whole woeful tale. But the damage had already been done.

"You know you shouldn't have written that letter," Brenn spoke into my thoughts. *"Someone could've found it."*

"It doesn't matter now."

Brenn was quiet then. For a few moments more there was just the wingbeat every so often and then the wind.

"Might I suggest, her Majesty stops moping?" Brenn added. "Frown lines are not becoming."

"I'm not moping," I replied. "I just wasn't counting on us being discovered so quickly – the foolish part of me wanted us to gain allies in Draig."

"You are nothing if not stupidly optimistic," Brenn replied. "But this was never going to be easy."

"I know that."

"Do you?"

"I have a strong resolve about this, Brenn. I'll do it – or I'll die trying."

A moment passed.

"Can I eat you then?"

"How could I possibly say no?"

Eventually, we neared the edge of one of the ports on the east border of Dion. Fishing was one of the main trades this far north of their land so we would hopefully be able to find passage to Wist discreetly aboard a cargo ship. Of course, Brenn was not impressed by my plan - but he couldn't fly to Wist when we were trying to be discreet. Not now they knew we were together. Brenn had to hide in clouds a few times as dragons, armed for war, barrelled past, no doubt looking for us. He evaded them, of course, but it would only be a matter of time before a rider with Hector's skill caught up to us. The dragon-kin's forces, when prepared, could launch lethal airborne attacks. The risks were not worth it, and I wanted to avoid unnecessary bloodshed.

Lights glowed from what I assumed was the centre, though the sky was black as pitch. I couldn't see where the land ended and the ocean began. Judging by the sun's descent, I believed it was early evening – summer meant long days, which I was thankful for. The smell of the sea was strong with salt and made me think of the Isle once more.

Brenn had bragged that a normal dragon would've needed to have at least four days in total to complete such an arduous journey, but Wraiths were made of sturdier stuff: like souls of the dead.

So, we'd been able to make it within two. Only stopping once for me to sleep in a deserted stable that was home to bats. The temperature had warmed considerably as we headed south which made it easier for me to rest but I found myself missing the picturesque snow-filled scenes of the Northern country.

Hector had filled his jacket for me on the off chance I got hungry between the hefty meals he prepared for us. I found small, wrapped loaves, slices of cake, and hand-sized cookies among the multitude of pockets. Brenn too had stolen odds and ends from the kitchen that materialised on the dragon's back once every so often. Even though they were delicious, they sat like lumps of stone in my gut, and I found I couldn't finish them. Instead, I used the cloth they were kept in to bind my hand until I had enough energy in me to cast a healing spell. I was no healing Mage, so it made my palm itch but thankfully the gash looked less fearsome as the heat from the magic melted away.

It was warmer than it had been in Draig, but a chill breeze was enough for me to keep Hector's jacket on; it still smelled of him, hay, and dragons. It was strange seeing the darkened ground instead of frosted snow even though it hadn't been that long. We had seen the inside of the tower just over a week ago, though it felt like a lifetime had passed since then. Sounds of life drifted through the summer air; faint inklings of music and laughter were audible, even from this distance.

Brenn landed in a wheat field with a thud; long wispy sheathes crunched under his feet as his tail swept long stretches behind him flat. I slid off his back and landed softly among the beaten rows. Brenn's dragon form swirled back into that familiar black mass of writhing wispy shadows; he emerged, unsmiling, in the tall, lithe form he'd worn in Clawton. He shook his head as he readjusted his hair.

"Your Majesty, I doubt we will find suitable accommodations here," he said, giving me an expectant look as he stomped towards me. He sniffed as his lip curled at our new surroundings. "This place is a dump. It smells like fish guts, pipe-smoke, and manure."

I gritted my teeth as I headed to the edge of the field. I hoisted myself over the weather-beaten fence and landed with a grunt as Brenn stepped through it, his body reforming on the other side. His eyebrows raised at my expression. "If I don't eat soon, I will have to stay in my Wraith form."

I shook my head – Brenn was sneaky when it came to hiding his power.

"Didn't you just eat like twenty people?"

"Thirty-six."

I waved my hand.

"You'll be fine," I replied. Brenn crossed his arms, his footsteps getting louder as we joined a road.

"Surely, I should be the judge of that."

"Find us somewhere to sleep," I said. "And some way to pay."

Brenn nodded and gave me a grin. The road to town was littered with remnants of what looked to be old watch towers and ruins. I recognised them right away– they looked like the ones that guarded the borders of Kya. I wondered why they had been left in such disrepair. A residential area had been abandoned too – what once were once houses, were now a collection of walls; reclaimed by nature, with moss and flowers sprouting across every surface, boards covering up doorways, roofs fallen in.

"I wonder what happened here?" I thought aloud. Brenn shrugged.

"Wasn't me." I gave him a deadpan look. "Like you weren't just wondering that."

The ruins gave way into woodland before we saw some newer buildings grow into view among glowing orange witchlights. The first homes were short and strongly built with carved stone bricks. Unlike Kya's uniform buildings, each here seemed a different size and shape. Some were high with multiple floors with just as many windows, while others were short and seemed to be descending underground. Torches filled the streets with light, couples walked arm in arm, and a group of youths only a few years younger than me ran past us, chasing what looked like a big, shaggy dog. I knew that because of the disruptive weather, shifters wore loose clothing – drawstring trousers and wrap-around tunics that were easy to put on and take off. It didn't seem like dresses were necessary here at all – I saw women wearing tunics and trousers just like the men. As we neared the centre the noise of nightlife grew.

Despite the time, the streets bustled. Many of the taller buildings doubled as businesses and the alleys between them led to even more houses. This space was condensed with people and thriving enterprises, not all of it savoury too.

"I believe this place was once called Agrieble," Brenn said. "Dion is shifter land – so everyone from anywhere comes from here."

"Why is that?" I asked as we walked through the town – there must be an inn around here somewhere. Brenn stared at me.

"Surely, you know the stories, your Majesty?" he said. "They are part animal the same way the werewolves are, but without the rich heritage. Outcasts tend to clump together."

Shifters only appeared a few centuries ago – no one quite knew how they came to be. Dion – which was originally a lawless territory – became where most of them dwelled. They accepted our rule because they couldn't stand on their own feet. But judging by the state of the ruins outside the town, I wasn't sure if I could say that anymore.

The town centre was livelier. Among the bigger buildings nearer the seafront, there were many repurposed official buildings, some of which had kept a few of the original Riachian stylings like the arched windows and the painted exteriors. One, which I assumed was once a town hall, had been turned into a fighting den, and another, originally destined for sea trade, had been repurposed into a busy inn. But they were not the only buildings that had once occupied very different roles. I spotted what was once barracks of some kind now being used as a house of indulgence.

The town was full: a circuit of taverns, a trading post, a few inns, a few stores that had closed for the night, but several tents with interesting wares ranging from card reading, and fortune telling, to a variety of things you could smoke, remained open. The alleys were full of bright witchlights and signs promising gambling or salacious company with golden signs wrought in iron hanging above doorways.

Kya had always had strict policies for this type of business that kept them away from prying eyes, but here they were out in the open. There was a florist who had closed for the night and was sequestered between two massage parlours, and no one batted an eye. Then, when I looked up, I saw rows of laundry hung between the houses. People drank on balconies overlooking the square despite the long summer sun receding – enjoying the temperate weather and the busy evening.

I caught Brenn snickering at me.

"Just look at your face," he chuckled. "Like you've never been outside before."

I shrugged my shoulders.

"Sometimes it feels that way," I replied honestly.

I never saw enough of Kya either. Exploration was coveted. So, when I found the catacombs, it felt like Celine herself had heard my prayers.

Despite the nature of our travels, I couldn't shake the thrill of adventure that still lingered in me. I wondered what Randall would think of all of this. There was no doubt in me that he would've loved it. Randall had family in Wist too – once upon a time I had dreamt of running away there with him. Too easily was that dream destroyed.

The colourful clientele must've been used to newcomers coming to town as they didn't glance twice at us. We found a boisterous inn parked a little way off the centre with stables attached. The planks that built it were made of old wood worn away by time. The sign hung above it rattled with the wind: *The Last Straw*. Men and women wrapped in colourful cotton clothes hung around the door smoking pipes and laughing, their faces red with alcohol. The smell of the sea was strong, and the sound of the waves filled any break in conversation with a lull of water.

I focused inward to summon my magic; as I had suspected, they were all shifters. Their presence wasn't anything to be afraid of – judging by the magic surrounding them, I would've assumed they were regular shifters – dogs, cats, rabbits, and the like. Irregulars were the ones we should be concerned about as they were powerful shifters. They couldn't control their powers and, according to Sorrel, it drove them mad. There were stories about them trapped in their forms forever that made my skin crawl.

"Any ideas, Majesty?" Brenn whispered.

"Acquire us funds from whoever has the worst mind while I find us a seat."

Brenn's lip twisted into a smile, and he quickly side-stepped away from me and headed back into the centre with too much spring in his step. Grimacing, I steeled myself and headed inside. I kept my face as impassive as I could as I stepped forward and through the porch.

The noise greeted me first: jeering, chattering, laughter, combined with the noise of glass smashing, and a drunken fiddler player swaying on his stool. The smell of mead, candle wax, and freshly baked bread filled the place pleasantly. An immense fireplace roared away, making the tavern as warm as a goose-feather duvet around my shoulders.

A colourful mix of all peoples filled the room. Besides the clusters of shifters, a few dragon-kin were throwing back spirits like they were water; a woman with a hand covered in blue scales used her tail to hoist a glass bottle high and pour the next drinks. I noticed some dark-skinned figures by the bar with intricate patterns around their eyes and across their faces; it took me a moment to realise they were Hydraen Fae, and I tried to hide my surprise. They must've been used to a much hotter climate than here, hence the thick robes and cloaks.

I hadn't realised shifters could sometimes have animal features too, but I spotted a couple making eyes at each other; a dark-haired girl's cat-like ears twitching as she blushed and the tanned girl sitting opposite her looking delighted. As the tanned woman tilted her head to come in closer, I realised her brown hair was actually a collection of feathers growing back across her head.

A lizard and a rat sparred on the bar top before the red-haired barmaid shooed them off and they continued the tiny brawl on the floor. The barmaid pressed her lips together and grabbed the broomstick.

There was a spare table in the corner furthest from the fire, tucked next to a curtain. I made my way over there quietly, shrugging off Hector's jacket which now was too warm to wear. I noticed the table closest to the fire had garnered much attention, people surrounding it with pints of mead in hand. The word "bets" was called out and met with groans or giggles but before I could listen, a whoosh of cold air brought Brenn sitting back next to me.

Unnervingly, he had a wide grin on his face.

"I learned a few fun things," Brenn said, dumping a full leather skin of coin on the table which I quickly swept off into my lap.

"Do share." Surreptitiously, I opened the bag. Gold coin and plenty of silver filled it – not a bronze in sight. I frowned and Brenn simply shrugged.

"There were plenty of people with bad minds," he said simply. "This town has been claimed by pirates."

I blinked. Suddenly, the boisterousness of the people made much more sense. Brenn wiggled his eyebrows.

"For how long?" I asked, suddenly feeling more aware of wandering eyes that sneaked a look at the pair of us.

"A few years," he said. "The locals renamed this place, Newt," Brenn smiled. "All of this coast from here to Riach's border has been claimed by pirates."

My stomach dropped. We had signed a treaty with them years before I was born – they were under our protection. How could this have happened?

"What about the Shifter Council?" Surely, they couldn't have allowed this.

"It seems that Dion has been divided for a while now – Dion to the East with Rynd as the capital and the pirate state, the *Republic of the Free* to the West."

My jaw fell.

Brenn chuckled at my face. "Your father was more than willing to kick the shifters to the margin when it suited him. No wonder they let the Fynix invade."

My mind ran back to the scenes of despair back in Kya. I hated the feeling of helplessness – the bloodshed and the smell of fire and magic taking over. And now this? So much for the honour of a pact with a warlock. I shook my head. How could I even call myself a Princess when I knew so little of the world? I'd convinced myself that learning forbidden magic made me even – maybe even better than them. Outlawed magic gave me an edge but how much more of my education had been adapted for me? I gritted my teeth as I thought of my father – I bet Sorrel knew all of this.

I rubbed my temples. What else had changed while I rehearsed my dancing or did needlepoint? How had hiding the truth from me helped?

"Why did they give up Dion?" I pressed.

Brenn gave a wicked, all-knowing smile that set my blood boiling. Perhaps I should read more minds since the upheaval in Clawton.

"Alongside general prejudice – it seems like they weren't taking as much money as they were giving the people of Dion anymore. The treaty was adapted to peace and independence."

I thought of the remnants lurking outside of Newt. Of course, peace meant giving them nothing. Withdrawing support from a country that had depended on it. No wonder it had changed so drastically. I felt shame creep up my neck.

Brenn huffed, clearly having read my mind or seen it on my face. "Oh please. What could you have done?"

"Say something. Do something," I retorted. Brenn crossed his arms and gave me a deadpan look.

"Of course, your father valued your input intrinsically."

It didn't make any of it right.

A riotous laugh went up from the table to the right of us, pulling me back into the room. Now I knew who they were I could see the cutlasses next to the coat stand, and the pistols stored under the table. But perhaps they could be of use to us? Pirates knew ways around the sea and land that even the most experienced seafarers would pale in comparison.

We could avoid the General that was now on our tail, and no doubt bypass any Fynix forces sent our way. And then we could head to Wist. Where my aunt, if she still had any faith left in me, would be ready and willing to help muster support.

Everything came into focus: I knew what my plan was.

I glanced over to the loudest table and then back to my companion. Brenn's smile fell as he shook his head.

"That is a terrible idea." He crossed his arms. "Pirates are not trustworthy."

I got up from my seat and went to the bar, leaving Brenn burning holes into the back of my head. I smiled at him as I ordered two pints of mead from the busty redhead behind the counter. She had dark eyes and pretty freckles all over her nose and cheeks; she smiled happily when I gave her a tip.

"Where are you from then, mister?" she asked sweetly as I rested my elbows on the countertop between us. "I haven't seen you around town before."

"Just passing through," I replied. I took a sip of my mead – it had a strong, wheat taste with a sweet hint of honey that ran through it. It was also alcoholic enough to make me briefly forget what I was saying. "I was wondering who is in charge around here. My colleague has some enquiries to make," I referenced to Brenn, who looked like he could stab me.

The barmaid looked at Brenn with a smile of amusement.

"Well, Captain Bennett isn't with us this eve," she said as she glanced over to the table causing the racket. "But his first mate is here with some of his," there was a smash of glass, and a cheer went up as the barmaid winced, "crew."

"Captain Bennett runs this town?" I asked.

The barmaid shook her head.

"Officially, the Pirate Lords do – but I don't think Bennett sees it that way. Truthfully, I don't think the Lords do either."

I thanked her and returned to the table to give Brenn his mead.

"Do you have a death wish?" he hissed, he tried to grab my arm, but I moved beyond his reach. I picked up the other mead as I headed over to the centre of the party. The sodden floor made squelching noises under my feet as I joined the edge of the fray. Burly men and even burlier women were cheering on a group of individuals chugging a bubbly amber liquid at the same time.

In the middle of all this was a woman with beautiful brown skin and short black hair cropped just below her delicately pointed Fae ears. But most arresting were her eyes; a mesmerising colour that was so blue they looked like the sky at dawn. Wearing a weather-beaten brown leather jacket, white shirt, and breeches that were laced up at the front with her long black boots, she looked every part a pirate; especially given the savage-looking cutlass resting in a leather-bound holster hooked over the edge of her chair.

She wiped her mouth with the back of her hand and slammed her tankard down first.

"And she wins again!" she yelled, to a cacophony of cheers and applause from around her. She grinned smugly as she crossed her arms and watched the rest of the crew finish up.

Second to finish was a slender man with a length of long blond hair that went down his back. Parts of it were plaited back but I noticed the marks around his eyes – flowers delicately drawn, as if with a fine paintbrush, circled his eyes and fell upon his cheeks. He had the ears of Fae too – though he looked very different to his companion and those I had seen by the bar. He wore a light blue tunic that was embroidered at the collar and sleeves, along with a midnight-blue draped waistcoat tied across his back. I realised the style was that of the Dean Fae which explained the lack of wings but didn't explain the markings. Despite his speed, he placed the empty tankard down gracefully.

"If anything," the Fae drawled in a voice as soft as spun silk, "this just proves you have a bigger mouth than the rest of us."

Suddenly, a belch exploded from the end of the table, along with the next slam of the tankard. The blond ground his lips together and looked away. "You are repulsive, Evan."

"That was a brilliant one. Excellent execution and depth." The belcher was shorter than the other two, with a rounded, tanned, freckled face and unruly brunette curls. The dark-haired Fae gave a little applause. "I must please my fans, Caden." His voice had a twang to it I didn't recognise. His dark eyes glittered as he grinned at his companions' disgust.

"You're as bad as Regan," the giant woman to his left declared. She was very clearly dragon-kin with one half of her face studded with dragon scales the colour of embers. They matched her flowing red hair which shimmered in the candlelight as she leaned away from the offending smell. Her broad shoulders looked as if she could crush me easily and she wore a pale green dress in a floaty crepe fabric with an auburn leather bodice laced at the front.

"Where is that damn troublemaker anyway?" the blue-eyed Fae said looking about the bar. Her eyes skimmed past me as she shook her head.

"Probably nursing her wounds in the cabin," the dragon-kin sighed. "You know how her ego is particularly vulnerable when the moon is out."

105

"That's what you get for challenging a legend like me to a drinking contest," the blue-eyed lady replied. She flicked her hair over her shoulders – I noticed the ends of her hair were a lighter blue. Maybe a Dean Fae too?

"Poor Regan," the man with curly hair replied, shaking his head. "Losing is not in her vocabulary."

The dragon-kin's lip twitched. "It wasn't until she met Aoife."

The first lady tutted as she looked about the bar.

"Well, this night seems to have reached an impasse." Her accent was strange, and I didn't recognise it – well-spoken and refined as her voice was. "Will no one challenge me? Or must I claim my victory once more?"

The crew laughed as people around them shook their heads or diverted their gazes. I had my pint in hand, and quickly bought another before I edged through a gap in the crowd and placed them both down with a small thud. A dribble of mead ran onto my thumb, so I licked it off. This didn't seem to be the kind of establishment that would mind for manners.

"I think I could take that challenge." The room's bustling atmosphere quietened as people craned to get a look at me. No doubt I still looked dishevelled in my Draigian gear, but at least I didn't stand out here; this place was a jumble all by itself.

The blue-eyed woman smirked and laced her fingers together ahead of her on the table.

"Oh yeah, kid?" she said. "Are you even old enough to drink?"

"Sure," I replied. She looked older than me by a few years. She started shaking her head – her smile remained unchanged.

"It wouldn't be fair," she said nonchalantly. "It wouldn't be a challenge."

The curly-haired boy snorted into his new pint and the blond fae watched me carefully – my skin prickled. I could taste the searching spells on my tongue, but I knew with Brenn keeping me under his glamours that I was safe, for now.

Look, you've embarrassed yourself now. Well done. Now come back before they decide to stab you, Brenn snapped in my mind.

I crossed my arms and tilted my head, unimpressed.

"I might surprise you," I replied. Those blue eyes didn't move from mine. "Unless you're scared…"

The dragon-kin giggled as she shook her head. A few chuckles went about the bar, and I could feel people staring at me. Even though I couldn't see him, I felt Brenn's scowl.

Flashing her pearly white teeth at me, the first mate grinned and gestured to the spare seat to her right. Then she kicked its leg, and it jutted out at an angle.

"Well, we can't have that now, can we?" She reached over and pulled the pint across the table to herself, keeping eye contact with me while people around the table snickered.

"On three?" she said. I nodded and lifted my tankard, but before I could move any further, she looped her arm around mine, so we rested in the crook of each other's elbow. She caught my surprise before I could maintain my cool exterior. "It's a duel, isn't it?"

"If you say so," I replied.

"Count down please, Don." She tilted her head to the dragon-kin, who still looked bemused.

"One," Don started. Her right blue eye winked at me. "Two. Three!"

She was quick but so was I. I chugged like I had never chugged before. I was almost impressed with myself with how much I could down the mead. The strength of the alcohol made my eyes burn.

Randall had secretly taken me to parties when we had started courting. Nothing fancy like the family of the courtiers who studied in the Royal Academy; no, parks filled with kids our age drinking and playing in the green fields. We played silly challenges like this, had competitions with cards, and stayed out until the sun came up. No one knew who I was back then – before everything fell apart. But, after having grown up with two brothers, competitiveness was a vice of mine.

After the last drop was gone, I slammed my drink down just as the first mate did the same. The thud was loud enough that I worried I might have dented the table. People muttered, eyes flicking back and forth between the woman and I.

The dragon-kin shook her head and raised her arms. The curly-headed man clapped the table with one hand in glee. With an intrigued expression, the blonde fae quirked an eyebrow.

"A tie, Aoife," the dragon-kin said. "I couldn't call it."

The blue-eyed woman, Aoife, as the dragon-kin had called her, wiped the corner of her mouth with the tip of her thumb.

"Shall we go again?" she said, a challenge in her voice.

"Are you paying?" I replied.

She grinned.

After three pints of mead, a purple liquorice fizzy concoction, something bright yellow that tasted fruity, and three tiny black glasses an inch high filled with something smoky, the room had slowly but surely started to spin. At some point, Brenn had moved in closer to watch the proceedings: we had gained quite a crowd before the curly-headed one, Evan, told them to clear off. The dragon-kin, Donna, was so impressed I could go toe-to-toe with Aoife she had bought our last round herself.

I waved to Brenn, whose glower was strong enough that even my inebriated self could tell I was in for a scolding later. The drinking finally stopped as the night drew into the early hours of the morning. The tavern was nearly empty beside us; but despite my lack of sleep, I felt full of energy. Even the barmaid seemed to have gone to bed, leaving the keys on the side of the counter for us to lock up when we were done. The trust she had for the crew was surely a testament to their reliability – or just how dangerous they were.

"So, kid," Aoife said, looking at me and then glancing at Brenn who was leaning on the counter with a bored expression. He eyed me every so often and demanded in my head that we leave. "What's his deal?"

I waved a hand. "Nothing – he just needs a nap."

Brenn scowled at me he bridged the gap between us and sat in a chair close by.

"I don't remember a drinking contest being on the agenda," he drawled. He eyed the crew with a wary expression.

"Live spontaneously," I replied. Aoife grinned at me. Donna's eyes flicked between us.

"Lovers' quarrel?" she asked. Brenn's face didn't change, but I laughed.

"We're brothers," he said snippily.

Evan's eyes lingered on Brenn for a moment and then he shook his shoulders and took a slurp of his foamy pint. Donna seemed to be looking at Brenn with fresh eyes.

"So, what brings you to Newt?" the blond Fae, Caden, said, glancing towards his drunken companions. "I assume it's not the sterling company."

"Hey!" Donna objected as Aoife made a rude gesture with her fingers towards him.

I opened my mouth to respond but wasn't quick enough.

"We are looking for a ship to take us to Wist," Brenn spoke. "We have business there."

Evan's eyebrows shot up. "Wist? You'll be lucky. Those waters belong to the wolves now."

My heart jumped. Werewolves being involved was not good news.

"The Syrees?" I pressed. "Since when?"

"Technically, it was theirs originally," Donna said. "The Wisterians just claimed it and thought because their council was run by a Wryfirth they could get away with it. But now that the family is wiped out, they have claimed the Blue Pass and the Southern Depths.

"Who is running Wist now?"

"The Council still is," Aoife said. "Just they've been boxed in from all sides. And the Wryfirth there gave up her position and retreated." Aoife's face was quizzical. "How do you not know this? It's been everywhere."

I suddenly felt sick.

"We were at sea for a time," I said, feebly.

"Fishing," Brenn added, his voice as unconvincing as ever.

Aoife didn't say anything, but her bright eyes were sceptical. Donna met her eyes, lifting an eyebrow. I held onto the edge of the seat tightly, so I didn't fall off.

"So, what is your business there?" Donna asked. She had swept up her red hair and was tying it up with a strip of leather. "Wist is crawling with refugees."

"Our family lives there," Brenn lied smoothly. "We were fishermen before we shipwrecked outside of Draig. Since then, we have been making our way back there."

The short one, Evan nodded eagerly. "Have you heard about the Wraith of the Wastes?" Brenn tilted his head. "It escaped and is roaming about in Draig as we speak."

The blond groaned, "Not this nonsense again."

"Oh, shut it, Caden," Evan retorted. "Apparently, the king of Fynix sent the Princess of Wryfirth there to meet her end. And when she died the Wraith had enough power to destroy the tower once and for all."

Some of the tension eased from my shoulders. The news clearly hadn't travelled here just yet. I didn't doubt that we had hours – if that. People would send hawks, fire messages, or even spell letters back and forth between each other. Enchanted paper wasn't a rare occurrence.

"That's all hearsay," Donna waved him off. "Anyway, the Princess is long dead."

"Most likely," Caden said slowly.

The first mate waved a hand.

"Donna's right," she said, rubbing her head, her words a little slurred. "We'll get the full story when Cap arrives, I'm sure."

"Princess, I think we should leave," Brenn said quickly in my mind.

"We're getting somewhere!" I replied.

Suddenly, Evan's head snapped up from across the table. His eyes were accusatory, and all softness had gone from his demeanour. He met Brenn's eyes, who had gone still next to me.

"Did you just-" Evan spoke through gritted teeth, but it seemed Donna was the only one who had noticed.

"Speak of the dog," Caden said.

A fierce look appeared on Evan's face, and he moved slightly forward, covering Donna. His eyes had turned dark – all the sparkle had gone. Through my arcane senses, I felt the magic surrounding him change; his aura turned dangerous and foreboding. My stomach knotted.

"What's wrong?" Donna said, poking her head around to look at Brenn. I turned too. Brenn's face was drawn tightly and furious. His eyes had gone black, and I couldn't see the white anymore.

Evan stood up and immediately a pair of long, dark talons shot from his hands. His eyes were just as dark, and his lip curled to reveal a set of elongated fangs. He growled lowly and Brenn matched him with a savage growl of his own, now on his feet too.

At that moment, Aoife acknowledged the demon and wraith staring dangerously at each other and sighed. The door creaked open behind us, but I couldn't bring myself to turn around.

"You couldn't hold it for another second, Evan?"

"Typical Evan," Caden said. "Blowing a perfectly good plan by being a hothead."

My stomach tightened as the realisation hit me. Each of the crew members brandished a weapon. Aoife was spinning two curved blades in her hands. A shining ball of green smoke had bloomed in Caden's palm. Donna held a cutlass of her own and Evan's claws were ready.

I finished my drink before crossing my arms. My thoughts were racing through the murky alcohol swamp, so I decided stillness was the best choice for now.

"I leave you alone for less than a day and you acquire a wraith and a royal," a deep masculine voice said. There was the noise of a chair being dragged across the floor. A tall man wearing a tricorn hat and a long leather coat sat down next to me. He had a worn sword in a decorated leather sheath and a crossbow hooked to his belt, and he was smiling. "How do you always bring trouble to my door, Aoife?"

Aoife shrugged her shoulders.

"They found us," she said. Her eyes flicked to Brenn. "You move an inch, and she dies."

Brenn hadn't moved but his eyes flicked over to me. A word and he would go. I know he would. But could he take all of them? The power coming off all of them was intense. But even their combined power paled in insignificance compared to the man sitting next to me. His smile was arrogant, but his magic was beyond anything I had felt in a while. He was easily a Warlock – maybe even a Mage. His eyes were a deep navy with a long scar down his cheek, hooking the corner of his mouth.

"Hello, Princess," the man said. "I am Captain Courtney Bennett – and you are both under arrest."

Nine

"Can I kill them yet?" Brenn asked as he surveyed the cell once more. Thankfully, dungeons here were cleaner than the ones the Fynix had kept me in. This one had a shabby bed with a simple wooden frame and a couple of thin grey woollen blankets.

The pirates had taken over one of the townhouses looking out onto the dock for their base. The group had escorted us down here, a short-barrelled pistol pressed against my back, accompanied by Brenn's seething sarcasm as they locked us in, leaving the demon to stand guard.

Opposite us, Evan was leaning against the wall with a scowl on his face – his eyes still pitch, with elongated fangs poking through his lips. "I could do with a snack," Brenn growled at Evan. He hissed back and I saw his tongue was forked.

"No." I reminded him for the hundredth time that hour. I had a plan, of course. Brenn just needed to be patient – I was waiting for the right moment. I was also waiting to feel less drunk.

"They are going to sell you back to Fynix, your Highness," Brenn said. He turned his back on Evan and leaned against the bars. Evan's hiss filled the air. "Then, the King will cut your head off and dance through the streets of Kya with it – just like he did with your father."

I scowled at him. Brenn could easily tear this cell down – it was warded against magical beings escaping, but not something as powerful as Brenn. Or me, for that matter. But they didn't need to know that yet. After all, I had to convince Brenn that killing them was a bad idea – they knew the seas and that was exactly what we needed.

But how much did they know? Surely, news had travelled fast, but what exactly did they believe? After all, they'd left Brenn down here with one guard. Surely his powers hadn't diminished in their eyes. Did they believe I wouldn't fight my way out? My head was swarming, but I focused on my plan: surely, I would be able to convince them.

"He didn't dance, and it won't come to that," I started to say before he jumped in.

"I saw inside that tiny half-demon's mind," Brenn said, and a growl rumbled through the stone dungeon quarters.

"Yeah, and got yourself rumbled." I crossed my arms. He'd explained on the way over – under command – that he had gone snooping through Evan's mind. The half-demon noticed and was not happy about the intrusion.

Brenn waved a hand dismissively. "We were trapped the moment the barmaid slipped the blond one a note about the killer glamours worn by an idiot and an attractive man."

I smiled at him.

"You're not that much of an idiot, Brenn."

His eyes narrowed.

"Just let me eat them – problem solved!" He whipped round to Evan, Brenn's face shifted, and I saw the rows of bone-mangling teeth that had appeared in the tower. His face contorted as Evan's jaw clenched, so I elbowed him in the side.

"We need a way to Wist, Brenn," I returned. "I can't sail, and you can't fly us all that way."

Brenn's form returned to normal, his teeth straight and mundane. He pressed his lips together and shook his shoulders.

I used the peaceful moment to reach out with my mind to Evan. My escape plan depended on getting into the half-demon's head. But I had to be discreet, and he had to be distracted. Unfortunately, he was still too focused; if I wasn't so determined, I would've been impressed.

"You could always try rowing again?" Brenn said, deadpan.

"Stop being an ass."

Brenn frowned.

"Why do I even bother trying to reason with you?"

"Honestly, I don't know," I replied.

I went up to the bars where Brenn had been taunting Evan. He hadn't moved.

"So, Evan," I started. "Any idea what the next move is?"

His dark eyes turned to me, and he shrugged his shoulders.

"Your Wraith friend hit the nail on the head," he said indifferently. "Probably sell you back to the Fynix king." Evan had pushed the sleeves of his black tunic up his arms and the taut muscles of his forearms moved as he gestured. "It's nothing personal, *Aaron*."

My faux name made me smile. There was no chance in hell I was going to be sold to anyone, but that didn't mean I couldn't be polite about it.

"You can call me Bryony," I told him. "Is your real name Evan?" The half-demon nodded.

"I would rather not be sold, Evan," I told him. "Even though I suppose the coin would be great for you guys, I would much rather have my freedom." Evan tilted his head to the side. "Brenn is very hungry too," I added.

Evan looked to Brenn and then back to me. "Do you seriously think you can convince me to release you?"

"Brenn, do you remember what you did in the Tower?" I whispered through our mind-link.

I showed Brenn my plan as I opened my thoughts to him. As usual, he said nothing. But then he started shifting into the humanoid white figure he attempted to frighten me with when we were in the tower. Now it just needed to work on Evan.

"When you die, your Majesty," Brenn said in a horrible, guttural growl, "I will kill them all anyway."

His bottom half turned to a snake, whilst his arms turned into claws. He paced the floor of the cage, whipping a fierce tail back and forth with a haunting howl. Brenn gauged great swathes of the floor and left jagged marks in the stone.

With my psychic magic, I stretched out towards his mind, I could feel Evan's horror ripple through me as I advanced further in. He feared Brenn, I could feel it, coursing through me like an icy wave. I whispered the words to tighten my grip on his mind, and Evan's consciousness suddenly fell under my control. I felt the whoosh of magic siphon through me as I eased into Evan's thoughts. His being was at my command. I clenched my jaw, and I saw the darkness in Evan's eyes fade back to just his brown irises. His whole body went slack and relaxed. He wasn't in any pain; I was simply redirecting his thoughts with my own will. Brenn let out a low whistle beside me.

"And you snap at *me* for holding back?"

"How else was I meant to get away with *anything* in the castle?"

I could feel Evan try to resist me, but I was already aggravated by spending an hour in a cell with an irritable Brenn. I felt bad for Evan, but I knew he'd have more hope of surviving the next part if we got out now. Waiting wasn't doing me any good at all.

"You want to let us out, don't you, Evan?" I spoke clearly. The magic on my tongue made it tingle, but it felt good to sense it coursing through me once more. I could feel Evan's fears for the future swirling around, Brenn, his crew, and his crewmate Donna for whom his emotions seemed to be a complicated bundle. Those feelings were tied like a thread unravelling on a jumper. Puppeteering was a total invasion of privacy, beyond illegal, and it made me cringe, but I shoved those feelings away and drove him forward. "You want to show us to your friends, don't you, Evan?"

I could feel his strength fight against mine, but it was no use. Clearly, despite noticing Brenn's presence in his mind, his talents were outside the realm of psychic magics. I overwhelmed him with a sense of calm and peace.

Evan stepped forward and I willed him to find the key and open the jail. He pulled a bronze key from the lock and turned it – a click sounded, and I pulled the door open. I stepped through the door and sensed my magic restored to its full power in my belly. The cell repressed magic, preventing any magical enhancements from being made to the body and people using it to break out of the cell by changing forms or pulling the bars apart. Not that the bars would've stopped Brenn had I let him rage.

The wraith skulked out behind me, the frown deepening on his face.

"If you had let me kill him," he started to say. "I could fly us out of here."

"I need a crew," I told him determinedly.

"You say that like it has to be this one."

"I like this one. They seem nice."

"They locked us in a cage," Brenn hissed behind me.

"I would lock us in a cage if I were them."

We followed Evan through the underbelly of the house. This time, I took a moment to fully take in my surroundings. The smell of wood, polish, and iron filled my senses as we passed rooms filled with barrels of rum, cones of sugar, and unmined salt rocks. Silks of all shapes and colours filled another room. I guessed they must've been

115

for trade – pirates were merchants after all, just with fewer rules.

We headed up some dark wood steps and Evan pushed open a trapdoor that led us onto a landing. I could hear voices coming from the next room over. This space was much more furnished than the dungeons had been, the walls painted cream and drapes hung across gashes in the wall as if someone had used the place for knife-throwing practice. I noticed the ancient Wryfirth crest carved into the masonry had long been defaced and felt my heart clench, just a little.

Instead, there was a new silver crest painted there: a rotary wheel crossed with two swords – a steel longsword and what looked to be an enchanted blade with a twisted handle. The blade was a deep onyx colour. I recognised it but I couldn't pinpoint where from.

Other than that, there was a closet overflowing with clothes and a chest next to it with a varnished oak finish that seemed to be snoring. The door to my right had been left ajar and I could hear the familiar voices drifting through. I still had Evan under my control, and an idea came to me on how to make an entrance.

I sent Evan ahead and commanded my words to his tongue.

"Evan, you didn't let the prisoners go and get your rum again, did you?" I heard Donna's voice. "I'm not sure I can deal with another rum-based fiasco. It's bordering on stereotype now."

Evan cleared his throat and then spoke in a monotone voice.

"Presenting her Royal Highness, the reigning Sun of the Kingdom of Magics, Princess Bryony Wryfirth of Riach."

The room fell silent as I stepped in. I smiled at the dropped jaws of the crew, and I bobbed a little curtsy. The captain and first mate stood next to each other by the open fire.

The walls, painted a deep green colour, were full of items hanging on nails, along with paintings of impressive landscapes that I didn't know. Trinkets and ornaments of all shapes filled the mantle, including a number of ancient-looking weapons. There was an oval table in the centre of the room where Caden was sitting, alongside a hulking figure of a woman I didn't recognise.

Donna stood immediately, with an axe in her hand. Caden too jumped up, and I saw his green fire muster between his fingers. Aoife's hand twitched toward her blade, but Captain Bennett stayed still.

I swanned over to settle in a free purple armchair near the door. After I sat, I noticed Brenn didn't follow me, and I turned my head to see him waiting. I rolled my eyes and then made Evan say.

"And Brenn: The Wraith of the Wastes." Brenn came in, but instead of sitting down next to me, he changed his form back into a shadow creature, keeping the monstrous jaws from earlier. I heard the scrape of his long talons on the floor and the sweep of a spiked tail.

He sat next to me, blocking the door.

The room was silent – no one moved. I cleared my throat.

"Sorry about breaking out," I said, crossing my arms. "But I have spent far too much time in cages in my life thus far." Next to me, Brenn growled deeply, enough for the eyes around the room to widen. "My companion feels the same way." The crew members turned to their captain, who stared back at me. "Don't do anything stupid – I just want to talk."

A tense beat passed, and I wondered if this would be our last moments together.

Captain Bennett was the first to speak.

"I did wonder how much you were holding back, your Highness," he said, that familiar Southern accent twanging on every word. He sat down at the table and put his feet up on the surface. Had my governess been here, she would've been aghast. "Not just anyone can escape the Tower with an ancient monster under their control." He glanced at my scowling companion. "No offence."

Brenn said nothing – I was more than sure it still annoyed him enough too.

"I'm surprised the royal court would teach you psychic magics," Aoife said, a little impressed. She joined the captain at the table. Donna and Caden though, hadn't moved.

"I could've sworn that kind of magic was…unlawful," the captain said with a knowing smile. He and Aoife shared a look. "Now, if you wouldn't mind freeing my gunner, we can talk."

Donna, could not move her eyes from the still figure of Evan, shook her head.

"You need to let him go," she said, her hand tightening on her axe. "Now."

Her face was hard, her amber eyes were blazing.

"Of course," I said, gently releasing my hold on his mind. Magic tingled through my senses as my full control returned. Evan stumbled over breathing hard; then he pressed his hands onto the table and twisted his head to me. His eyes turned to horror as he saw Brenn for the first time. "Sorry about that, Evan. But I did ask nicely first."

His eyes darted back between Brenn and I.

"Also, Riach laws prevent women from learning anything besides performative magic and basic healing," I clarified. "That applied to me as well. But I couldn't resist, so I learned other magics in secret."

Evan frowned furiously and his eyes darkened as they set upon us. But this time, Brenn didn't hold back. The wraith swarmed over to him; Brenn's dark magic made my skin prickle as the temperature dropped. I watched my breath fanning out in front of me.

"Try anything and I'll consume everyone here and make you *watch*," Brenn seethed.

For a moment, I thought Evan might try. His hands, now clawed in dark tendrils, shook at his sides. Then the Captain cleared his throat from the table. Evan's fangs rescinded, but nothing about him relaxed. Instead, he moved to where Donna stood and put distance between them and us.

Brenn seemed to consider this a concession and returned to my side.

"Yes, very scary," I said. "But the reason we didn't just escape – as we very easily could have – is because we have a proposition for you."

"Don't rope me into this madness," muttered Brenn.

"Very well then. *I* have a proposition for you."

The captain tilted his head; he had long hair that was tied back at the back of his neck and a shadow formed across his eyes under his hat.

"Proceed, then your Highness," he said. Despite the joking tone, there was a certain grandeur in his voice – he must've been of noble birth, no doubt.

"My aunt is still in Wist – and she is the last remaining family I have," I began. "We have been trying to travel there but we have run into a few, um, problems along the way." I thought of the Bonekeeper, red eyes glinting like fresh blood on snow. I thought of the Fynix and their war drums outside my chambers. Then, finally, of the Tower and its lone inhabitant.

"We would like passage there. I have supporters in Wist, and I want to be with my people. From there we can figure out our next move." My words were met with blank faces.

"You wish to reclaim Riach?" Donna said incredulously.

"I want peace and safety for my people. By any means."

Evan snorted as the captain raised an eyebrow. Aoife's face showed a flicker of something like sadness.

"Bit late for that, Princess," Evan added — his face still stony.

"Wist is under the control of the Horned King now," Aoife said. "You'd be walking into a more permanent death sentence."

"Not if we don't get caught," I said. I glanced at Caden, whose face was unreadable. "I thought pirates were good at being stealthy. And if all the bragging I heard is anything to go by — I thought you guys were the best."

At that point, the huge figure sat next to Caden scowled. They'd been quiet this whole time, observing proceedings with an impassive face.

"We are the best," she said, her accent neutral but familiar. Syree perhaps? I noticed the gruff turn of the vowels. "But that doesn't make us foolish."

"You could've fooled me," Brenn rumbled next to me.

"What's in it for us?" Captain Bennett asked. "Unfortunately, Princess you don't have many bargaining chips."

"You won't die horribly and painfully," snarled Brenn.

"We have a business to run. We're not a charity for wayward Princesses on missions of self-destruction," Captain Bennett said with a shrug. Aoife gave him a flat look. "Especially, when that Princess and her companion are wanted all over the world,"

I glanced up at the flag of the rotary wheel crossed by a long sword and the enchanted blade among the collectables above the fire. Then the memory came back to me, and I remembered where I had seen that blade before.

"I like your flag, Captain," I said. "That sword is the Blade of Kazaan, isn't it?"

The Silvian hero had wielded it long ago — it was said to have only been wielded by the finest of swordsmen and blessed the user with incredible powers. Silvia was the home to ancient magic practices – Mages of all races would travel to study there. At least, that was before it became consumed by dark magic and the shadow realms were born. Now it lay abandoned. "It belonged to the Cavalier of Silvia before it fell."

An odd tenseness accompanied the silence then. The Captain's smile sharpened.

"Maybe once, but then it was mine." Bennett's expression turned to a grimace. "It was lost at sea."

Next to him, the corner of Aoife's mouth quirked. The Captain noticed, and he clenched his jaw.

I nodded. That was the common knowledge of the item. But alas, the Wryfirth historians knew a little more of what became of it.

"It washed up in Dean," I said, evenly. "But now it's in the catacombs under the Sapphire Palace. I know because I used to practice magic down there. Forbidden magical items were my only company. Along with the dead, of course." Obviously, Randall had been with me sometimes, but they didn't need to know that. "Should you accept my mission, you can have it back," I told them. "It might need sharpening though – I'm sure I used it as a doorstop once or twice."

The captain winced at that, and Aoife giggled. That noise broke the tension in the room.

He whipped his head to her.

"It's not funny!" She looked away, her shoulders vibrating. "It's an ancient weapon! The heirloom of my family."

"Hey, *I* didn't drop it," Aoife replied, and the captain pressed his lips together in defeat.

He turned to me.

"You're sure it's the one?"

I nodded.

"All the relics in the catacombs are treasures – it's the safest place for them. Not even the treasury is so highly warded."

"I didn't realise the Wryfirths kept a secret store of goodies under the castle." The larger lady brightened at the thought and rubbed her hands together. She had dark skin with short brown hair that was short on both sides but longer on top. "Perhaps we should pay it a visit."

I shook my shoulders.

"You need to be a Wryfirth to find it," I told her. "Even if you destroyed the castle, you'd never be able to access it without someone living with royal blood."

"And it would seem that you are the last," Captain Bennett said.

"You can have the sword, but I decide what happens to everything else." I spoke. "You will be rewarded though, I assure you." There were treasures galore down there but I was sure I would need them to broker any sort of peace. The Captain looked to Aoife who shrugged her shoulders and chuckled.

"You know you want that damned sword back or I'll never hear the end of it," she added.

"Hold on," Evan interjected. "There is no way on this realm that I am going on a boat with that thing."

"I must second the short one's opinion," Caden said, crossing his arms. "I grew up with stories about the Wraith of the Wastes. What's stopping it from devouring all of us in our sleep?"

Feeling it was his turn to become involved in the conversation, Brenn's form began to shrink. Black glittering smoke transformed into the small, lithe snake once again. He wrapped himself around my shoulder, lifting a serpentine head and tilting it to the side. He innocently stuck out his forked tongue.

I raised my hand to show them the pact scored into my skin. Caden raised his eyebrows.

"Brenn can't harm anyone unless I permit him to, or they are going to damage me," I said. "He's the ultimate protector."

"How did you ever get him to agree to that?" Donna said, looking at the snake.

"It was just something I thought of while I was in the Tower," I replied.

"Plus, her royal highness is very good at mental magics," Brenn added.

"Thank you, Brenn," I replied, ready for the barb that was sure to follow.

"Terrible at everything else."

"I'm still a novice at many things," I told the table. "Unlike my brothers, who had a full education, mine was limited to whatever I could smuggle out of the library or what was in the catacombs."

"How do you expect to take back your throne if you don't know much magic?" Aoife said. "I assume that is what you want — eventually."

"I have a wraith on my side," I replied. "We can handle it."

Aoife's blue eyes sparkled.

"So, your ultimate goal is the throne?"

I felt the eyes from the table on me.

"Of course. It's mine, and my people need me."

The group stared at me. Even Brenn held his forked tongue.

"My country has never had a queen rule alone," I told them. "It's time."

Donna's hard exterior seemed to have ebbed away, and she smiled. Aoife too.

It was the giant woman who responded first.

"I'm in," she said, crossing her arms. "But we get a reasonable monopoly over the catacombs." I nodded and she seemed satisfied with my answer. "I could use a challenge. And if I get to kill some Fynix bastards, that's a bonus."

"For the record, I think it's a bad idea," Donna said. Evan's eyebrows had shot up in surprise. "But I can understand wanting to help one's people. I'm in."

"I'm in too then," Evan added quickly. "Who else is going to put the Wraith down when she dies?"

Brenn snickered from my shoulder.

Caden sighed and threw his hands up.

"Not like I have an option," he said. "I like Wist and I'm down for a little trouble now and then."

"As long as when you get your throne back you accept Newt and the pirate states as new independent democratic cities," Aoife said. Next to her Captain Bennett looked delighted.

"Done." I glanced at the captain whose dark eyes were still staring at his first mate. "What do you think Captain?"

He took off his tricorn and dumped it on the table — the scar on his right cheek was more visible than ever with the light from the fire.

"I want my sword back."

Aoife rolled her eyes.

Ten

After that, it was as if we resumed the earlier conversation from *The Last Straw*. The girls welcomed me over to the table and I made an effort to be lively despite the tiredness nagging behind my eyes. We stayed up a while longer, the warm glow from the fire burning down to the embers by the time we thought about going to sleep. During that time, Caden and Captain Bennett had been speaking about the logistics of the journey to Wist. If we headed south through the Pass of the Fae, the seas that divided the Fae lands from the rest of Nos, we ran the risk of interception from Fynix forces. But the alternative route would take us through the Divide and past the Wastes. A prospect no one other than Brenn found promising.

"There's also the issue of the Bonekeeper," I said. I had crossed my knees on the chair and rested the mug of cocoa that Donna had made me on one of the plush arms.

Unlike Donna, Evan remained snappy and never left her side like an angry shadow.

Aoife's eyebrows shot up.

"An issue, indeed," she said, her long, dextrous fingers gripped around a red clay mug. "How did you escape? They're truly wicked fighters." She looked at my arm – I had a feeling the veins would never lay flat again now. Their colour had faded from the angry red spindles, but I could still feel the ridges if I ran my hand over it. "Did he do that?

The giant lady with beautiful dark skin, Regan, pulled a face.

"I met a Bonekeeper in Arge when I worked in Qicog for a bit," she said. "Nasty buggers – I saw her take down a whole fort of dwarves." She shuddered – her hazel eyes wide. "Came out wearing red."

My stomach flipped over. I thought of the traveller with Coesau and those scarlet red eyes. Of course, I hadn't found him frightening at first – though maybe I should have. I had consumed a lot of mead – the Fynix king could've been standing right there, and I would've probably asked him to dance.

"Avoiding is definitely the best option for us," Evan interjected.

"I could take one," he added quickly. "I'd just rather not."

"It's no secret that the Demon King loves his military," Donna said. "Let's not go picking fights unnecessarily. I mean, we don't want to have to tackle an even bigger force."

I imagined the demon homeland: Raive. As it was past the Divide in the Shadow Realms, its presence in my education had been stifled. I knew the lay of the land – and its reputation, of course. But my lack of knowledge had been filled with rumour and hearsay. Monsters lurked in the streets. Worship of the Night Gods prevailed in the absence of sunlight's touch. Darkness held endless depravity and disorder.

The artefacts in the catacombs from their people were very old indeed. No successful conquests had been undertaken since ancient times. Books lay bound in chains that, no matter what I did, would not open for me. Gems shone in colours that Riachian didn't mine – and sometimes, in the darkness, I would swear I heard them whispering. My blood chilled.

"What is Raive like?"

Evan shook his shoulders. "I haven't lived there in years," he replied. He struggled to find the words. "There is no place I have ever been that is like it."

"So, it's not a den of infamy, ill morals, murder, and chaos?" I asked, to which Evan's steely expression broke.

"I didn't say that," he added with a smile. "Besides, there is a beauty to chaos."

I saw him rest a hand on Donna's thigh. A pinkness filled her cheek, and it might've been the light, but the scales covering the other side of her face seemed to have more of a shine to them.

Unaware, Regan suddenly cleared her throat.

"Tell you what, demons make the best lovers in Nos," Regan said, clapping her tankard on the table. "Let me tell you of some acquaintances I met in Rangathan."

Regan launched into a tale in which she had accidentally initiated a clan war between two demon families by seducing the daughters of opposing houses. It was so filthy I didn't think I would ever think of the demon's forked tongue without blushing again.

"You are traumatising, Her Royal Highness," Aoife laughed.

"You are traumatising *me*," Evan groaned.

"Oh, don't be ridiculous," Regan said. "I've heard some royal tales that put all of that to shame."

"Sorrel had quite the reputation," I agreed.

The big parties my brothers threw invited every corner of the nobility for drinking, gambling, and other such scandal. Of course, Abel was just as bad, but my father didn't care unless they posed especially big problems. Several times, the parties were so riotous the royal guard had to come in and put them down.

I was strictly banned from these events. I always snuck in, of course, but I took no joy in drinking myself to oblivion and being sick in one of the fountains in the castle garden. My brothers used their soirees to entertain certain ladies too. Of course, there was a fight for the crown and Sorrel had a whole harem harking at the chance of becoming queen. Abel, who could barely hold a conversation, had numerous lovers too of all genders. People really would do anything for power.

My stomach twisted as I thought of our family halls as I had seen them. Full of death, gore and ruin. I pushed the thought aside. "He was the heir apparent, and everyone knew it."

"Saying that, your reputation was that you were as pure, meek, and passive as a lamb," Aoife said. "But now I've met you, that doesn't seem correct."

Reputation was everything to my father and thus none of my disappearances or trips outside of the castle were ever mentioned. I was a princess of stained glass – an art piece ready for someone's window. It felt good to be rid of that ridiculous image. I was never passive or delicate; I mean, there was nothing wrong with that, but for me, those words didn't fit. I was never going to choose to be that person either. That choice had been taken away from me.

"What was real, and what my father told people were different things," I replied. "He was never happy with how I turned out."

"Does that mean you have conquest stories too?" Aoife said, nudging my arm. Her blue eyes sparkled. "Please tell me you've got some sexy lover tucked away somewhere safe." She wiggled in her seat.

I shrugged and tried a smile. My stomach had twisted

126

uncomfortably.

"None as vibrant as Regan's, I fear. But I had a partner for a while," I started to say. "It didn't end very well."

"A Prince?"

"A stable hand."

Suddenly, I felt a cold presence sliding onto my lap. He drew his tail up into a circle, his beady dark eyes looking up.

"You do not control your feelings well, Your Majesty," he hissed, a forked tongue slithering out. "I could feel the tale of woe bringing down your heart from over there."

I raised my eyebrows.

"And you came over to check on me?"

Brenn's onyx eyes looked bored.

"Only to observe your discomfort," he said indifferently. I sent him a half-smile: what a strange creature.

Aoife's eyes were only full of questions now.

"Now I have to know," Regan declared, rubbing her hands together.

"You don't have to tell us anything, Princess," Donna said, elbowing Regan in her muscled arm.

"No, it's okay," I said. "It was a long time ago."

It had been years now – even though the wound still stung like had happened yesterday.

"He was called Randall," I said. "He worked in the stables, but he was actually training to be an alchemist."

I smiled at the memory, even though my heart was growing tight like spring. "I liked him for years until I said anything." Of course, a princess and a servant couldn't be seen interacting like that. Any level of informality was disgraceful for both of us. "I was meant to ignore him, and he was meant to ignore me." Aoife smiled, but it didn't quite reach her eyes. "Of course, I couldn't very well ignore the most handsome boy I had ever seen."

"We used to sneak out into town and explore together. I showed him the catacombs, and we fell in love." I thought briefly of the nights we had spent together. Between the silk sheets of my bedchamber, or underground in a den we'd made from stolen palace blankets. We filled the cavern up with candlelight and the jewels

127

down there would sparkle like stars on the walls.

I bit my lip: maybe I was too tired for this after all. I never got the chance to say goodbye. I swallowed hard. I couldn't think about this anymore.

"My father didn't want me disgracing us, so he had him killed," I finished. "One of his finest hours." My chest felt unsteady. Perhaps Brenn could feel it as he wound his way up to my shoulder. Their faces were mixed with empathy and sadness, but I couldn't rid myself of the sick feeling in my belly to say anything more.

"Your father was the worst," Regan said first. Aoife nodded.

"At least you're free now," Donna added.

"Yeah, make a new reputation for yourself," Aoife said encouragingly. "The renegade Princess who harnessed the Wraith of the Wastes, beat a Bonekeeper, and escaped out of Draig – that's not a bad place to start."

I nodded and patted Brenn's head next to me.

"'Harnessed' is a very optimistic word to use," he grumbled, his dark face frowning.

I yawned. "Mind if we retire? He might not need sleep," I gestured to Brenn, "but I do, and today was too much when I got up this morning, let alone now."

"I'll lead you up," Donna offered as got up from her seat, the wooden feet scratching against the floor. She towered over me and I thought of the giant dragon-kin in the headquarters and realised it must be a hereditary trait. Evan moved to follow her.

"Oh, sit down, you berk," she told him. "Unless you want to lose a limb."

Evan crossed his arms; Captain Bennett had an amused look on his face and Caden smirked. He gave them both a rude gesture with his fingers.

"Goodnight, guys," I said to them.

"Goodnight, Bryony," Aoife called as we left the room. A cacophony of calls followed her, and my heart felt a little softer in my chest. "And Brenn!" she added, to which I swear Brenn flicked his tail.

Donna led me up to a small, white-panelled room with a window, a bed, and a wash sink. I spotted a tub tucked into the corner for washing in and found myself longing for a bath. She waved the witchlight on, and it sputtered out a muted yellow glow.

"Sorry, it isn't much," she murmured. "Our guest rooms are all full of merchandise now. This one was for the old staff when this place was run by the shifters."

It had a door that I could close and that was all I needed right now.

"It's perfect," I said.

Donna gave me a half-smile.

"Let me know if you need anything," she said, but she paused before she closed the door. "Also, I just wanted to say, I'm sorry for before." The dragon-kin's orange scales glinted against the rest of her pale skin. She had beautiful hazel eyes that seemed to possess all the colours of autumn leaves. "For pulling an axe on you – and everything before that." I chuckled.

"It's fine," I said. "Trust me, it's becoming part of my routine at this point."

She smiled a little, then added.

"Goodnight, Bryony."

"Goodnight, Donna."

With the close of the door, I flopped down on the bed. The sheets were old but not dirty. The aches I had been ignoring from this never-ending day had been wreaking havoc on my knees. I kicked off my boots and curled my legs on the bed. Brenn slithered up next to my head.

"You ducked out of that chat, your Majesty," his words were curious. "I didn't need to read your mind to know how you were feeling."

I shrugged. Brenn had already seen Randall in my head when I let him in within the Tower. The cavern cored into my heart caused by Randall's death hadn't gone away. Only over time, I learned how to traverse the stones better. My regrets had long been etched into those rocks.

"There are no wounds deeper than those caused by love," I said.

Brenn tilted his head.

"What about if you lost all your limbs?"

I didn't reply. "It was a legitimate question."

129

"Maybe then it would be a little worse," I said. Brenn hissed with his forked tongue in response. I eyed the Wraith: a strange being indeed.

"You were a human once," as I spoke the Wraith stopped moving. "Did you ever fall in love?"

"I lived in a time and the very beginning of your line," he said indignantly. "If I remembered anything about my life then – I wouldn't tell you, your Majesty."

"Why not?" I asked, crossing my arms. "I tell you everything."

Brenn narrowed his eyes.

"Yes, I know – even though I never ask." Brenn stretched his slippery body long. "You would never stop asking me questions and would be irritating."

"Rude."

I could feel my chest getting tight. It was too late. My memories refused to be pushed away. The room was quiet, and eventually, my exhaustion got the better of me.

The drapes had been changed in my room. The pale pink swathes of chiffon and embroidered satin were now a delicate shade of lilac, the colour of fresh lavender. I was thirteen, Sorrel was teetering on manhood, and Abel had terrible spots across his face.

I was perched on my windowsill. Our city was abuzz as any weekend was, but it was extra special this weekend. Even the castle was busy – my maids, Emmeline and Frieda, had been hijacked to attend Sorrel's victory party.

The noise emanating from downstairs was enough to tempt me into sneaking away from my bedroom and to the great hall. On many occasions, like the start of the season or one of the hundreds of balls we threw, the palace was dressed to perfection. However, with Sorrel at the helm – the painted walls with the sculpted golden trim looked very different.

Drapes of silk hung over every window. Someone had bewitched the chandelier to glow red, and feathers filled the floor between forgotten garb, ribbons, and shoes. I looked about for my father, but he wasn't among the revellers for once. Instead, there were around a hundred aristocratic men in various stages of undress and scantily clad women drinking and dancing to sensuous music.

When he wasn't on the battlefield, or bullying Abel into training with him, this was Sorrel's scene – where the ladies of the court would try their luck. Sorrel's handsome face was enough for many a lady to forget their maid's warnings about how my brother treated women. He viewed females in the same manner he viewed his servants: useful at certain times of day, but ultimately expendable.

All the talk at court surrounded a band of rogue werewolves who had stumbled across the border. I didn't know much about the extent of them, but rogues were usually dangerous; unaligned werewolves who had lost control of their animal instincts and no longer bowed to an Alpha. Sorrel had gathered an eager hunting party and there were no survivors. My stomach turned over when I saw what he had brought back from the hunt: seventeen pelts. A few of which were oddly small. I nearly vomited.

"That's vile, Sorrel," I exclaimed when he had presented them to me. Had the Syree Royals found out what he had done, hell, had any Werewolf found out, he would've easily caused a war with our neighbours. Even the worst criminals had death rites – a burial ritual. But stealing a wolf's coat was beyond insult: it was their skin.

Sorrel smacked his lips together before shrugging his shoulders. His embroidered royal blue tunic was hanging open and his white shirt underneath was splattered with wine. At least, I hoped it was wine. He still wore his riding boots and his Crown-Prince coronet rested at a wonky angle on his head. His ice-blue eyes met mine.

"Father loved them."

My head was pounding. Sorrel reeked of wine and smoke. The smell of alcohol could've easily emanated from a brewery. It was still early – had I come in later, no doubt I would've seen other things that would've turned my stomach further. I spotted Abel, red-faced and languid on a collection of cushions surrounded by men and women with feathers and flowers in their hair. He loved to be doted on, and they loved being paid.

"You better put those away," I told him. The pelts had been thrown at the foot of the throne like some grotesque tribute. One of Sorrel's right-hand men was lying across one as if it were a goose feather cushion. "I'm not being torn apart by wolves when they find

131

out."

Sorrel waved one hand and used his other to finish his glass of red wine. His face contorted as he glanced back to his entourage and raised an eyebrow arrogantly. His ego could overshadow Kya entirely.

"I needed a new cloak," Sorrel replied. Around him, his friends laughed, but I wasn't cowed. "They're only *animals*."

"You're the only animals I see," I retorted. People in conversation around us dropped to hushed voices to listen in.

Sorrel's eyes turned nasty.

"You're no fun," he sneered. "Beat it before Father catches you."

Sorrel's friends were all rich snobs – I would've rather had my teeth pulled out than enjoy their company a moment longer. The older I grew, the more their eyes would linger on me as I walked by. On more than one occasion, I heard one of them joke to my brother about taking me off his hands. My skin crawled.

Had nothing changed, I had no doubt I would've eventually been shipped off to one of them. I sighed. At least this story had one silver lining.

I remembered heading down to the kitchen, where great fancy delicacies were being constructed for the feast; I stole a cake shaped like a palm-sized sun and then shimmied out of the stockroom window. It was a fast way to get into the gardens after hours. None of the kitchen staff ever ratted me out. I knew they had been around when my mother was here, so maybe that played a part of it.

Anyway, back then, I clutched at my skirts and hoisted myself through the grate up onto the gravel. The guards were either at the border or minding the party from the front entrance. No one stopped me as I headed out down the gardens at the back of the palace. The noise from the party drifted away the further I got, replaced by the songs of crickets and owls. I headed to one of my favourite spots. Its best feature was that it was away from the palace and a comfy spot to sit and be alone.

The glade was hidden just behind the stables. Once upon a time, a few members of the Dean Fae had come and blessed the garden for the royals here. They had such excellent green fingers; their gardens were always filled with the most marvellous blossoms and blooms. Such good relations hadn't been seen in generations of my family's reign and yet the flowers always returned. Bright, lovely, and thriving with life. And in the evenings, just before dusk, fireflies filled the air, and moon lilies began to glow.

Of course, I shouldn't have been out unsupervised. Princesses weren't meant to go anywhere without a governess. Fortunately for me, my current governess at the time, Nanny Gill, a beautiful blonde woman with a voluminous figure, had been won over by one of Sorrel's cronies. And, well, she couldn't very well say no to the Crown Prince of Riach – could she?

Thus, for the next few hours, I was free.

I sat under my favourite tree in the glade and closed my eyes. I could still see the glowing lights of the fireflies behind my eyelids.

Someone cleared their throat, and I glanced up. I recognised the floppy brown hair from the stables; he had his cap screwed up in his hands. He wore dark trousers, boots, a brown loose shirt, and a beaten jacket.

"Your Majesty," he started to say. "Shouldn't you be in the palace?"

I frowned at that.

"Probably. But 'Your Majesty' is for when you are addressing my father," I told him. "Bryony will do." The boy looked surprised. "But 'Your Highness' when you're around anyone who it will matter to."

The boy looked back at the stables; the lights had gone out now. The horses had been put to bed until morning.

"You can go if you want," I said, sensing his worries. "I'll be fine."

The boy put his hands in his pockets.

"I feel bad about leaving you here," he said.

I grinned at him. Perhaps the boy had not expected that reaction – his brown eyes went wide. "I'll worry."

"If I could come with you, will that quell your worries?"

He laughed a little at the idea but then realised the sincerity of my question. He quickly opened his mouth but shortly closed it again as his expression changed to bafflement.

"Won't you be missed?"

I chuckled at his concerned expression.

"They won't even notice I am gone."

133

He realised he was still holding his cap, and he hastily put it back on.

"You know the city, don't you?" I asked, climbing to my feet.

"Yes, Bryony," he responded, trying out my name.

I brushed down my dress. And as I looked up, I realised he was smiling back.

"I've never spoken to a Princess before," he said, bashfully.

I shrugged my shoulders.

"That's definitely your loss," I said. "Because this one," I pointed to myself, "is great." His surprised grin made my heart flutter unexpectedly.

I set off in the direction of the gate, pulling my cloak up over my head. When I didn't hear his feet behind me, I turned around. The amusement on his face was lit up by the night lilies that had started to glow.

"Come on then," I called, waving him over.

"But where are we going?" he asked, speeding up to catch up with me.

Our feet tapped as we walked along the paved stones of the yard. I turned to check we weren't being followed, but as expected, there wasn't a soul around.

"On an adventure!" I replied. "You need to give me your name since I traded mine."

Somewhat bemused by my energy and happy to be swept along, he chuckled.

"I like an adventure. And it's Randall."

I felt a warm tear run down my cheek before I swiped it away. Meeting him had been the best thing in my life thus far – yet, knowing me, is what doomed his.

"It wasn't your fault," Brenn said quietly next to me. One might have even assumed that was kindness in his voice – if they did not know him well. "You cannot blame yourself for the stupidity of others."

I half-smiled as I sniffed and wiped my face.

"Can one being in love really be called stupidity?"

"I think love is the definition of stupidity."

I sighed. "I think I might agree with you on that."

Brenn raised his head and noiselessly slid off the bed.

"Might I take a moment to investigate this place?" he declared. "I want to see if the whole thing is a dishevelled mess or if that is just the crew."

I shrugged my shoulders.

"I'm not sure they would take too kindly to you just wandering about on your own." I couldn't see that kind of behaviour going down very well with Evan in particular. "Can you do it without being seen?"

Brenn closed his eyes and his snake form evaporated. There was no black smoke this time – there was nothing.

I sat up.

"Brenn?"

A waft of cold air floated onto my legs.

"I'm still here, Your Majesty," he replied, his voice now a sort of echo.

I guffawed.

"So now you know invisibility magic too?" A rumble chuckle followed soon after.

"How do you think I did all those murders before?" His voice sounded eerily like wind through the gaps in a windowpane. "I didn't knock on the door."

If I was fazed by this, I was too tired to feel it.

"Can you teach me?" I asked. "I want to learn. I want to learn more magic."

Brenn didn't respond for a moment.

"No."

I frowned.

"Why not?"

"I don't want to."

I looked at the space where I presumed Brenn was.

"I'm sure you'll be great."

There was another beat.

"Things are different for me, as I'm not human anymore," Brenn explained. "I'm ultimately more powerful than you, and the process for me is entirely different from it was when I was a human." He

135

spoke fast.

"So, you do remember being human, then?" I quipped. "That's interesting."

Brenn groaned and I couldn't help my smile.

"Leave me alone, you curious creature." I heard a rustle of the sheets as Brenn must've flown to the door. "May I go now?"

"Yes, but return if I call you using the link or you see anything that requires immediate attention," I said. "And get me some books on magic – if we're going to sea, we will need something to occupy the time with."

Brenn grumbled as he left. I only knew he had gone when the room was completely silent, traipsing the halls like a strange, spirit guard dog.

I kicked off my boots and pulled off the trousers, which were now so muddy they could've stood up by themselves. Then I unravelled the bands around my chest. Even though the crew now knew my secret, I figured I must keep up the act until we were at sea, and I was settled in Wist. I made myself get up and wash before deciding to just sleep in my shirt and underpants. I could've asked to borrow one from one of the other girls, but I didn't have the energy to move.

Hopefully, Brenn would bring back books on glamouring or shape-shifting, then I wouldn't need to be so concerned with what I looked like. A glamour worked like a smokescreen for editing appearances. I remembered some of the financially well-endowed of court paid handsomely for such a service.

If only the practice was forbidden – I would've learned it myself then. However, my cluster of talents were illegal at the best of times and deeply unethical at the worst. But they were still talents.

I huddled myself beneath the blanket. The soft sheets were stiff at first, but as I warmed up, so did they. I felt my shoulders finally ease and then I closed my eyes before drifting away into the warmth and the darkness. Randall filled my thoughts once more, and I prayed he was at peace.

Eleven

Aoife made climbing rigging look easy. She scaled the mast with ease, ran to the crow's nest before she launched off onto a rope with the grace of an acrobat and then swung to safety on the deck. I itched to have a go myself, but I doubted I would have the dexterity of the first mate. Of course, Brenn told me that was the worst idea I had that morning and that I should stay exactly where I was unless I wanted to die.

The blue ends of her hair flashed as Aoife moved, and she wore a red leather buccaneer's coat – just like the captain's but in a deep scarlet. With her tan breeches and high boots, I felt like my wardrobe was in serious need of adapting for a life on the seas. Next to me, Brenn's scowl deepened on his face; his new human form, the same masculine face from Draig, had mimicked the outfit the captain wore but seemed to be in better condition and he skipped the tricorn.

We stood at the docks beside The Siren's Promise. She was a great wooden ship with an impressive number of guns and the figurehead of a siren at the bow; her head crowned in a spiked tiara as her peaceful face gazed on at the waves. The dark brown of the wood was weathered with the lower levels carrying barnacles and seaweed in the scuppers.

The carved woman at the front cast an eerie gaze across the water. A strange choice for a figurehead, really. Beautiful women who lured unsuspecting sailors into dangerous waters where they met a watery death. Not exactly a fate anyone would wish to tempt. People tended to put a goddess or saint at the front – to guide their adventures across the waves – not infamous sea creatures.

I knew from my reading that sirens were a race that dwelled in the waters of the Shadow Realms, among other monsters of the deep. The coves near the Wastes and Silvia were rumoured to lead to their underwater lairs, though the truth from any alleged survivors was as flimsy as a jellyfish's leg.

"So, Bryony," Aoife said, calling to me from the deck. "What do you think of her?"

"I think she's marvellous!" I called back. Her freckled face lit up.

I looked at Brenn, whose face hadn't changed at all.

"It's a boat." I elbowed him. "A *big* boat."

The Promise towered over the rest of the boats and fishing vessels in the dock; its impressive masts casting imposing shadows in the morning sun. The residents of Newt watched the ship prepare to depart. The potent smell of fish and the noise of the morning flow of commerce filled the air as the dock bustled with life. Other vessels had already departed to make use of the clear weather, or perhaps just to get out of the way of Captain Bennett's vast ship.

Aoife and Regan lowered a big wooden ladder down the side of the boat to the dock so we could climb aboard. Brenn went first so he could laugh as I wobbled my way up. I gripped the plaited hemp rope hard, and its bristly fibres dug into my palm. Heights were not something I usually struggled with, but the wind was strong today, making the blue frothing waves take height beneath the boat. It made my knees weaken as I climbed the different rungs, feeling the rise and fall of the deck with the waves.

The deck moved a little underfoot as we traversed the ship, causing my stomach to lurch too. Now higher up, the wind whipped the saltwater air across my face, and I was thankful for once for the loss of my hair. Perhaps that explained why both Aoife and Regan kept their hair short, and Donna plaited hers back tightly.

Aoife gave us a tour as we reached the deck, explaining everything from the masts to the helm. As we reached the bow, Aoife opened a small wooden door that led down a short flight of narrow stairs. Then she set about showing us the underbelly of the wooden beast. I knew very little about ships or sailing, but I was determined to become a master of all things nautical by this journey's end. We descended two-gun decks and a galley before reaching the lowest point of the orlop deck just above the hull of the boat. The galley had been full of strange mechanisms with oar-shaped arms attached to the outer case of the bow through off portholes that somehow kept the water out. I wondered about the purpose of the machines and the first mate explained it would be easier for me to see them in action. I tried my best to not look too surprised by the vastness of the space below the main deck, and Brenn said very little while looking unimpressed.

138

When I asked how such a small crew commanded such a giant vessel, Aoife shrugged.

"The Siren's Promise is special." She didn't elaborate and evaded all my further questions. But even so, I could feel magic running through this place like a lifeline. It was strange though – I couldn't pinpoint a source.

Aoife concluded her tour by showing us the crew quarters in the forecastle at the front of the ship below the deck. Regan and Donna shared a bunk, as did Caden and Evan. But Aoife's room was next to the captain's at the helm end of the ship. Our bunk consisted of two bunk beds and a short set of drawers that had latches to keep them shut when the ship was moving about. Everything was nailed to the floor to accommodate any poor weather and Aoife added it was very unlikely that I would fall out of bed, but if it was something I was concerned about, I should choose the lower bunk.

Bad weather be damned, I immediately hopped up to the bunk on top and claimed it as my own. Brenn didn't test out his. He only remarked that the height of the bed did not make it more or less comfortable, and he didn't accept my answer when I said it was still better. It had a tiny porthole window by my feet and if I pressed my head against it, I could hear the sea rumbling outside.

A knock on the door had me sitting upright. Donna and Regan poked their heads in, and Aoife lingered in the doorway.

"I guess this is the first time you've bunked up on a ship," Regan said, looking at the cabin. "You're lucky with your height. Poor Donna and I have to sleep curled up like prawns."

"It's a time of firsts," I said delightedly. "This is my first time on a like this boat too." I swung my legs off the side of the bunk before hopping down.

"Ever?" Donna asked. Aoife's eyes had gone wide.

"Pretty much," I replied. "I never went on any big expeditions. This is all new to me."

Brenn just shook his head at that and turned to Aoife, his voice a bored drawl.

"What's the plan? Or are there any sea rituals we must partake in before we can leave?"

I glared at Brenn, but before I could say anything, Aoife

responded.

"We will depart when the captain is ready," she said with an unbothered smile. "In terms of rituals, we dump any deadweight, so keep it up and you'll be floating."

Brenn didn't reply. Aoife turned to me.

"Come up for a moment. Captain Bennett has something he needs to discuss."

I told Brenn he could stay in the cabin if he wanted to rest, but he grimaced and followed me up on deck. Evan was swabbing the planks clean near the bow, but stopped to scowl at the Wraith. Brenn deliberately walked right over his newly tidied area and went to sit on the gunwale railing of the boat, ignoring the growls that Evan was sending his way.

I followed Aoife to the captain's quarters, which lay under the quarterdeck. The two rooms were the only ones above deck: a main wide and long one, with a smaller room to the side. I knew from the tour that the smaller one was Aoife's. Just from the doors, the rooms seemed grander than the other cabins.

Aoife knocked on a polished mahogany door with a bronze circle window in it.

"Come in," came Bennett's reply.

The room was an oval shape. The walls were full of shelves that contained books and trinkets in a gloriously untidy fashion. A wide row of windows behind the desk looked out on the blue horizon and to the right was a printed cotton folding screen – covering I assumed what were the captain's sleeping quarters.

The hefty wooden desk was loaded with a huge map and tools that looked like they were for drafting courses. The captain had hung up his buccaneer's coat and wore a black waistcoat, a white shirt, and black breeches. He had tied his dark hair back, making his scar more prominent in the daylight; his dark eyes flicked up to me and the corner of his lip quirked into a smile. There was a roguish charm about him, something I was sure had not gone unnoticed by the first mate standing next to me.

However, Bennett wasn't focused on mapping our journey; he was fixing the hilt of what looked to be a blunt training sword. The kind I was used to seeing when Sorrel first started training in the militia.

"Ah, your Highness," Bennett said with a smile as he finished fixing the handle in leather binding before laying aside. "I just wanted to run something by you. That Bonekeeper you encountered – do you remember his name?"

How could I forget? Those deep red eyes were burned in my mind.

"Aegius DuVale called him General Titae," I replied. "Huge man. Dark Hair. Red eyes."

Bennett grimaced. Slowly, he placed his hands against the desk.

"Blast." He brushed his hair back out of his face. "I hoped we could avoid this."

Instantly, my teeth were on edge. I cast a look down at the sword.

"Your Highness—"

"Please, just call me Bryony," I told him. "I prefer it." My stomach was sinking.

"Bryony, we have some bad news." His voice was apologetic but Aoife narrowed her eyes.

"We? You." She replied. "Our dear captain has a confession."

The pair shared a look; the captain clenched his jaw, but Aoife didn't back down. Those dark eyes were glinting – flicking between me and the beautiful blue of hers.

"My *bold* first mate has decided that this incident was my fault," he said reluctantly.

Aoife groaned.

"So, it turns out we are already familiar with the Bonekeeper that attacked you," Aoife interjected. The captain threw a hand up. The first mate scoffed. "Oh please. It would've been the next moon cycle before you finished!"

"We were at the new port opening in Hook and there was some nasty business over something being stolen from the Demon King," Captain Bennett went on. "It was very unfortunate."

"Someone shouldn't have stolen a royal diadem…"

"How was I meant to know they would miss it?" Captain Bennett grumbled. "Plus, I thought it was romantic."

141

"So, it was your fault?" I concluded. Aoife crossed her arms next to me.

Bennett gave me a flat look and crossed his arms too.

"It was Evan's idea." He cleared his throat. "Anyway, his Royal Demoness was very upset with this and sent the best Bonekeeper for the job, his own son, Prince Kyan." Aoife's expression seemed to have darkened, and the captain had noticed. "And judging by your depiction of his person – and the information I received via my friends on the border of Draig in Delth, I worry that it is the same Bonekeeper that we ran into those few years ago. He doesn't go by his father's name when on foreign missions he goes by his mother's: Titae."

"The prince?" I asked. Perhaps I had misheard. Captain Bennett nodded.

Prince Kyan? My blood iced over. The general I had incapacitated was the Prince of Raize? I remembered the feeling of his core through my magic – the heat and fury. Those scarlet eyes that would surely haunt me for the rest of my days. Suddenly, I felt very unwell. This was not the way I had ever imagined beginning diplomatic relations. Not only had the Demons sided with Fynix – they had been instrumental in the destruction of my capital.

"The Demon prince," Aoife said with a sigh before she sent the captain a pointed look. "If only someone hadn't got caught."

Captain Bennett guffawed. "What a ridiculous spectacle that was," Aoife added, grinding her teeth together.

"He almost took my hands off!" Bennett exclaimed. "Plus, if we had just given it back, they would've known I'd stolen it."

"You did steal it."

"It deserved life outside of the royal collection," Captain Bennett finished. Aoife waved him off with an unsurprised expression.

"Anyway," he continued. "If it is the prince looking for you, then being with us is just going to complicate things for you. If you want to live, that is."

I sighed and shrugged my shoulders. I'd knocked out the heir to the demon kingdom. My infallible sense of courage was straining a little with the thought of the Demon King. Who knows what he would do to us should we be caught?

142

"Now the world knows I'm alive and working with the Wraith I'm not sure working with pirates will prove me less irredeemable than I already am," I said with a sigh. "As for staying alive, Brenn and I are in a pact together. If I were to die, he would be unleashed on the world – free to do whatever he fancied doing. Thus, killing me wouldn't be the brightest idea."

Aoife weighed this with a shrug. "Besides, they have to catch us first," she said. "The Siren's Promise is the fastest vessel on the sea. It's what we're famous for." Her voice was full of pride.

Captain Bennett stretched his arms above his head.

"That's not the only thing we're famous for," he added smugly.

"Yes, we're rather infamous for having a drunken womaniser as a captain," Aoife added. Bennett's jaw dropped. "Very impressive."

"Then I'm sure we have nothing to worry about!" I replied. "If that's all, I should probably go check that Brenn hasn't chewed through Evan."

Aoife nodded. "Sorry about the extra worry – he's a turnip."

I shrugged my shoulders.

"It's okay. If I worried about everyone who wanted to kill me, I'd never get anything done," I added. "Thanks for the heads up though." I was doing my best to ignore the wriggling of nerves in my stomach.

A demon prince would surely complicate matters now I had attacked him. Surely that was treason in Raize? Even if it was done in self-defence? Perhaps he wouldn't have attacked me if he had known who I was.

"Go rest up," Aoife added as I passed her to the door. "We've got a beast of a journey."

I nodded.

"See you shortly."

I headed to the door and before it shut behind me, I heard Bennett speak to Aoife.

"A quiet shop in Raize," Aoife said. "That's what you said."

Captain Bennett hummed appreciatively. "I'm very romantic."

"You're nothing but trouble."

"But you look so lovely wearing it."

She *giggled*.

I found Brenn lounging in cat-form on my bed when I returned to the cabin. He was covered in dark fur, much like a feline shadow, and showed no effort to get up once I entered.

"That's a new one," I remarked as I came into the room. I clambered up on my bed and was careful to not sit on him. "Would you like your belly rubbed?"

"Would you like to lose a hand?" It was most unnerving to watch the cat's mouth move and words come out instead of a tirade of hungry meows. "This form fits this atmosphere," he declared.

"So, nothing to do with the long-haired ginger tom roaming around then?"

Brenn flicked his tail. Earlier on deck, the ship's cat had shown no hesitation towards the Wraith. He walked right between his legs and mewled noisily for attention. Usually, someone would pick him up for cuddles, and since Brenn had not bent to the cat's whim, the cat decided he no longer wanted to play: he wanted to fight.

"That cat is far too entitled," he ground out. "Plus, in this form, I can eat any mice before that cat does."

"Naps?" I mused. Brenn got up and made an effort to walk across my legs heavily before he dropped to the floor.

"Don't name the beast," he seethed. "He will rue the day he ever crossed me."

"Don't kill it," I called as I saw his midnight fur vanish down the corridor.

I lay back on my bunk – you could barely feel the waves here. Besides any incoming storms, I doubted I would have any trouble sleeping here. I looked up at the door that Brenn had so thoughtfully left open and groaned.

Then the idea came to me. I'd seen Caden move things upstairs with such ease. Cargo boxes floating from platform to platform carried by swirls of green light in the air. Surely, it couldn't be as difficult as summoning lightning. I lifted my head and raised my hand. Magic grew in my chest – I pulled it to my fingers. I knew none of the spell movements, so I adapted my forward bolt into what I thought would be a soft gentle motion.

The magic in my fingertips zipped out, and immediately I knew I had made a mistake. The noise sounded like a small cannon going off as it whipped through the air and burned a hole straight through the waiting door. Smoking wood filled my nose as the edge around the gap faded from a glow to a dark crisp.

"What the hell was that?" Donna yelled from down the hall.

"Nothing," I replied, getting to my feet and shutting the door. The recent addition was no bigger than a bronze coin. Tentatively, I reached out my fingers and they poked straight through.

I swore loudly through my teeth.

"Oo-er, Her Royal Highness has a foul mouth," I heard Regan say from down the hall.

"If you'd had to live with my brothers, you'd end up with one too."

I abandoned the hole – hopefully, Brenn would be able to fix it. Groaning, I flopped onto the lower bed. I looked at my lightning-burned hand – the red strikes seemed to say, "Look what a mess you've made." I wasn't bothered about how the veins looked now, but when compared to my other hand, the redness looked angry.

At that moment, I wondered if I could glamour it and I remembered the bag that Brenn had stashed under his bed and the books he had collected. He told me that I should wait until we set off for the voyage as I would want something to do.

Bored, I leaned over the side of his bunk and reached out a hand. Upon feeling nothing, I craned my neck and looked under. The sneaky whatsit had pushed it right up at the back. A mewl from behind me made me turn – ginger hair and wide golden eyes watched me. Naps came up to me and sniffed my leg, his long whiskers twitching, his fur glowed from the light streaming in from the porthole. The cat watched as I curled myself over and pulled the bag forward.

The leather sack was stuffed full of books and as I yanked the biggest one free, the rest spilled out onto the floor with a thud. It was a beaten copy of *Basic Motion: Spell Work* by Angelo Sloe. The spine had been well and truly broken in and I ran my fingers down the ink-blotted pages. The next was a lean purple book with silver lacing work along the cover and the back. Printed on it was *The Art of Masquerade* by H. Ding. It didn't look worn like the other. In fact, it looked brand new.

145

I sighed. I had hoped he would borrow books that wouldn't be missed. However, I assumed that was my fault for being optimistic. At least now I had some books for the journey that was ahead.

Glamouring and motion were a good start: perhaps Brenn was listening to me after all. I took the motion book and clambered to my feet. The boat seemed to be swaying side to side now, my shins working harder to keep myself upright.

I tucked the book under my arm as I headed up the wooden stairs to get onto the deck. Over by the forecastle, I saw Regan's massive arms heaving at the capstan as a great silver chain connected to an even bigger, heavier anchor was raised from the side of the ship. I heard the noise of metal and wood grinding against each other as the device turned slowly. As she moved, I saw that Donna and Evan had joined her in pushing the other bars in a clockwise direction. I went over to offer assistance, but Regan shook her head before I could even offer.

"I've seen your arms, Princess."

I gasped with feigned offence.

"What? These muscles?" Then I flexed my arms, which produced nothing but squishy flesh. Regan laughed lowly.

Watching as he flicked his tail back and forth was Brenn. He sat at the centre – being slowly turned around and around.

"You know, you could always help, Brenn," breathed Donna in as upbeat a voice as she could manage. Evan's face scrunched up like it always did whenever anyone spoke to Brenn.

Brenn tilted his head and then hopped off the device.

"But I am a lowly cat," he padded across the deck before sitting back on his hind paws and raising his front ones. "No thumbs."

Regan snorted at that. With a final wrench, I saw the anchor hoist to the side of the ship. It was full of seaweed and bitten raw with rust. Regan secured the rest of the chain and straightened it back up. Evan and Donna panted with effort, but not her. She simply clicked the chain in place and brushed off her hands.

"You should've let me help," I said as she came up to me, realising that I only came up to her shoulder. Donna was a giant – but Regan was the tallest, even taller than Caden and the captain. She grinned. Now in the sun, I could see her hair better. She did it in a

146

strange fashion – long down the back but shaved at the sides. Her hair was dark at the roots but almost fair on the ends, perhaps from long hours in the sun.

"And let you pull every bone in your body? No, thank you." She wore a white vest top and sandy-coloured breeches with multiple pockets around the hips. "This is hardy work."

I frowned.

"I can do hardy work. I'm very hardy."

"I don't doubt that, darling," Regan replied. "However, you need actual muscles if you want to work aboard this vessel."

Donna sent Regan a reprimanding look.

"You don't need to do anything, Bryony," she said kindly.

"Thank you but no," I declared – behind me, Brenn sighed. "I'll pull my weight."

"Reason is optional to her Majesty," Brenn said. "Best save your breath, dragon-kin."

"That's not true," I retorted. Regan crossed her giant biceps in front of me. "Besides, I was never planning on just sitting like a plant pot during the voyage. If I don't keep busy, I'm sure I'll go mad."

Brenn mumbled something about how he was sure my mind couldn't get any worse than it already was.

"I want to be useful."

Regan eyed me for a moment before shrugging her shoulders.

"Sure," she said. "Maybe then you won't look so weedy." Donna looked mortified. "Oh please, Don. She's a Princess, not a *Priestess*."

"Werewolves have no tact," Evan said, leaning back on the banister. A growl sounded from where Regan was standing – her eyes flashed dangerously. "It makes them so easy to mess with."

"You're a werewolf?"

Regan turned to me, a strange expression on her face.

"I thought it was obvious."

Donna's eyes flicked between us – a colourful history had befallen our two kingdoms – even before the war. We were natural enemies. Both from ancient cultures with proud traditions – only now my people had fallen to ruin and the cultures of the Syree remained unbroken.

"My observation skills clearly need work," I said. "Maybe if you

rolled in the mud some more and let me scratch behind your ears —
then I would've noticed sooner."

Evan chuckled next to them, and Donna's eyes widened as
Regan, after a beat, laughed the loudest.

"Cheeky witch," she laughed.

"See, at least your observational skills are better than mine," I
replied.

She wiped her eyes and clapped a hand on my shoulder, which
nearly sent me flying.

"We'll make a pirate out of you yet, Princess."

The action took the wind out of me and made my book clatter to
the floor. I ducked to pick it up as Regan walked to the helm.

"Please don't tell me Donna has already convinced you to join
her smutty book club," the wolf groaned from the top at the dragon-
kin, gesturing with a hand to me. "She's only been here for five
minutes!" Regan stamped the floor twice — I realised then the helm
was right above the captain's quarters.

Donna flushed furiously.

"I have done no such thing!" She fumed. Regan raised an
eyebrow and the moment her back was turned Donna mouthed
'Later!' to me. I grinned and nodded. I had never been part of any
club before besides a sewing circle and dancing lessons, which were
part of my education as a woman of the court.

Evan was headed to the bow but inspected the book I had in my
hands.

"This is a spell book," I explained as I showed the battered
cover. "Brenn picked up some for me when we were in town."

"I love shopping," Brenn added.

"Motion magic, yeah?" Evan said next to me. "I haven't seen
books like this since I was a fledgling demon."

A small part of my chest sunk a little, but I wasn't to be deterred.
Everyone had to start somewhere!

However, it must've shown on my face somewhat as Donna
swatted his arm which made his face fall. Before he could say
anything more, a door was flung open and the captain, in his leather
buccaneer coat, strode into view. His black waistcoat and white shirt
that seemed a little dishevelled, but were all fixed as he took his place

148

at the helm with Aoife in tow.

"Right, troublemakers, get your asses in gear," he called. "We're off."

Finally, we pulled away from the dock with Regan at the helm.

The great white sails were let loose by Evan and Donna who climbed the rigging on either side, and we took to the water as the white lungs filled with wind and pulled us from the dock. The creaky boards that made up the walkway drifted far from us as we took a new course.

The colourful town of Newt started to shrink into the distance as the Promise sailed easily over the waves, leaving the smaller vessels rocking in her stead. The tall stone buildings on the front started to shrink before my eyes as the wind picked up the air in our sails. Flags from the Shifter nation and some I didn't recognise waved between the old and new buildings surrounding the sea front. Perhaps the Pirate Lords were looking after this place better than my father had after all?

I suddenly felt myself overwhelmed by the feeling that I was leaving something unexplored. I made a mental note to come back here and just explore once things were right again. When I had my throne. When my people were safe – whenever that may be.

The water streamed behind us before the ripples resumed the pattern of the waves. I looked down and saw the churning of the water under the boat. In the glassy reflection, I could see my dark hair merge with the wood of the Siren's Promise.

"I hope you aren't thinking about jumping in, your Majesty," came the familiar drawl of my immortal companion.

I looked down to see the black cat form of Brenn, his onyx eyes looking up at me. He hopped up onto the railing beside me.

"I wasn't going to."

Brenn looked at me in disbelief.

"I don't fancy getting wet right now," I told him. He didn't look convinced. "Plus, I don't feel like that would be the wisest thing I could do."

His whiskers wrinkled. "Surprising that logic came from you, Your Majesty."

149

"Insubordination! I'm full of logic."

Brenn lay flat, padding black paws in front of his body. He seemed appeased by my answer.

"You do strange things."

I frowned.

"And I can't swim." Brenn's eyes snapped open but as he began to speak – Regan boomed over him.

"Come here then, Princess! You're getting a crash course in sailing!"

Twelve

The boat seemed to be flying through the sea as it leapt across the waves. My tongue tasted of salt and, even though it freaked out Brenn, I loved to stay close to the edge, watching wild kelpies appear – all shimmering aquamarine and just as beautiful as they were dangerous. The fish below danced in all colours, and I swore I saw the tails of some bigger creatures swirling in the currents below.

Donna and Evan scaled the rigging like pros as they looked after the masts. They took me up to the nest at the top and I got to see the sprawling countryside that surrounded Newt. The houses seemed to shrink until there was nothing left but long swathes of green. Brenn watched from the ground; his tail sweeping across deck with impatience. He didn't seem keen on me being up so high, or himself for that matter.

I helped them tighten the thick hemp ropes which made my hands burn; Donna had showed me the hard calluses she had built on her normal hand. Her other was hidden beneath impenetrable amber scales, and I recalled Astyanax's hardened skin under my palm.

Donna and Evan swung back to the deck using the mast's holding lines. At the bottom they would secure the lines with great wooden rods. Evan told me it was called a belaying pin and it was used to keep the rope taut which in turn stabilised the masts. I took the slower route down the rigging after being yelled at by Donna for not being careful enough on the top beams. Fearing her wrath, I descended with as much care as I could.

Despite his initial hesitation, Evan seemed to have relaxed around me, even though his smiles seemed a little forced at times. On more than one occasion, I caught Donna sending him a stern look, to which he would throw his hands up in the air or send back a glare of his own.

At least we seemed to be set on a definite course. Aoife explained to me that avoiding the Eastern Isles would be a wise decision. Last time the Siren's Promise travelled there, it was caught in a spot of bother. Apparently, it included the Vampire Princess, her dwarf-half-brother, her werewolf love, and seventeen warlocks who

151

had pledged their loyalty to her. When I asked about it, Aoife just sent a fierce glare to Captain Bennett, who began whistling a merry tune.

It seemed though the captain was at the helm, Aoife was the navigator. She carried what looked to be a leather-bound parchment roll case up to the deck, then she knelt down on the highest part of the gangway and pulled out a swathe of light-coloured fabric. She rolled it out like a mat next to the captain and immediately, small yellow and blue lights glowed from the centre; like fireflies, they started to dart about the map, outlining the land and waters ahead, as well as our current alignment.

I joined them and knelt beside her. A tiny compass figure in the corner pointed North-East. The magic emanating from the object was vast; I could feel the layers of spells washing over me as I came closer. Whoever had enchanted it must've been very powerful indeed.

"Where did you get this?" I asked, letting my fingers run above the glowing lines of the Hook - a curved piece of land that had been reclaimed along with the rest of the coast as part the Free realm. But this map didn't look like the maps I had seen growing up. This map was bigger than I had even expected. I recognised Riach and the Wastes but so many islands and provinces I had never heard of. The Shadow Realms were far vaster that I had realised.

"Is this real?" I asked, gesturing to the expansive countries that made Riach look ever so small in comparison.

The first mate quirked an eyebrow at me.

"Of course," she said. "Riach and the West keep to themselves and don't teach about the rest of the world. But it is far bigger and more dangerous than they would like to believe."

Then Aoife gave me a private smile and glanced a look at the captain who kept an even gaze ahead. I tried not to seem dumbfounded, as if my world hadn't just grown exponentially.

"This was a gift from the most notorious pirate lord," she replied. "It's a wickedly handy thing."

I couldn't agree more. Magic items like this one were rare.

"Who are the other Pirate Lords?" I replied. "I didn't realise that the Republic of the Free had rulers."

Aoife opened her mouth to reply but before she could the captain spoke.

"Lousy beggars, the lot of them," he said with surety. "They'd chop your hand off for your rings and use it to wave to you." He was grinning at the idea.

"They control different lands and waters." Aoife must've noticed my confused expression. "There are six of them in total."

"Let's hope we run into one on our journey," Bennett said. "Many of them have things I would like."

Aoife didn't look impressed.

"If I recall," she began. "Stealing from the lords is, in fact, a serious crime."

Bennett didn't take his eyes off the horizon.

"I don't recall you complaining when I brought Naps back."

"I'm not talking about Naps," she retorted.

Before I could question this, I saw Brenn sauntering up the deck – he held the book I had brought to the deck curled in his tail.

"Your Royal Majesty needs to not leave her possessions lying around for just anyone," he called from the bottom of the steps that up to the helm.

Aoife didn't look up from the map. "I don't suppose he gets less annoying as time goes on." Her fingers ran along the fabric. A new stream of blue magic joined the map and I realised that she was plotting a route.

"I think he gets more confident," I replied.

The dark cat somehow managed to maintain a perfectly bored expression.

"A little politeness wouldn't go amiss."

Brenn didn't even blink.

"Forgive me, your gracious, righteous, divine, Majesty," he drawled. "I thought you wanted to learn motion magic."

Opposite the helm was the bow, but before that there were a few storage boxes that were bolted to the floor at the prow. I went and sat on the widest one; if I really leaned back, I could see the waves just beneath me. Brenn sat opposite me and cleared his throat.

"Motion magic is –"

But before he could continue, I spotted Regan with Donna on her tail. A grim-faced Evan followed them.

"Aoife said that you were learning magic," Donna said excitedly.

153

Regan had her arms crossed and observed me and the book. "I know I have some capability, but I never had a chance to learn."

"Mind if we watch?" Regan added.

Brenn narrowed his eyes as the pair of them sat on the boxes next to me. "You are a werewolf. You cannot perform magic if it's not in your blood," he spoke decisively.

Regan pulled a face.

"Oh dear," she said, deadpan. "That never even occurred to me."

Brenn remained unswayed. "Don't you have jobs to attend to?"

Donna twisted to the helm.

"Captain?"

"Go ahead," he called back between quibbling with Aoife over the course.

Donna turned back and grinned. "We're a very efficient ship." Regan nodded.

I waved off Brenn. "Let them stay – it'll be fun."

He scowled. "I didn't join this boat to be a teacher, Your Majesty."

I gave him my best optimistic smile. "Please." After a moment, he quietly used his two front paws to open the book and lay it in front of us.

Evan joined us too – the deep scowl now permanently etched on his face, it seemed. He did not need lessons. He easily manipulated magic from years of practice. Brenn's eye twitched, but he said nothing.

"Ready, Majesty?" he pressed.

"Born ready."

Brenn read slowly through the first chapter of Sloe's book. The forms used for spell casting seemed simple enough and the terminology was clearly made for younger ears. It was shape-based magic and all about channelling a pull or a push through magic currents. Circles drawn in the air made threads which enabled manipulation.

Initially, it seemed to be going well. But unfortunately for him, Brenn demonstrated the motion magic with Evan who was not very happy about it. Soon, the gunner was sliding around the deck like a banshee on a string. The girls and I tried to catch him, but Brenn

154

seemed to be enjoying flexing his magical muscles at Evan's expense.

The continuous swearing brought Caden up from the kitchens. He had a black apron tied around his middle with his long blonde hair swept up behind his head. His face was thunderous and his cheeks were pink.

"Someone better be dying to warrant all that noise," he yelled. "We only just left port and I have a headache!"

Evan was upside down now and scrambling.

"Brenn! Let him go!" I snapped. The pact pulsed in my hand. My command was clear, but it made my insides feel strange with an unfamiliar, unwelcome sensation.

Brenn let go of the screeching demon and dropped him near Captain Bennett and Aoife. The Wraith shot me a filthy look. It was easy to forget the nature of power in our relationship, but my use of the pact clearly infuriated him. For him it must've felt like I leeched his power, but for me it felt like my senses had been submerged in darkness. I could feel his emotions better and it was all rage.

Evan stormed back over.

"You try that again Wraith I will have fun pulling you apart," he snarled, his fangs peering through his lips once more.

Brenn tilted his head to the side.

"Is that supposed to frighten me?" Brenn hopped off the cargo and immediately transformed to a copy of Evan.

"Tiny demons like you – noble, higher, or lesser – *I devoured them all*." The real Evan's face did not change, but Brenn's was enough to make the steeliest person quake. He must've been mad because the sky began to darken around us, and the temperature dropped. "I ate you all – I decimated villages, towns, cities all for my own amusement and you," he met his eyes, "wouldn't have a hope in hell." Evan growled viciously; his eyes black as Brenn finished.

I didn't even see Captain Bennett move as he joined the pair on the deck and got between them. We seemed to have picked up a gale and the captain had to yell to be heard over the powerful wind.

"Evan, walk it off, and Wraith, shut your face or you can swim to Wist," he shouted over the wind.

A chill had passed through the air and made me shiver. On the top deck, Aoife frowned.

"Turn the lights on, Brenn," I said.

Brenn looked up and cold pellets of rain began to fire on the deck, making my hair stand on end. The icy weather was something from the winter months rather than summer.

"The weather isn't my doing," he retorted. The clouds blotted the atmosphere, like someone had just spilled black watercolour paints over the soft sheets of the sky.

"I think I know who it was," Donna spoke. I turned to see her flaming hair getting soaked by the pouring rain, her jaw tight. When I followed her eyes, I saw a trio of red-masted ships growing larger upon the horizon.

"Stations!" the captain shouted, making me jump. "We're under attack." Evan immediately backed away from Brenn, his face still furious as he rushed to join Regan downstairs. I rescued the book from where Brenn was still standing in Evan's form and quickly stashed it below deck.

When I caught his eye, he scowled but stayed. My shoulders eased at once. At least he'd forgiven me for using the pact to command him, though I knew that once I was alone, he would have something to say about it.

"Can I help?" I said to Donna as she wound a large rope that had secured a cannon nearer the front.

She gestured to the other cannon, and I started copying her movements. She quickly showed me that the mechanism the cannons sat on enabled them to change direction and to be turned quickly.

"Hopefully, we can outrun them or it's going to get bumpy!" she called over the wind, which had begun to howl. Already waves had made the deck rock alarmingly. I gripped the railing tightly as Donna continued. "They must have a Sky Magic Warlock, or if we're super unlucky, a Mage!"

Warlocks were commonplace in the capital – half of my life had been surrounded by the stuffy voices of men with beards that travelled past their stomachs. But Mages – they were on another level. They had obtained total mastery of one or many sources of magic; indeed, their talents were highly sought after in the Capital and in the ranks of the army. So, people practiced in secret to avoid conscription, much to Sorrel's dismay. Thus, naturally, it was one of my dreams to be a Mage.

At the centre of the world, my tutors had always told me that Kya turned out the best wizards, warlocks, and mages. We had the best schools, the best universities, the best colleges, and the crown funded it. However, it was true that the Royal Academy of Magic wasn't the only school that taught magic at a higher level.

"Who's chasing us?" I yelled to Donna.

"They're wearing Fynix colours – either they know our reputation and want to sink us or someone at Newt sold us out," she replied. "Probably the first."

My mind was whirling – we'd only been on the Promise for a couple of hours! Was this an omen of things to come? How exciting!

The sea seemed to be whipping itself into a wild frenzy, the water rose up the sides of the ship and crashed over the deck. Brenn let the water pass straight through him and the water soaked me, making my skin prickle all over. He smiled.

"The pact says nothing about a little water."

My shirt and trousers were now soaked through – thankfully, I had left Hector's jacket downstairs. But the rest of me was now freezing. I heard a giggle from Donna as she took in my expression too.

Of course, she looked perfectly ferocious and beautiful, even while soaked. After I pushed my hair out of my face, I spotted droplets of brown-coloured dye on my fingers that I wiped on my trousers.

"You'll get used to being wet," she said cheerily.

Now they had gained on us, I recognised the Fynix flag, a red gold standard divided by two flaming golden swords under a crown. I heard noises of feet running about below deck. I realised there was another flag under that one: no decoration, just red.

"What does the second flag mean?" I said, my voice straining over the gale. Donna glanced back at the ships.

"All red means no prisoners," she replied.

I heard the captain stomp his foot hard from the helm. Beside him, Aoife was gripping the railings of the quarterdeck as she watched the incoming fleet.

"Brace yourselves!"

Suddenly, the ship seemed to start to thrum underneath us. I assumed the mechanisms in the galley were at work – but for what purpose? I looked to Donna who had stopped preparing the cannon.

"You might want to hold onto something," she yelled. She knelt by the cannon, and I joined her on the other side with Brenn tucked in behind me in his human male form. A great cracking noise filled the air and for a moment, I thought the boat was being broken by the waves. Then we lurched forward like a whip across the waves. If it had it not been for Brenn catching me, I would've smashed my head against the iron casing of the gun. I thanked him in my mind and he simply nodded.

Magic was coursing through the vessel now as the boat picked up tremendous speed, as if we had just caught a current. The ship groaned under the force before it eased into the action. I climbed to my feet, the motions from the lower decks making the wood vibrate. I looked over the railing and a fierce wind whipped at my face. We climbed the waves with ease, surging forward at a hardy and unstoppable rhythm.

"We're the fastest vessel on the seas." Donna was grinning at my expression. "Go have a look downstairs. You might not get another chance."

Donna didn't need to tell me twice. I immediately shot towards the stairs before descending the ladders to the galley.

It was truly a sight to be seen. The mechanisms inside had started to turn, causing the arms on the outside to reach and contract in great strokes. No wonder we had picked up such a pace – there was much power being generated right under our feet.

Regan was standing among the arms next to another device that looked like a capstan. Her chest was heaving and there was a sheen across her forehead.

"Don't touch any of them, Bryony," she said between breaths. "The mechanisms will crush you."

"How does it work?"

"Honestly, I'm not sure," Regan said, putting her hands on her hips. "The warlock whose ship this was originally packed in a lot of surprises you don't find on other boats." She cleared her throat and made her way back to me, careful of her path. "These machines need a little spin to get going, but after that, they'll work until we stop them."

I watched in awe at all the wooden rods working in unison. If I focused, I could see the enchantments tangled around some of the machinery, but most of it was beyond anything I could decipher. "They're amazing!"

Regan slapped me on the back as she passed, a wide grin on her face.

"Come on kid," she said. "We're not out of the woods yet."

The distance between the Promise and the Fynix had started to grow but the rain to hammered down all the same. Whoever was casting the magic aboard their ships truly had an incredible amount of power. I wondered how hard it would be to learn. Lightning had taken me a few years to truly understand and, despite how dangerous and unruly it could be, I couldn't say I had mastered it. How different would rain be?

"Very, Your Majesty," Brenn said in my head. *"You have years of study ahead of you if you wish to accomplish anything to that scale."*

"Then you think it's possible?"

Brenn gave me a deadpan look.

"As if you would listen to me if I said otherwise."

The speed of the Fynix ships was still impressive despite the new pace set by the Promise. They loomed in the distance, their dark ships like islands on the ocean. I had no doubt that we would soon lose them among the waves, but who knows how long that would take. Normal vessels would've had no hope of catching us, but we had been very unlucky with the magical support in their crew, Donna explained to me. The captain's brow was furrowed in thought.

"Aoife?" Bennett called, a hopeful smile on his face. The first mate turned her head and immediately her face soured.

"We're outrunning them," she replied. "There is no need for *that.*"

"Aoife." The first mate didn't even look at him. "Aoife, it would be one less unit to worry about?" She gave him nothing. "Aoife, *please.*"

Aoife groaned before shrugging off her coat and tossing it over the captain's head.

"Only because you said please so nicely."

I watched in confusion as the first mate took off her boots and belt before stretching her arms out and heading down the stairs to the main deck. She shot daggers at the captain, who gave her a merry little wave as she quickened her pace to a run to where there was a gap in the rails for the ladders. Then, with all the grace of a bird in flight, she jumped off the boat.

I couldn't hold back my gasp as the splash sounded from the waves. However, the next second, a tremendous watery howl sounded like a great machine whirring with a high and twisted pitch. I sprinted over to the other side of the deck to see the head and body raised of a giant sea serpent, its wet scales glistening in pearlescent tones of blue, as it moved with an ungodly speed. It raised its head momentarily above the water and before diving under the waves with dangerous grace and speed. Slippery flouncing gills surrounded its neck like a ruff, and it had pointed ears atop a long, sinuous face. And above a terrible mouth of needle-like teeth, its eyes were the colour of moss.

I stared, open-mouthed, as it twisted and turned in the water, churning the sea white as it made its way towards the first ship. An unfamiliar noise howled from its mouth – sharp enough to make me wince and press my hands to my ears.

Even from our distance, you could hear the screams of the men aboard. The serpent had sprung out of the water and mounted the boat. I noticed it had two sets of webbed feet along its lithe body, which it used to climb and a great whip-like tail which bashed everything behind it.

I watched as it tore the red masts into ribbons with its powerful claws before using its body to snap the supports of the mainmast, which caused an almighty crack. I watched as the support poles went down one by one, but the serpent was far from finished. From the deck, it dived back into the water, its head rearing on the opposite side. Its body encased the entire deck of the ship and then the serpent squeezed, pulling its muscles tight. As it did so, the boat was crushed under it and the hull cracked away in chunks. The vessel, guns and all, took on water and started to sink rapidly. The crew that hadn't already dived into the sea jumped for their lives and frantically swam away from the wreckage.

Detaching itself from the sinking vessel, the beast made its way towards the next one. The guns were heavier on this one – forty of them, if I were to guess – but it did nothing to deter the serpent.

Having seen the way the creature had annihilated the first ship, the second had already prepared cannons. They aimed and fired, but the beast weaved through their attack with ease and speed. For this was the creature's domain, and they were the trespassers.

Instead of climbing this boat, the serpent dived beyond view under the water. For a moment I thought it might've fled, having been spooked by the cannon fire, and then I saw it: the ship had started to rock. First it was slow, but it sped up until the crew aboard were thrown off either side and the vessel capsized. Now immobilised, the serpent clambered upon the downward deck and tore holes in the hull as great swathes of wood came away under blue, jagged claw. It snapped parts of the bow off and destroyed the helm with ease. Throwing its head back, it released another howl that had the crew in the water clutching their ears.

It darted through the water until the final ship was within its reach. It did not take long for the creature to climb aboard and claw down from the deck to the hull and sink it. Pieces of wood and metal floated away or sank as the serpent dived under once more. The wind had finally died down, letting us move at full speed away from the wreckage. The rain too, had pattered to a stop as the sun returned to our sky.

Their fearsome reputation made sense as the captain hollered our victory and the crew gave a cheer. The serpent then returned to the side of the boat and shot a beam of water up onto the deck.

I turned to the captain, who looked on with a proud smile.

"That's my girl."

Even Brenn had a face full of surprise.

Another screech went up from the serpent. But now its watery call was joyous.

"It is always so handy to have a siren on board," Evan said, something of a chuckle in his voice. He had returned to deck as was leaning over the side.

"That's a siren?" I asked. Evan nodded. "I didn't know sirens

161

could do that. I didn't think sirens even looked like that."

"Not all of them," Evan explained. "They vary depending on waters."

I thought of the drawings I had seen in the books in the catacombs. Beautiful aquatic women: breathless, and utterly ruthless. I recounted this to Evan, who frowned.

"Why were they in the catacombs? It's not like their existence is a secret."

I shrugged.

"I guess they didn't want women getting any ideas," I replied. Before Evan could reply, there was the noise of someone climbing up the side of the boat. A bare arm reached for the rope near the top of the railing, but before she fully emerged onto the deck, the captain was there with her coat ready. I glanced to the helm to see Caden manning it. I assumed he came up from the lower decks during the stormy weather I just hadn't noticed due to the incredible ship or surprise siren.

Aoife was soaked but her eyes were as wide as her grin.

"Mother, that was fun," she beamed. "I love frightening men."

She wrapped the coat around her tightly as the captain smiled back at her.

"I love you frightening men too."

She looked to him and breathed through her teeth.

"You owe me new clothes," she reprimanded.

"If I owed you clothes every time we destroyed some I wouldn't have any money left."

"That sounds like a 'you' problem," she said, slapping his waist-coated chest as she passed and headed to her quarters.

Barely a moment later he followed her in.

I heard a low chuckle emanate from Regan. "You get used to the lovebirds," she said.

"I don't think I have, and it's been *years*," Evan retorted with a grimace.

"A siren and a human," I wondered aloud. "I want to know *that* story."

A raspy sort of laugh came out of Brenn, and I wondered what I had said. Donna opened her mouth, but Regan shot her a look.

162

"Get Captain Bennett a couple of bottles of rum and I'm sure he'll tell you," Evan jumped in. "If Aoife doesn't beat him to it."

"I love it – it's really romantic," Donna said, clapping her hands together. "Book-worthy."

Evan pulled a disgusted look.

"Hopefully not one of your books. No plot, just sexual dalliances by moonlight—"

Donna flushed furiously.

"You wouldn't know romance if it hit you on the nose, Evan," she snipped.

"I'll have you know I was the most romantic at the academy," he said coolly. "I had three dates to the Royal Lunar Dance."

Donna waved a hand with an unimpressed expression.

"Being romantic and being available is not the same thing, pint-size." Regan laughed.

Caden who was manning the helm in the captain's absence hummed in agreement and nodded. Evan whirled on him with a fierce expression.

"You can't say anything, Caden," he snapped. "You're about as romantic as a dead fish."

Regan raised her eyebrows at this, and Donna shook her head.

"No, I think Caden wins – I remember Friderick," she said. "And Quentin, Fuegi, Dylan, and Bill."

Caden looked impressed with himself. "Don't forget Will, Haden, Aaron, and Litus."

Donna nodded.

"Prolific lover," she said to me.

"A Master at romance," Caden finished. "And I think you'll find that I am undefeated."

Evan rolled his eyes at this and flapped a hand.

"Just because I haven't been playing," he declared.

Caden scoffed loudly. Evan retorted and the pair bickered.

Regan sent a look to me, casting her eyes between the demon and the dragon-kin. The werewolf took over the helm so Caden could go and prepare dinner for the crew. Evan followed the Fae down the stairs and their raised voices disappeared below the deck. Donna and I sat at the railings at the bow, watching the boat begin to slow to its

163

usual knots.

Brenn however was restless. He changed back into his cat form and paced.

"We have barely been travelling a few hours and we seem to have half of the Fynix fleet already on our tail," he snipped. "We would have been better off walking to Wist."

"Don't be dramatic." My hair was still damp, so I slicked it back quickly with one hand to get it out of my face. "We're alive, aren't we?"

"I told you we should've taken a more subtle form of transport."

Regan called a reply from the helm.

"I doubt those ships even knew you were on it," she said in an upbeat voice. "The chances are they just saw the colour and assumed we were coming to them."

Brenn scowled deepened even further if such a thing were possible.

"Our work has varied," Donna said. "But our captain is rather notorious. Pirate Lords always get this kind of reception."

I frowned.

"I didn't realise," I confessed. "It certainly makes our voyage more special."

Brenn scoffed.

"I'm having a nap," he snippily, as he stalked away from me.

"Brenn!" I called, knowing full well that wraiths don't sleep.

He ignored me and walked faster.

I sighed as he disappeared to the lower decks. I decided to leave him be a moment – my stomach was all nerves and adrenaline. I needed to ride this one out.

After we'd dried off, Donna suggested we keep reading on about the basics of motion magic.

This magic was nothing like anything I had learned before. It started with drawing strings of magic into a circle. After an hour or so of me trying and failing to make a bottle wobble, I couldn't do anymore and lay on the deck like a beached whale. The feeling reminded me of how it had been to practice the lightning first in the catacombs, the tiredness aching from my very bones. Donna seemed to be feeling it too and joined me in laying down.

164

It had turned dark as we headed north but the cold wasn't bothering me like I thought it would. Perhaps it was one of the ship's enchantments.

Captain Bennett had come up later and he looked positively ruffled. He greeted us politely before resuming his post. I couldn't believe he was a Pirate Lord. I imagined such Lords to be ancient, beardy creatures with hooks for hands and missing legs. Not spry handsome gentlemen.

As the night drew on, Regan noticed my yawns.

"Go to bed, Princess," she said before yawning too. She shook her head fast. "No, no, no. I don't go to sleep at this time." She rubbed her eyes. "I am one with the moon; a child of the night; a beast in nature..." she trailed off before pinching the space between her eyes and releasing an almighty yawn herself.

"I'm exhausted," I said before rolling up and stretching my hands over my head. My back clicked as my shoulders relaxed. Donna gave me a half-hearted wave as she rolled to sit up too.

"Don't worry, Princess." She swept her red hair to one side and began to plait it down her right shoulder. "Your stamina will get better on a journey like this one. After a few weeks at sea, you'll get used to things."

"Yeah, in the hot countries we barely use the bunks – we just sleep on the top deck," Regan said, getting to her feet. "Fynix is hot enough to melt your skin off."

"Last time we headed there, Evan wouldn't wear clothes for four days," she added. She pulled a disgusted face. "That mission left more than physical scars."

Donna turned to her.

"If I remember correctly, you were wearing a skimpy swimming costume during that entire time too!"

Regan shrugged.

"I'm a wolf! My blood runs hot."

Yawning, I headed to my bunk downstairs. The calls of goodnight came from all over the deck.

Thirteen

I woke up to the sound of many feet aboard and someone yelling. I turned over to see if I could feel for the fluffy soul that was now Brenn. I found the fluff and patted his head.

"Good to see it's not you causing trouble." Maybe he was maturing – could wraiths mature? Maturity surely came with age, but Brenn was ancient. Perhaps he was just learning to be more considerate?

A pleasant meow sounded from next to me and I opened my eyes. The warm bristly tongue of Naps was affectionately licking my fingers, his soft whiskers brushing against my hand.

I heard another yell sound from upstairs and then a bang like a cannon ball being dropped.

I groaned. Naps' wide golden eyes blinked at me. I rubbed his head and he purred. Clearly the only well-behaved cat aboard the vessel was this one.

I climbed down from my bunk and quickly put on the clothes that the girls had lent me. I had a fondness for the green trousers and the loose white shirt was better than anything I had been shoe-horned into in the palace. Regan had also lent me a woollen jumper of hers that was made out of a collection of orange, red, and brown wools. I pulled that on over my head too before heading up.

The boat continued to be abuzz as I ascended the steps into the brisk morning air.

"I can't believe you want to take us back to the Wastes," Donna said – a surprisingly solid note of fury in her voice. "What happened to going West?" She saw me and her voice softened but her face did not. "Morning, Bryony."

"You saw what happened, Donna," Captain Bennett said in an unaffected voice. "My bet is that the Fynix didn't even know who we were carrying then – they saw the colours and wanted to attack." Donna ground her teeth together. "Now we haven't pissed off anyone on the East for a long time, and, with the war now over and the hot season taking place over there – we could easily slink past and end up in Wist in a few weeks. Only a couple extra if all goes to plan."

"I for one don't mind the East," Caden said decidedly. "I could use a more relaxing journey – and we could always stop in Qicog for supplies."

Regan's eyes brightened at this.

"Oh yes," she rubbed her hands together. "Time to trick some engineers into making us more trap balls."

Aoife, who was dressed in a short blue shirt, dark trousers and boots, shrugged her shoulders towards the captain.

"I'm not sure the supplies we need are worth the danger we would be in," she said. She noticed Donna's expression continuing to sour. "Obviously, we'd have to be extra careful around Raize but maybe it is the only way."

Donna nodded. Evan sent her a look of gratitude.

"Do we really need to fear the demon homeland?" Brenn suddenly spoke and then I spotted him. He was sat at the top of the stairs, near Aoife. His expression looked stern as if to ask where I had been.

"You could've woken me up when you got up," I sent to him through our thought link. *"I didn't mean to sleep in."*

"You're no use to anyone tired," Brenn replied. *"Plus, you were snoring loudly, and it amused me greatly."*

"We do when there is a Bonekeeper after our Princess, yes," Aoife said. "If they spot us – there is no way we can defeat a demon fleet."

She sent a smile my way. "Go get some breakfast, Bryony," she added.

Caden blinked at me, as if he just remembered something.

"Yours is the blue plate with a bowl over it to keep it warm," he said. "Don't break anything."

Evan who seemed oddly bristled by this conversation stepped forward.

"I'm going to steal a sandwich," he announced as he headed off.

Donna shot a sharp look at the captain, but Aoife crossed her arms.

"For the record, I think this is a stupid idea," Donna announced.

The captain clenched his jaw as he locked eyes with her.

"I don't see any other way around it," he said and then waved a

167

hand. The conversation was done. I noticed Donna's shoulders ease as Evan, and I descended the stairs.

The kitchen was quite a small room; oak cabinets ran from floor to ceiling on one side and then what seemed to be a stove; a tap and sink, and a collection of cooking implements filled up on the other side. A porthole, like the one above my bed, looked out onto the rolling waves and let in the sunshine. There was a table big enough for six tucked in at the end.

Evan found my food behind the stone stove's door. It was still steaming hot, and I could smell the floral scent of Caden's magic lingering behind like perfume. He found me some cutlery too and told me to have a seat.

The food smelled divine. Thick slabs of crispy but tender bacon, a huge helping of beans, a tiny army of mushrooms, two whole fried tomatoes, toasted doorstop bread, three sausages, and a weird circular black looking slab.

"Goodness me!" I exclaimed as I headed to the bench. The loaded dish was way heavier than anything I had expected. "Did Brenn eat this morning? Maybe some of this is meant for him?"

Evan snorted.

"Brenn had double that and then some." Evan pulled a plate from under the sink. It had flowers decorating it in a delicate pattern. "Caden is a total feeder – he thinks you're too skinny."

"That's what prison does to you," I joked. Thanks to Hector's feeding, I had been slowly getting back to my regular shape. But I was still bony when I took my clothes off. My breasts had come back first though – my body clearly had its priorities in order. I nodded and sat down at the table, "I won't be able to finish this though. I'm not Brenn – he's a pit."

Evan knew his way around the kitchen well enough to find a butter dish and a box of cheese labelled '*DON'T YOU DARE EAT THIS EVAN*'. He helped himself as he found a rounded cob loaf and carved into it.

"What was that all about?" I asked. Evan sliced the butter and then the cheese into generous proportions. "Did something happen in Raize?"

168

"Donna is a total hot head," he said affectionately. "She's just worried about me that's all."

I started on my mountainous meal as he took a breath. He sat down opposite me and tore into his sandwich.

"I used to be in the demon army – the higher one – not quite a noble yet but my parents were in court enough," he confessed. "This was years ago now; I was still a fledgling – I didn't even have my full demon form yet. Things had just started kicking off with your father and the Fynix Fae, about five or six years ago, I guess. I was part of a unit that was collecting information."

"So, you were a spy?" I asked. Then I remembered something my brother said about the East having a force of their own. "Part of the Brigade of Shadows?"

Evan smiled and I gawped.

"That's amazing! Your people were a massive problem for our court," I said, scooping beans onto my spoon.

"I didn't realise our rep had reached the West," he said. "That's not very good for spies."

I waved him off.

"Everyone has spies," I said. I knew very little about our own secret service. That was reserved for my father and only my father: red cloaks who lived in the shadows. That was all I knew about any of them. Only Sorrel had managed to elbow his way in there. Abel, despite his whining, never accomplished it. "But you guys had stories about you – I'm sure I saw a few romances in the bookshops when I went."

Evan stopped eating then, a bashful red climbing up his neck as he blushed.

"People romanticise everything," he said quickly. "The real shit was brutal and not at all book-worthy." However, something about his expression looked pleased. "Anyway, I was sent to Draig to spy on the leader, Aegius DuVale," he continued. "At that point in time he wasn't a spineless fool and actually cared about protecting his people."

"Still, I can't believe they've been invaded."

It was still fresh in my mind. Moving forces into a place is a pretty direct way about going about it. It's a bloodless way of going

169

about it too. Unless the Draig people rebel – but clan culture up there is pretty strong and the DuVale's have been in charge forever.

Evan had nearly inhaled the rest of his sandwich.

"Anyway, being up in Draig, away from court had been the best experience of my life," he said with a grin. "I met the Captain and Aoife who were on a 'holiday' excavating some ancient, buried treasure. And Donna was travelling with them." His shoulders eased a little.

"Defection was the easiest decision I had ever made. And the best one I have ever made. Despite some of the ridiculous missions the captain gets us tied up into."

It was my time to look bashful then. "Sorry about that."

Evan shrugged.

"Believe it or not, you're not the weirdest mission I've ever undertaken." He brushed the crumbs off his lap. "Just wait until you hear about the Elves."

Elves? Real Elves?

Before I could question him further though, a more relaxed looking Donna entered the kitchen. "Cooled off now?"

She shot him a sharp smile.

"I have a plan, it is all under control." She seemed to be telling herself this. Her eyes fell on me. "You're not scared, are you? The East is just like the West really – just with more monsters and the fact that it's dark all the time."

"I'm not scared. Just excited, I guess," I replied. "Should I be?"

Evan shook his shoulders.

"If you can befriend the Wraith of the Wastes, I doubt anything over there would scare you."

I smiled.

"When I met Brenn, I was stunned rather than scared," I put my knife and fork down. My appetite had been well and truly sated. But my plate was still over a quarter full. I offered it to Evan who took it immediately and even used my knife and fork. Donna didn't look surprised to any of this. "He was in his original form – smoke and teeth." The thought of our first meeting made me shiver – being back in the tower reminded me of the dread I had felt. "But once he started speaking, I knew I had a way in."

170

"How did you escape the Tower?" Donna asked as Evan hungrily devoured all the food next to her. "It was meant to be inescapable: a cruel and awful way to go, no doubt."

I explained about the blood and how the original spells were placed by my own family. The Fynix King must've not known that when he sentenced me there. Donna's jaw dropped when I said I had learned blood magic and even Evan looked impressed.

"I don't remember you telling us about that when you first arrived," he said, poising a fork with a sausage loaded on it to me. "Blood, psychic, lightning…anything else?"

I shrugged my shoulders.

"I feel like my magic skills are a need-to-know basis."

Donna smiled, "You know when we get to the catacombs and see all these forbidden books – we'll be able to figure it out ourselves."

I sighed, "Probably." But my heart felt warm in my chest. That Donna had faith that we were going to get there. Sometimes it felt like a pipe dream. "But until then – I think it is best that I keep those to myself."

Donna and Evan went on to muse to what other forbidden skills I might have. Necromancy was bounced around, along with a few other crazier suggestions like mutation magic or irregular shapeshifting.

"Shapeshifting isn't illegal magic," I started to say. "It's just hard – you have to be very powerful to change and keep a new form." It was why Brenn liked to do it a lot during the day. He loved to show off.

"Speaking of magic, my new plan involves that fancy pink book of yours," Donna said, with an excited gleam in her face. I had shown her my new books yesterday – she was just as interested in learning magic too.

"Glamouring?" I asked.

"I thought we could come up with a suitable disguise!" She said unbeatably and smiling over at Evan who was focusing intently on his food.

Evan looked between her and I.

A look of realisation dawned on his face.

171

"Absolutely not."

There was talk of taking one of the through rivers to Wist, but being so close to the Fynix homeland and their new occupancy in Riach seemed unwise thus we resigned to travelling via the open sea. There was talk of islands and ports that I hadn't even heard of but, oddly enough, I didn't feel in any great hurry.

A few weeks had passed since we climbed aboard in Newt, and I had found myself at ease with life on the Promise. Many of my days were spent practicing motion magic until I could move bottles around the deck with ease and then, after what felt like an eternity, I could move larger objects like cargo crates or people. Now I had nothing but time to practice, I felt my magic change form easily inside of me – ready to be used at a moment's notice.

Being on the ship too, besides the occasional outrun of a potential foe, I found to be relaxing. I helped where I could with jobs on board, but most of the time the crew were so efficient in their roles didn't need extra support. Leaving me somewhere on deck either practicing new magic variations or enjoying the view.

I loved to watch the waves lap at the side of the hull as we crossed the ocean. Occasionally, a kelpie tail or serpent nose would rise among the rippling surface but disappear again as quickly as it came. I wondered what creatures the foreign waters would hold and if I would know any of them.

"Princess, keep that up and we'll have to fish you out," Regan spoke dryly from the floor next to me. "Come tamper with my face some more – it was actually a pleasant sensation."

Donna was lying next to her. Dusk was fast approaching and after a day of studying *The Art of Masquerade* by H. Ding, we were all conked out on blankets near the forecastle.

Unlike drawing magic in threads, as was the way with motion magic, it was concentrated into the fingertips and the features that you wanted to manipulate were gently tugged, pushed, or coloured anew. You could make hair grow or disappear. There were sheet glamours like those Brenn had cast on me – a subset of illusion style casting and base glamours which were temporary physical adjustments. This was another level of difficulty – even Caden, who had always wanted to learn despite his own astounding Fae beauty, struggled with the more complicated manoeuvres. Evan resumed his usual spot, watching the proceedings and making the occasional sarcastic comment though initially we had tried to rope him into being a model for our practice attempts.

The practice required a great deal of energy to move the features and a great deal more to keep them all in place. Donna successfully gave me a long nose like a woodpecker, so in return I gave her a pointed chin. We looked at each other before we realised how ridiculous we looked and started howling with laughter.

They eventually wore off and the skin fell back in place accompanied by an itching sensation.

"Oh, thank the Gods," Donna yelled as she felt her chin. "I have missed this chin!"

The next few days followed the same pattern. Eventually I could conduct base changes for hours and now I was trying to master hair.

I practised giving myself all the trappings that Brenn had given me. Bristly eyebrows, stubble, sideburns, thinner lips – I even practised giving myself a moustache. Firstly, it was short and stubby, like a teenager trying hard, then it was full like a cat's head, then it was long and wispy enough for me to twirl in my fingers. It came out blonde like my natural hair.

"You were so fair," Donna said peering at it. "Not that I don't love the brown – but I think one day I would like to see it its natural colour."

I smiled.

"It's already coming through if you look closely," I dipped my head down so she could see. Close to the scalp the fair hairs had grown from the root. "When it's long enough to cut I will cut the dark off."

I felt the magic tickle under my nose as my moustache receded.

Regan had closed her eyes a moment and I grinned to Donna who nodded eagerly.

I pulled my magic into the tip of my finger, feeling it fill with heat and pressure. Quickly I tapped just under the werewolf's nose. She didn't react as a magnificent curly moustache grew, matching her dark hair. She opened one eye and gestured for Donna to hand her the hand mirror we had been using to practice.

She pursed her lips as Donna, and I giggled.

"Damn," she said, impressed. "I make a handsome fella." She nodded at her reflection. "Nice one, Bryony."

Donna decided to try and add a beard. Then later we discovered if we both focused, we could make a little mat of curled hair over her chest.

I turned to Brenn, who was watching the proceedings with a bored expression. I gestured to Regan with a proud smile.

"Well?" I said, smugly.

"A hairy werewolf? Ground-breaking." Was all that he said.

"Don't mind the wraith," came Evan's voice. "You guys are doing great."

Donna looked up at Evan like she was seeing him for the first time. Then she turned to me - eyes glittering.

"The answer is still no."

I joined Aoife up on the quarterdeck as she explained the next few days of the journey. The map was incredible now I knew how to use it. Aoife had explained that it was connected to the leylines that ran throughout Nos so it could pick up the incoming storms, high and low tides, dangerous waters, and occupied territory. She explained that the map had picked up Brenn's presence too – she directed me to a small red dot on the page.

"*That* is a vicious killer currently pretending to be a cat," she said, hovering a finger above it. A line of magic grew from the page, stretching out like a cord of wool – the same shade of red that Brenn was on the paper. It travelled off the leather, ran along the deck, down the steps, all the way up to where Brenn was watching Donna attempt to change the scales on her right side.

It stopped as it reached him, and the magic seemed to go taut.

"Usually, people can't tell if they are being tracked. The magic line is only shown to the map's users."

Brenn, however, seemed to sense it and turned around from where he was sat. He looked at the line and then at us. "Usually, anyway."

I guess that didn't apply to ancient wraiths.

"I didn't realise it had such strong tracking abilities," I said, as with a wave of Aoife's hand, the magic dissipated. "Did the map pick up Brenn when we left the island?"

Aoife shook her head.

"It is tuned to the wayfarer's whims, and I wasn't looking for the Wraith of the Wastes then," she replied. "However, the Captain sensed that something was afoot the day you escaped."

"Really?"

Aoife shrugged.

"We just thought he'd eaten too much fried eel again," she went on to say. Blue eyes glanced to where Caden and Captain Bennett were. "Maybe it was a coincidence."

But before she could continue, Brenn strode up onto the deck. He looked down at the map; the red dot glowing brighter than ever.

He sat down, his tail sweeping the floorboards behind him.

"We're getting closer," he said. "I can feel it."

There was no cynicism in his voice and no sarcasm.

"To the Wastes?" I spoke. Brenn looked up at me – onyx eyes shining in the afternoon sun.

"Home," he stated. And with that, he came and curled up next to me on the floor. He didn't speak another word for the rest of the evening.

Caden made us chicken dumplings with vegetables for dinner which we all ate at the helm. The Captain and Aoife were going to sail through the night for us. Evan was relieved to have the night off as it was his turn. Caden secretly told me as we headed downstairs that it was only because last time, he had fallen asleep at the wheel and the boat had sailed into waters infested with wild kelpies.

"Since when has a demon had trouble staying awake in the dark? The whole of the East is under shadow," he finished as we reached our quarters. Brenn had been perched on my shoulder and hopped off onto my bunk, his paws padding around in a circle until he was settled. Right in the middle.

Evan and Caden had stopped in the doorway as I climbed up to bed.

"Look, I was still feeling the aftereffects of that Fae wedding. I had a whole barrel of fae wine," he said shuddering at the memory.

A look of equal horror passed over Caden.

"I do recall you dancing naked on an altar to their star Goddess with a hollow pumpkin on your shoulders and a rainbow painting on your ass," he said with a grimace and then gagged.

Evan grinned wide and then said to me.

"Best night of my life."

A violent sky. Darkness splintered all around – a storm raging on with flashes of gold and white as rain poured. Before me, waves crashed onto a beach of black sand. But I wasn't wet – I was warm. Like I'd laid in a sunbeam behind glass.

And there I was on the beach. Standing with my toes in the sparkling black sand as the moon's glow made everything glitter. Somehow, the rain hadn't disturbed the shore; like the sea had trapped the thunder within it.

I looked behind me and saw the edge of a lush green forest; plants with leaves that bloomed the colours of gems and glowing roots painting patterns across the floor. I could hear voices coming from beyond, echoes of laughter and stringed music filtering through the air like wind chimes before they seemed to disappear, as if it had been carried by the breeze.

I noticed there was a pathway of pale stones that seemed to be reflecting the moon, verdant shades of sapphire and purple.

The leaves seemed to whisper as the storm raged on.

Come here. Come.

Come here. Come.

It went on and on like a heartbeat. I matched it with my feet pacing forward, the forest seeming to beckon me.

Come here.

Come.

As I walked, I saw all manner of wildflowers I didn't recognise blooming at the feet of the ancient trees. I spotted some silver blossoms bordering the path with long slender leaves that filled the air with a delightful musky and calming fragrance. Besides all the unfamiliar flowers, the smells of lavender and jasmine filled the air pleasantly.

As I walked, I tilted my head up and realised some of the trees were not trees at all: they were towers. Homes built among the tallest

176

trees, some curving around them, and others surpassing them in height. And as I ducked under a roping chain of carnations, a short burst of light flashed in front of me, and I saw a figure so small I could've missed it.

Carrying a light so small it was barely the size of my littlest finger's nail, was a tiny spirit. Her eyes were wide and green, but her face was forlorn.

"You're too late." Her voice was as soft as the petals among her red hair.

I wanted to ask what I was too late for, but the sensation of longing grew inside of me. I couldn't even open my mouth to reply. Something was pulling me forward – my feet were moving but I didn't know where I was headed.

Come.

I walked on, the spirit, dressed in what seemed to be a collection of leaves woven together, flew beside me. Her face didn't change but as she flew faster, I was running to keep up with her.

Suddenly, we came to a clearing – the storm had ceased and only the rays from the moon and her companion stars filled the sky. The trees here seemed to be alight with spirits alongside the tiniest of winged fairies no bigger than a feather. Their light-as-air voices seemed to cease as they noticed me – many faces fell, and I felt a deep pit start in my stomach. This place was fit for the gods – how could they possibly be unhappy?

Come.

The voice spoke again and the spirits that filled the glade seemed to gasp, and exchange looks of delight or surprise.

The fairies parted to reveal a pool at the centre of the glade, the surface of which was shimmering gold. Above the pool was an altar of sorts, a stone table with a round top. From this, a small golden waterfall cascaded into the waters below. Behind that stood a great tree, it bore scarlet red leaves and small white blossoms. A sheen covered the trunk. Blood-red stones seemed to be growing from it – as natural as any of the leaves. It seemed to come from a gap in the wood, like part of it was missing.

As I moved closer, I could feel the magic in my chest embracing me like a breath of fresh air. Strangely enough, the air tasted like home.

I stepped forward and saw my reflection – my old self stared back. Long blonde hair, oval face, blue eyes, golden skin: my mother's daughter looked back at me. Then the scene changed, and I could see beneath the surface of the water – a face as big as a house – eyes wide with horror, hair that was wild, a mouth caught in a scream. Immediately, my chest seemed to tighten – the pull pushed me forward and before I could stop myself, I felt myself submerge me. Water filled my lungs, but I couldn't tear my eyes away from hers. Her open mouth was ready to swallow me. I was drowning.

Gasping I shot up in my bed. I could feel my mouth opening and closing, but my heart was racing so hard I could feel my magic heating up in my chest in response. I was heaving and felt myself fall forward as my body shuddered. Brenn looked up at me – his eyes were wide.

I touched the wall next to me and looked out the window – still aboard the Siren's Promise. Not drowning and choking on water. I scrambled forward to the window and loosed the screw under it to let in a slice of air. I took deep breaths until my heart slowed and my magic stopped humming like an engine inside of me.

Finally, I felt my shoulders ease. Brenn hadn't said anything – he had only watched and now was sat up.

"Usually when one experiences a sex dream the response doesn't leave the dreamer in such a state of panic," he said, factually.

"No, it was a nightmare," I said. "There was a glade…" I let my voice trail off. I opened my mind to Brenn and showed him the dream. The green sprite and the tiny fairies. The altar – the tree of red and white blooms that seemed to be growing rubies between its bark. The face at the bottom of the pool. "Who was that?"

Brenn's brow furrowed.

"How strange," he said. "That was an ancient depiction of Celine – the all-seeing." There was a pensive tone in his voice. "Before she was just the sun-goddess, she was the patron of many things – the truth being one of them."

I stared at him.

"But what does this mean? I've never seen that place before," I thought back. There was an ancient temple in Kya for Celine – every

178

surface glowed with gems. A white marbled statue of her looking north. She wore a diadem – her expression was peaceful. "I barely even left Kya before the invasion."

Brenn seemed to be debating something as he didn't immediately reply. But then he rolled over and stretched out like he was done with this conversation.

"Perhaps she wants to talk to you," he said.

"A goddess wants to talk to me?"

"Surprising. Considering how dull your usual conversation is." I frowned at him, but he'd already closed his eyes. "Perhaps she has something to reveal to you."

I had heard of the Gods' involvement before, but not since before I was born. Yet, every folktale had some piece of divine intervention at its core. And there were whispers of miracles among my people. Unlike the Priests of Kya who kept the temples clean and helped worshippers, I was not the most devoted servant to our Pantheon. It was hard to pray to a God or Goddess who you debated the existence of.

I looked out on the waves – the face still burned into my mind.

"I wonder what she has to share?"

"Well, hopefully, it's more interesting than this conversation."

Fourteen

The following days were blissfully uneventful until we started to reach the eastern oceans. As we drew closer to the edge of the Wastes, the waters became ever more turbulent. Powerful waves threw us about the deck and on more than one occasion, I had found myself hanging off the rigging. Caden crashed into the mast and needed to bandage up his wrist. It was hard not to think of Hector back in Draig and how easily he could've patched him up. Regan helped me knot the cables of the masts while Evan and Donna ran up and down the rigging to adjust the sails and provide a lookout.

Brenn had decided that helping was beneath him and that he was going to stay with the captain at the helm as he wrestled the ship back onto its course. We'd come into rocky waters and that combined with the weather required concentration. A storm had really picked up within a matter of moments, and I found myself clinging to the cables with all my might. Aoife was beside me too after she'd come to help.

"Couldn't we have gone around the storm?" I yelled over the whistling of the wind. "Why didn't it show up on the map?"

"I don't know!" she screamed back over the howl. The boat lurched forward, and we bumped into each other. "The storm I saw earlier was way past our trajectory."

Thunder cracked and suddenly a yell came from above.

"We've got company!"

I looked around for any ships but all I saw was the raging grey sea. But being up so high I wasn't surprised they had spotted ships on the horizon that I couldn't see. But Aoife's expression wasn't the determination I had seen before. She looked horrified. Suddenly, water exploded from the right of the ship, a great geyser of grey fury shot upwards and drenched the deck. Regan didn't react as she got soaked – her feet firmly planted on the floor as white water crashed aboard and swept me and Aoife off our feet. Immediately, the same thing happened on the left of the ship too and I gasped.

The noise of cracking filled the air as a tremendous wave swept across the floor. I struggled to find my footing and slipped to the ground. A gleaming metal hook wrapped around the mast, and it crunched as it embedded itself in the wood. Demon warriors, in bronze armour or battle leathers descended upon us from above.

"Battle formation," I heard Aoife scream from somewhere nearby.

I wiped the water from my eyes and suddenly the boats aside us came into view. I was near the bow at the front of the ship, and I saw how the boats had us wedged between them. Magic must've concealed their presence from us. We couldn't escape without damaging ourselves.

The ships were adorned with towering masts and the black and gold flags of the Raizian people. Just as I thought it could not get any worse, figures dressed in black abseiled aboard the ship.

I saw Donna slide down the rigging with her axe in hand, her red hair stuck to the side. Evan's claws and fangs were out, and his eyes looked filled with a dark rage.

Given the talons and teeth they possessed, I knew our attackers were lesser demons. But the familiar brush of scalding magic still filled my blood with icy dread. Everything seemed to be happening too fast for me to comprehend.

If we hadn't been a moving vessel, I guessed he would've portalled aboard but instead, he came via the railing of the ship. The Bonekeeper I had met in Draig was now aboard the Siren's Promise and this time he had not come alone. Two other hooded figures flanked him; one with striking red hair like spilt blood, the other seemed to have no hair at all, but was covered in tattoos, their eyes a ghostly white. The bottom of each of their faces was masked. My heart was racing.

"Don't you have anything better to do?" I yelled over the racket, but around me the crew of the Promise seemed to have sprung into action.

The deck quickly became a battleground between the crew and the invaders. I couldn't keep track of how many there were among the weather and the fighting. I heard the sound of cotton tearing like paper and then a savage, animalistic growl. I thought for a moment that it might be Brenn but then saw a flash of black fur patched with brown around the face and flanks. Regan had changed into her wolf form – tearing into the first soldiers she had seen with ease.

181

Donna and Evan worked back to back as they fought. I couldn't see the Captain and Aoife on the quarterdeck only figures moving quickly. I felt my magic stir inside me – no way was I not being involved in this battle!

"Stay back, Princess," I heard Caden yell from the hull. He had a grimace on his face but brandished his magical threads between his fingers. I felt Brenn beside me, in shadow form.

"For once I agree with him," he hissed as he swarmed around me. As I went to move forward to join with the fray, I felt his scales dig into me. Then a demon with a long sword ready for me hurtled towards the mass that was Brenn. With a joyful hiss Brenn's serpentine mouth took the demon's head in one swoop motion. Blood sprayed across the deck but not for long before the Wraith of the Wastes consumed the rest of the soldier. He was more than a snake or lizard: his body formed a great length of scales ridged with sharp tusks along his spine. A shadow-feld wyrm – I remembered seeing it in one of the books in the dark of the catacombs.

The weapon the demon had been using clattered to the floor. I retrieved it – a long blade with a leather-bound handle and onyx edged blade. Then I heard a cry that made the blood in my veins ice over. Donna was becoming overwhelmed, and I couldn't even see Evan. Caden's vantage point from the hull had been overrun with demon soldiers. Even worse, the Bonekeepers seemed to have disappeared.

"Brenn! Attack them!" I yelled. "I can protect myself."

Brenn eyed me dubiously. "Free food!" I added.

"Don't do anything stupid," he snapped, before I saw his wyrm form slide dart forward, mouth wide at the incoming fighters from the right. I turned before I saw their blood spill across the planks. I pulled my new magic from my core into my hands, and a circle with glowing thread spilt over each of my fingers.

Breathing in, I outstretched my hands and felt my magic reach out like ropes, wrapping around two demons closest by. I heard a cry behind me, but I had my hands bound in magic before me. I focused hard and lifted the pair of them into the air, the threads holding their weight well. Then I flung them forwards off the ship and into the waters below.

I surged forward to find Donna wrestled to the ground. With a yell, I grabbed the soldier above her, feeling the magic surge down my arm like a breeze. Then I yanked him up high and threw him overboard. Donna saw me do this and gave me a look of approval before using her axe at one short-haired demon's knee.

To one side of me, I could see Evan using his claws to tear into a demon twice his size, black blood spilling all over his face. Meanwhile, Brenn was decimating the soldiers near the helm. I saw more than one rogue limb strewn across the deck between us.

Donna slumped as she swung her axe twice more into a lanky intruder, kicking his body over the side.

Suddenly, red hair materialised in front of me. The Bonekeeper was much taller than I was but still I met violet eyes glowing around tanned skin. I lunged back and positioned the sword in my hands. The Bonekeeper wielded two short-swords, the ends of which were curved and savage-looking. I had some experience with swords thus far, from lessons the captain had given on board. I had prioritised learning magic, but I was a fast learner.

I saw the Bonekeeper move towards me, but Evan got between us and went in for a slashing attack. He moved like a blur, but then so did his opponent. I looked for the other Bonekeepers, the Captain was locked in a brawl with the white-eyed individual. The other, who I knew was the general, was fighting Regan nearer the bow. There were only a few soldiers left on board besides from the Bonekeepers but I noticed reinforcements on the opposite ship and my heart sank.

It happened so fast.

A swish of a silver blades and blood splashed across the deck. Evan had dropped to his knees, crouched over, dark blood spilling from his guts. His forearms were covered, the gore pooling on the floor in front of him. Donna screamed.

The red-haired Bonekeeper appeared back in front of me only to be attacked next by a furious Regan.

"He asked for you alive," a deep voice said sharply, "but it wasn't essential."

Hot rage coursed through my veins, and I gripped my sword. I turned to the Demon King's son and met the Bonekeeper's dark red eyes. I saw Donna bent over Evan as he bled out. My stomach lurched at their faces.

I saw Caden bloodied at the bottom of the stairs against the tattooed Bonekeeper and Aoife and the Captain fighting like hell at the helm. My magic wasn't strong enough to fight like them. But that didn't mean I wasn't going to fucking well try.

I aimed the sword and lunged.

The Bonekeeper easily dodged it, so I used my magic to shove him backwards. He hadn't been expecting the sudden wave of motion magic which made him stumble and I swore I heard something like a chuckle. He zipped forward. This time he had his curved swords at the ready. I couldn't use my lightning here without frying everyone else too, so I needed to stick to my threads for now. He swung his left sword, which I was able to block with my own. He forced his blade against mine and my muscles strained against him as he swung his right.

I jumped up and planted a foot in his solar plexus, and he stepped back. I took his moment of instability to shove him hard. All I had to do was hold him off until Brenn returned to me, but the reinforcements had started to climb aboard from the opposite side of the ship.

He regained his footing, and I moved back to strengthen my stance. But as I stepped back my foot caught, snagged on a bloodied demon body, no doubt mauled by Regan. I tripped backwards and felt myself slip over the railing. I waved my arms to catch myself, but my fingers closed in on air as I fell off deck. And hurtled towards the sea.

The noise of the battle instantly faded around me and was replaced with the whoosh of water and then silence. I was lucky I hadn't been impaled on a rock in my descent and I opened my eyes to see endless blue before closing them. My head was dazed with the impact, and I tried to remember, kick legs, kick legs, swim, swim, swim. I commanded my body to get me back to the surface, but my arms were useless, and I seemed to be sinking deeper.

The surface above was blurry. Where was Brenn? How come he hadn't seen me fall?

The boats seemed to be shrinking – I needed to breathe. I tried to rise up through the water, but it was useless. Terror seeped through me – I was going to drown. I was dying.

I choked a sob and tried to get myself up. I'm not dying here. *I'm not.*

My vision blurred some more as dark spots edged their way into the rest of my vision. Then a shadow filled everything, and I knew this was it.

Suddenly, hands grabbed my arm then waist and pulled me tight. I didn't realise death had such a strong grip. I had the weird sensation of air on my wet head as someone placed me down on the deck. Someone was breathing close – voices drowned by the seawater in my ears and the gradually heaviness of my chest eased. Someone was beating on my chest hard and a spilt second later I felt water at the back of my throat.

I could feel the ache in my shoulders once again. My heart raced and my lips tasted of sea salt. Then I felt a lurch in my stomach and turned to vomit onto the floor.

The noise was coming back to me. I opened my eyes and saw the frothy puddle of my own insides.

"You can't swim." The Bonekeeper next to me stated. His long hair had come loose from where it had been tied before – every inch of him was soaked. He was standing above me.

I wiped the water from my eyes. I realised I was on a different ship. This boat was grander than the Siren's Promise, the deck was massive and instead of the two masts – this boat had four. A black and gold flag waved from the crow's nest. Our boat, the Siren's Promise, seemed to be drifting away.

Brenn...Brenn. Where was he?

The screams had followed me to this boat. I saw Brenn in his Wyrm form devouring the crew of the demon's ship. The red-head and the one with all the tattoos had whirled on him now – I could feel the bloodlust aching through him with his terrible power.

"You can't swim," he said again. It wasn't quite a question.

"Are you going to kill me?" I asked him, my arms and legs ached from trying to tread water.

"My father wants you alive."

"Ah, so Captain Bennett was right," I said, coughing until my

185

breathing evened out. "You are the son of the Demon King." His jaw seemed to clench. "Prince Kyan."

"Princess Bryony," he said, in his low timbre.

I laughed despite my raw throat.

"Please, introductions are saved for the dancing part of the evening," I replied. His expression didn't change, those red eyes fixed on me.

"Call the Wraith off and we'll let the crew live. If you don't, I'll send Jasper and Rion over there to finish them off." His voice was quiet and threatening: I didn't doubt his sincerity. I thought of the bloodshed over there and immediately called Brenn. No fucking way were any of them dying for me.

Water spilled over onto the deck from the waves that were slowly dying down now the battle had ended. I had no doubt the weather was due to a storm mage on board. I watched the Promise gain ground between us. As I climbed to my feet, Brenn appeared next to me. Baring his fangs at the General who stepped back at the Wyrm enveloped me.

The demon said something, but his words were lost in the great boom that tore through the air. The ground shook under us, and the crew stumbled. The next few bangs sounded like breaking wood and the smell of acrid gunpowder burned my nose.

The Siren's Promise was firing back.

"We need to get off this ship!" I said to Brenn as the incoming cannons tore into the boat. On deck, the crew were readying their own cannons once more. The other two Bonekeepers sprang into action to help the general as he regained ground and squared off with Brenn.

The Wraith lunged first, leaving me pressed against the railing as debris flew over onto the ship. A chunk of it sliced my shoulder as I raised my arms to protect my face.

In wyrm-form Brenn moved like a deadly snake, his tail swept at the general's feet and his fangs were sharp and ready to tear into him. Brenn's attacks were too fast for me to fully see but he moved in blurring jabs at any opening the demon had. The red Bonekeeper slashed down and the white one prepared to fire a weapon that looked like an enhanced crossbow.

186

However, what was more impressive, was that the General held his ground with forms unparalleled to those I had seen from the soldiers at home. He moved like a shadow with all the grace of a deadly panther that roamed the forests near the mountains of Riach. Brenn finally landed a clean hit at the demon's wrist, his teeth locking on. Black blood dripped onto the deck, but it didn't slow the demon at all. In fact, his momentum didn't slow as he sliced into the Wraith's serpentine stomach. Brenn growled and let go but only to change shape into his male form once more, his fingers dark onyx claws.

"I have a plan," I raced out. *"Is there any alcohol on this vessel?"*

Brenn didn't slow down as he and the general slashed at each other. Blood splattered the deck between them. He knocked the two others into each other with a vicious tail whip and bared his fangs.

"Now is not the time for a drink," he snapped back.

"Brenn!" I showed him my idea briefly and after a beat he replied. *"A barrel of spirits in the stock bay by the smell of it."*

"I need it." I went to run past them, but the General leapt back and turned his sword on me.

"Stay there!" Brenn's voice echoed in my head. Immediately, he summoned the brown barrel above the deck. It floated above the heads of the crew, but no one seemed to notice. Perhaps he had glamoured it too. That tricksy Wraith, keeping all his skills to himself.

"When I say, drop the barrel and change form to that eagle you were before," I said, I could feel the power of the pact hard in my head. Perhaps my adrenaline had summoned it.

"Sorry we can't stay," I said, quickly climbing up onto the railing. "You know how busy royal schedules are, right Kyan?"

I pulled my magic up into my core – the temperamental nature of it filled my fingers instantly. No motion magic now as I felt the familiar burn of my beloved lightning. I saw the crazed look of approval in Brenn's eyes.

"Now!" I yelled, launching myself off the ship.

The barrel smashed against the deck and coated it in shining brown liquid. Brenn instantly let Kyan go, dodging a deathly sword swing, as he too jumped off. His form became a mass of smoke as his great wings met the air.

Instantly, I leashed the bolt and sent it onto the deck. For a brief moment I was worried it was just water but then the heat took, and the flames sprouted rapidly. The bolt was far from finished though, it zapped outwards, the water aboard carrying it to the rest of the crew and the Bonekeepers. Loud cracks emanated as the bolts hit the soldiers with many of them dropping to the deck or falling overboard. Spider webs of lightning ricocheted through the ship among the flames, I saw the general throw his sword to the ground as it lit up with electricity.

Unfortunately, as I was still soaked from my unwanted swim, I felt the bolt snake its way up my arm too. My skin burned like iron needles piercing my veins, but I gritted my teeth. Surely, now we could escape. Despite the pain, I couldn't shake the smile as I found myself falling towards a watery death for the second time in a matter of minutes.

I didn't look as I felt Brenn pull me upwards, claws of his Riach Eagle form digging into my shoulders. The flames had taken over the enemy ship, but I was happily flying back to my own boat. From my height, I spotted the General storming his way to the helm to take over before the burning ship crushed into the rocks. The red-head Bonekeeper let out a shriek of anger but Brenn above me let out a loud laugh.

"You're crazy, Princess," he laughed. Smoke was billowing from it now, but I focused on landing as we reached the Promise once more. I noticed the vessel on the opposite side was in far better shape and my stomach twisted at the thought of the fight continuing.

Brenn dropped me on the ship, and I landed with a thump. My arm was still killing me, but I was content in the knowledge that all those demons felt that way too. It was an oversight that I had done that to myself, but the buzz in my head was making me giddy.

Brenn began devouring the last poor souls left on board. Regan and Evan had been laid out at the hull with Donna defending them.

"Nice of you to come back, Princess," called Captain Bennett from the helm which he was defending with Aoife. He still had his tricorn on, but his shirt was soaked in blood. Slices had torn at his chest and his arms – how was he standing? Aoife, looking as bedraggled but less bloody, was suddenly tackled from behind by a demon ready to slit her throat with a curved dagger. The captain's face changed instantly and quicker than I had ever seen him move, he drew a dagger. Then the air around him seemed to ripple – even from where I stood, I could see the remnants of magic.

The weapon zapped through the air, and I saw the soldier fly off Aoife with an unexpected force. He clattered to the floor, and I saw the dagger had gone straight through the man's eye. Aoife's eyes were wide but before she could respond the captain had extended an arm and pulled her tight against him.

I ran up to where they were on the deck. Brenn was finishing up those that had left. The boat that had been on the left had pulled away but not retreated. But the stupid Bonekeeper's vessel was gaining speed again despite the fiery wreck it was. I saw a dark shadow at the helm and knew the General hadn't given up yet.

"Can we lose them?" I asked, breathless. The sea was getting riotous again – no doubt an attempt to slow us down.

Aoife dropped from the captain's arms and instantly had the map out.

"Fuck! We're headed towards rocks," she growled. "Head North – that is our best bet." The captain shook his head, his expression was resolute.

"They will catch us that way," he ground out – the muscles in his forearms were straining as he fought to keep the boat going onwards.

"Those rocks will end us – you won't be able to navigate." Aoife retorted, shaking her head. "She won't survive the journey, Bennett."

North and we get caught or continue east and we die.

Suddenly, an idea popped into my head. A stupid, reckless and ridiculous idea that would surely be brilliant.

"Keep going straight," I called as the winds started to howl again. They both turned to me. "I have an idea."

I pulled my magic into my chest.

Come for me. You've waited long enough to be let out. This is your time.

I felt the whoosh of magic flood my senses as I stretched my fingers in front of me. The threads shone like silken moonlight as I kneeled on the deck. I drew a magic circle on the base of the helm; because it was so big the magic seemed to want to grow, to explore, and tiny strings of magic stretched out like roots around it.

I shut my eyes tight, my arcane senses flaring off on their own so

189

when I opened them, I could see my magic stretching out like a blanket over the deck. In my mind's eye I saw it run to the sides of the hull and cradle the boat. My heart raced as my magic poured out of me.

I caught eyes with Brenn who was slithering up the deck, once again a wyrm.

"Don't you dare!" he yelled.

I grinned at him and doing what he had told me, I held my ground, keeping my stance even, slowly raising my hands.

Instantly, the weight of the boat hit me – it was more than a bottle, a book, or even one of the crates. Trust the magic to do the work – I breathed deeply. Deeper than I ever had before. I felt some of the pressure lift – it was still agonisingly heavy on my shoulders, but my hands felt soft, like I had put them in a pool of warm water.

I kept raising my hands gradually and I heard Aoife let out a sound of surprise behind me – I didn't trust my focus to turn and look at her, so I kept on looking straight. The noise of the water whooshing out of the bilge and scuppers as we started to lift out filled me with confidence.

Slowly, we rose into the air – my arms were shaking with the effort, and I could feel the sweat starting to form on my back.

We were up – I leaned forward taking all the magic with me. And slowly initially, but surely, we started to move. Taking to the air like a swan to a lake we moved steadily onward.

Brenn had appeared next to me – he was in his human form again.

"You're a crazy idiot," he said but he extended his own arms. I felt the familiar surge of his dark magic next to me and the weight dropped immediately on my arms, but I didn't give. I used my magic to push forward as we moved the boat together. I felt his magic flood through mine making my chest burn with the effort of breathing.

The rocks that Aoife had been so worried about sailed away under us as we soared up into the clouds. The ships hounding us turned small as we flew. No doubt if they could've portalled up, the Bonekeepers would've joined us. Thankfully, you couldn't portal onto a moving object, and they didn't know where or when we would be stopping. There wouldn't be any unexpected surprised anytime soon.

190

"Guys we're fucking flying!" came Evan's voice. He was alright? I dropped my gaze to see a bloody Evan being carried by Donna below.

Her own face was covered in blood, her red hair streaked with death. But the marvel that passed her expression filled me with such joy that I laughed.

"You do realise if I hadn't been here to help you your arms would have burnt off," Brenn reprimanded in a short voice next to me.

I just laughed – the pain had turned to an ache but as we charged forward, I saw nothing but open sea. Not a jagged rock in sight.

"Do you think we're in the clear now?" I forced out in the lightest voice I could muster. Then I turned my head – their faces were in such a state of shock it made me giggle. I felt something cool drip from my nose, it tasted metallic. My nose was bleeding.

"Captain?" Brenn snapped in a stern voice.

Instantly the shock seemed to wear off and the captain cleared his throat, but Aoife spoke.

"You've done more than enough," she said in amazement.

I turned to Brenn who nodded, and I copied his movements.

"Slowly," he said as I lowered my arms. The boat started to gradually sink through the air – the storm had been passed through entirely and the sky was clear and blue. We landed with a splash – the boat rocked from side to side as it met the familiar waves once again. The magic coursing through my veins made the boards crack around my feet a little as I struggled to keep upright.

My hands were vibrating now as I let go of the threads of magic holding the boat. The ache seemed to grow as I let the magic dissipate in my core. Relax now – you deserve it.

As if that command applied to every part of my body, I felt the weight on my shoulders depart. I dropped to my knees and then lay with my back on the helm's floor. My fingers still seemed to be throbbing with magic despite me letting go of my concentration.

Aoife and the Captain instantly went to help me up, but I waved them off.

"No, no," I said as I regained the breath I didn't know I had lost. "Let me be."

191

The sky was glorious and blue, and the sheer craziness of what I had just done seemed to be dancing along every one of my veins. So, I laughed and pumped a fist.

"Fuck yeah," I said as my breathing turned to a kind of breathless laughter. The faces around me were smiling too. Even Brenn had a look that wasn't disdain – something that was not entirely horrified. Impressed?

The sun was out and despite all the pain, all I could do was laugh.

Fifteen

The medical wing was a short stub of a room with a collection of beds. Laid out on three cots were a grim-faced Evan, a green-looking Caden, and face-planted the wrong way was Regan. She wasn't in her wolf form and was buck-naked on top of the sheets. Her ebony limbs were sprawled everywhere – I noticed a few tattoos across the small of her back before I looked away. I wasn't sure she would appreciate me gawking. Donna dutifully placed a sheet over her behind.

"Are you sure you're feeling okay enough to do this?" Aoife said beside me. Donna was spoon-feeding Caden something that was glowing on a silver spoon. She'd explained that he'd been hit by a demon using toxic magic – she was administering the antidotes. Donna worked away like she'd done this a hundred times before. Even though Regan would heal fast as werewolves do, Donna was going to apply balms and stitch any of the bigger ones to prevent scarring. Were all dragon-kins just natural healers?

"I can do it," I said determinedly. Aoife gave me a grim-face smile before handing me a silver needle and some copper-coloured thread. Evan groaned as I sat down on the bed next to him.

I gave him my best smile despite the fact my hands were shaking. "Any preference on what stitch I should use?"

"If you don't use some fancy-ass stitch I will be disappointed."

I lowered myself to where the gash was. The skin was still viciously torn. Donna was certain that he was going to be fine – but judging by everyone in the hospital wing, we could barely say that we escaped unscathed.

I threaded the needle with more ease than I thought was possible. But then as I lowered to the cut – so diligently cleaned with rubbing alcohol from Donna, my hands started to shake. The cut would heal normally but the blade had been enchanted against any fast healing. Thank the Gods it had missed anything important.

Brenn's presence appeared behind me – he was ebbing power, no doubt from eating all the corpses of the dead.

"I could always do that," he said. "I'm good at sewing." I don't even know how he managed to make that sentence threatening.

Evan's jaw clenched.

"I would rather bleed."

Brenn snickered before he turned back into his snake form. He opened his mouth to reveal his long fangs.

"I am sure we can arrange it."

"Guys, please. *Please.*" I lowered the needle and went for the first stitch. The skin was ragged, but I steeled my breath and pinched the two sides together before gently pressing the needle through.

Evan hissed and instantly I felt terrible. "Do you want me to try to distract you?"

"What've you got?"

I shrugged.

"How about something funny?"

Evan gritted his teeth in response.

"Once upon a time, back before war was a massive problem," I started. I felt Brenn slither up my back and rest on my shoulders as he liked to do in his cat form. "There was a ball. A tradition held every year for Princesses – the Blossom Dance. When the leaves from the trees around the city of Kya would first go into bloom."

I had to keep the stitches evenly spaced but work as quickly as I could. I couldn't help but think of my governesses – how is my stitch-work, Lady Grimsby?

"The point of the ball was to find me a husband," I told them. I knew Donna was listening too; the only person who wasn't was Regan who was happily snoring away on her bed. "I started attending most balls after I reached the ripe old marrying age of twelve. They even expected me to attend the balls thrown in honour of when Sorrel killed something. The hope was eventually I would pair off with some man or another."

"However, I had no interest in finding a husband – especially those my father favoured," I could still recall them all now. Lined up around the ballroom that had been decorated in golden and white draped with ribbons ties between all the witchlights. Flowers on every surface imaginable and beautiful floral sculptures that the earth-based mages had made in the shape of deer, rabbits, wolves, or even one year, a dragon. "You could tell which ones had spoken to my father. They were always blanched white – having your life flash before your

194

eyes will do that. But anyway, those my father chose were always awful."

We were getting somewhere now. My stitches were halfway finished.

"Anyway, this one boy, a prissy, rich kid, far up his own behind, was so wealthy it was enough to make him rather popular among the ladies in court. An heir to a great fortune – despite being the son of a Baron." I went on. Evan snorted at this. "Money speaks – even to royalty. And thus, the donkey was top of my father's list for my potential husband."

"However, this particular ass-wipe of a man was so determined to win me over, he stuck beside me the entire night. He was exactly my father's kind of man. And my father left this boy with me while he abandoned the ball – as he liked to when he was suitably drunk. Don't get me wrong – I gave him a shot. I asked how he was, made pleasant small talk, but then his reply was hideous.

'When we are married, you will learn to speak when you are spoken to. Or not at all'."

Donna made a retching sound. "My sentiments exactly."

"I was about sixteen at the time," I added. Wearing a dress that was made from the palest pink fabric. The skirts gathered around me like they were petals, and I was the bud. "The guy was at least twenty."

"I digress. Anyway, the dancing had started, but this stuck-up twit would not dance no matter how much I hinted or told him. He looked very affronted I had spoken to him at all – so I kept at it. But as he had made himself my companion that evening, no other partner dared approach."

"Thankfully, eventually he excused himself to gather drinks for us, so I went to make my escape. Then I noticed the tables of girls near the back. Usually, I was kept nearer the front so my father could keep an eye on me. I realised that these were all the sisters. All the sisters of the boys my father had invited to come and try and woo me."

"The dance floor was filled with couples but usually, the same sex doesn't dance with each other. It's seen as common."

"But alas, my father was not there," I said. I grinned at the thought. I went to the back and after a little persuasion, I had the girls all pair up and we headed to the dance floor. We danced the quickstep together before a waltz and then a quadrille. However, then that turd from earlier came back. As it turned out, *I* had abandoned *him* to dance with his sister – who was far better company, by the way. He was furious and grabbed my wrist."

"Naturally, I pushed him into a table of desserts! Pie and cake went everywhere. Cream cakes were launched into the air. And my dress was ruined. A food fight commenced immediately, but I had underestimated my arm power as he knocked over one of those sculptures when I pushed him."

"And it went through an ancient stained-glass window."

Evan snicked and Donna gawped. Brenn shook his head.

"Once the disaster child, always the disaster child." He said, like it was a fact.

I finished up my stitch. It was ugly but at least he was now back together.

"Did you get punished?" Donna asked. Caden looked less unwell now – a colour had flushed back into his cheeks, and he had drifted off into a deep sleep. I nodded.

"Banned from balls or family events for a whole year," I told her. "But my father didn't like the idea of me having an unruly reputation – so he said I was away practicing dance in Hydrae. In truth, I wasn't allowed anywhere visitors could be. The dessert fiasco had been brushed aside with the explanation that I was not able to handle the physical affections of a man in public."

Evan pulled the shirt off over his head. He had other picket-like scars dotted around his torso that had healed, leaving pale patches of skin in jagged marks. Alongside them, he has several tattoos too, of various creatures of red and black.

"A year in solitude sounds like some kind of hell," Donna said to me.

I thought of all the secret picnics Randall and I would have. We'd stay out until late when my father was away and wait until the night was upon us and all the lights of the forest would glow. Randall taught me how to make basic potions and I taught him how to sew.

We explored every inch of the catacombs and all the treasures they had to offer. Time moved too fast when I was in love.

"It wasn't all bad."

The cold sheets covered my body as I lay down face first into my pillow, but I didn't feel any sense of relief. Instead, I saw Evan cut open and bloody – an exhausted Regan – Donna bruised badly – and Caden poisoned.

This was all because of me.

They were all hurt badly because of me.

"They knew what they were signing up for, your Highness," Brenn said, boredly. "You are not responsible for their actions."

"I practically blackmailed them into joining this quest – they hardly had a choice." My voice was muffled, but I didn't move my head.

Brenn climbed up onto my back and sat.

"Princess, you managed to pick the friendliest group of idiots in all of Nos, I have no doubt that even if you hadn't suggested the sword, they would've joined us for the adventure anyway." I still didn't move. I was letting the pillow absorb the tears before I rolled over. It was good to cry sometimes – it felt like a release.

"It was your mission – one you had to make through no faults of your own. Your family landed you in this mess long before you entered this world."

I wiped my face with the back of my hand as I turned over onto my side and Brenn slid off me. I thought of Kya. My city and home had been ravaged by the army that swept through our defences like they were nothing. I was just imprisoned – I knew that many of my people would've suffered far worse fates. Many texts about the Fynix had been banned for years, but down in the catacombs I had ready about ends worse than death at the hands of them. Their history was as colourful as ours, but it seemed like this war had lasted so long now history had ceased to recall what happened before.

It wasn't just the Fynix. Across the Divide, the Demon King had established a country so formidable people would add the weeks of travel around it instead of passing through. I felt the hatred curl in my gut like a venomous snake.

The way the Bonekeepers swept across the deck. My senses

tingled when they were around – something sharp, dangerous, and formidable was close. And then there was all that *power*. The stories I heard through my maids or gossip from the kitchens didn't compare. I hadn't even felt the full force of it yet, but it sent shivers up my arms.

"We can do this, Brenn," I spoke softly.

"No one else would dare to," Brenn said, "so it has got to be you."

It wasn't scathing or anything like his usual barb. When I looked at him, he'd closed his eyes. Curled up by my side.

"Now go to sleep. I understand humans need rest."

"Goodnight Brenn."

"Goodnight, your Highness."

Sixteen

The next day, Donna, Brenn, and I gathered at the helm as the Captain and Aoife explained the plan.

"We will stop at the northern coastline," Captain Bennett announced. "These lands have been deserted for hundreds of years, so there is no risk of us running into anyone –"

"Apart from the hordes of monsters," Brenn said, flicking his tail from where he was delicately perched on my shoulder. He had been unusually reserved at breakfast. I thought perhaps it was a sour mood brought on by my lack of cooking skills, but I didn't know how to use the strange magic-fuelled stove and Brenn didn't say anything as I helped myself to the bread, cheese, and butter. A cheese sandwich seemed a strange sort of breakfast, but I didn't want to disturb Caden's recovery to ask.

"I'm sure you would know about that more than I would, Brenn," the captain replied before continuing. "We will make repairs using whatever we can find. Hopefully, Caden and Regan will be up soon to help with this process."

Despite his seeming good health, Donna had explained that Evan was going to take a little longer to heal. The blades, demon-made, knew just how to stall the healing process. It was a grim tactic, but Evan had assured me that they were special blades and not everyone had them. He was sure he had a pair of daggers with that ability somewhere in his quarters.

Caden, whose icy eyes kept flickering open and closed, had groaned and then reminded Evan that he used them to clean his nails, so they were in the bathroom. He then told him to shut up so he could sleep. His blonde hair was unkempt for the first time in his life.

When we were out of earshot, Donna suggested that the added vocal nature of his recovery was most likely to be a response to the oak roots and jasmine blossom healing potions he was ingesting. More than once, he claimed there were three of me; that Naps was secretly plotting his demise; and then he found the very idea of milk hilarious and laughed nonstop for over an hour.

"We will be there a matter of days and from there we shall make headway along the northern border of Silvia, stopping in Qicog for supplies, praying we don't get stopped crossing Syree's borders, and boom – we're in Wist."

"Sounds plausible," Donna said optimistically. She looked my way. "I'll take you out in Qicog – don't let Regan hijack you for an evening. You'll lose all your money, probably half your clothes, and end up drunk in a tavern full of dwarves trying to wife you."

"Wife me?" I asked, laughing.

"Tall women," Aoife explained, "it's a very popular fetish."

I pulled a face.

"Let's get moving," the Captain said, signalling to Donna to lower the foremast sails so we picked up more speed. He smiled at me. "At least now you'll get to see where our favourite wraith comes from."

"You're going home, Brenn," I said as the wind whipped the mainsail as we caught the wind to herald us left.

"My home died a millennia ago," he said shortly. "I'll be visiting a graveyard."

The following day marked the time we would cross over into the Shadow Realm. The idea of a country with no sun seemed awfully sinister to me, not that I ever minded the dark, but sometimes you couldn't beat the sunlight on your face to begin your day.

I stood on the deck as the sky began to darken. The sun snuck behind the horizon and a chill travelled across my skin and brought goose pimples to my arms. The darkness didn't absorb us instantly; the sky faded from a midday blue, to a dusky grey, to a deep navy, and finally to a pitch shade of black. It took an hour until we had truly entered the Shadow Realm and by that point, I already missed the sun.

The coastline appeared too – a dark crust creeping into view like soot on the horizon. We headed north – but everything seemed oddly quiet. The only noise came from the familiar creaks from the Siren's Promise as it conquered wave after wave.

I peered over the side of the ship and the dark sea greeted me. I couldn't see much below beside a faint reflection of myself. But I was certain that more than enough creatures lurked below in these inkwell waters.

Captain Bennett had to carefully manoeuvre us around a great number of jagged rocks that protruded out of the ocean like fingers clawing at the sky. Aoife kept her eyes focused on the horizon and called out directions from the bow. She'd tied her hair back into a bunch at the back of her head. The wind kept a steady gale as we headed along the coast until we could find a suitable place to lower the anchor.

Finally, Aoife found a cove and called to us to prepare for docking. My heart pounded involuntarily when I saw the long stretch of black glittering sand. Suddenly, the dream drifted back into my memories.

But this place was a husk. There were no living trees left, only rotting stumps and dry branches that looked like they had survived on dirt alone. Here there were no flowers or forest. It was as if a dreary death sentence had been placed on the land.

"How long has it looked like this?" I asked no one in particular.

"As long as I've been alive," Captain Bennett called from the helm.

"And he is *ancient*," Aoife added with a nod of affirmation that made the captain roll his eyes.

Brenn spoke then. His voice was low. There was something unusually soft in his tone – something nearly vulnerable, or perhaps I was imagining it. Or perhaps his feline form was throwing me off.

"It used to be the best place in Nos."

I looked at the rotting wasteland that stretched as far as the eye could see. It was hard to imagine it.

I looked at Brenn and had an idea.

"Show me?"

Brenn raised one furry eyebrow, but then he released something like an exasperated sigh.

"Close your eyes."

I did so and felt the presence of his smoky magic waft by my nose. I knew if I opened my eyes now, I would see the streams of glittering black. "Now open them."

My eyes adjusted to the bright sun that seemed to be beaming down on a lush forest of greens of varying colours.

The trees and bushes were full of flowers in varieties I had only ever seen in books. Small glowing orbs floated around, and it took me a moment to realise that those were the fairies I had seen in my dream. People lazed on the black sand – nymphs, pixies, and lingering in the back was that spirit, the one in green, a kind smile on her face. My magic seemed to bubble inside of me. I could taste it on the back of my tongue.

"This looks just like what I saw in my dream," I told him. "Even the feeling."

I felt Brenn lose concentration and the scene in front of me glowed in vivid colours before blurring and then turning dark once more, as if a shadow had overtaken the sun.

Captain Bennett had activated the witchlights along the boat to give us more visibility as we landed on the beach. The anchor was moored and before I could say anything more, I saw Brenn materialise into his shadow form and leap off the boat.

"Brenn!" I called but he seemed to be swarming up the waters and to the sand. I shared a look with Donna who shrugged but then she gasped.

"We thought we better come upstairs to get some good air," Evan said weakly.

"As opposed to Evan's gas," Regan said as she strode over to the forefront of the deck and brought him a chair to sit on.

"Evening all," she said back to her big, bold, and beautiful self. "Glad to see in my absence, all reason was abandoned, and we made all the stupid decisions."

She gave me a proud smile.

"Proof they need my intellect."

"If we relied on your intellect, we would've already died," the familiar drawl of Caden came aboard. He seemed to be wearing the contents of his bed and then some. The Fae was bundled up in at least five different blankets and a woollen hat, scarf, and gloves.

I was happy to see them, but Donna raged about them leaving.

"Sorry D, but if I had to share one more minute alone with that blithering idiot, I was going to stab myself all over again," Evan said from across the deck. He'd managed to pry one of Caden's blankets off him and was now lying at Donna's feet.

"Yes, Donna, it was quite hellish having to hear that brute snore his way through the afternoon like a pig was stuck in his throat," Caden replied with a similar note of dissatisfaction. "How am I meant to heal if I will end up mentally damaged afterwards?"

Donna threw the pair of them an exasperated look. She got their pillows from downstairs and made them lay at the base of the centre, close to the mizzenmast.

She turned to Regan shortly after, but the werewolf wouldn't hear it; no matter what Donna tried to edge in about healing on the inside too. Regan was adamant that she was fine.

I turned to see Brenn waiting for me on the shore. He was back in his male human form that he had used in Draig and was waving both his arms.

"I think he wants to show me around," I said to Aoife who had joined us on deck along with the captain as the anchor had been dropped.

"You'll be fine with him – but try not to run into any monsters," Captain Bennett said. "And look out for anything useful."

I nodded and headed to where I knew the climbing ladder was on the side of the ship. "Donna and Regan, help us hunt for good lumber in case we run out of lead patches before we hit Qicog," I heard the captain go on to say. "We need to be able to survive another full-frontal attack and right now, the old girl needs serious patching up."

Donna lowered a small rowing boat from the rigging on the side of the ship and we stepped into it before descending to meet the waves. To the dragon-kin's dismay, Regan ignored the rowing boat completely and dove off the deck into the sea. Landing with a great splash, she swam to shore and bowed from the beach. Cursing loudly, Donna rowed furiously, churning up the water in her wake, and soon we mounted the beach.

Donna handed me a palm-sized witchlight to light my way with its blue glow, but thankfully the moon was strong tonight. My feet landed on the sand with a crunch and instantly water welled up, making inkwells form around my boots. It seemed to shimmer like crushed onyx under the torchlight from the ship. From where I stood, I could still see Aoife and the Captain at the bow, making plans to restore the ship and fix the worst of the battle damage, no doubt. Despite us sealing the patches torn in the hull by the cannon fire with lead, it was only a quick fix, and the ship would need sturdier fabrics to travel further once more. From what I understood, the plan was to dock as soon as possible for proper repairs – but until then we would have to improvise.

Donna furiously herded Regan along the brush to find lumber leaving me with Brenn once more. The noise of wind rustling through the dead wood made the hairs on my arms stand upright and for the first time in a while, I felt a sense of cold overcome me.

I found my immortal companion at the edge of the trees. Thankfully, the persistence of the moon and my witchlight meant my eyes had adjusted to the light. The tiny form of his feline shape had gone, and he was massive. I recognised the form from my books on monsters: a manticore. A beast with the body of a lion, wings of a dragon, a tail from a scorpion and horns coming out atop his head. The head originally looked like it belonged to the lion too, but as he turned around to look at me, those onyx eyes wide and watchful, it didn't look right.

"Wait for me!" I called hauling myself through the sandbanks as quickly as his giant form began to disappear into the vast brush of dead, draping plants. The dunes turned to curled leaves that crunched under me, and the smell of dank, rotting seaweed and dust filled the air.

I finally caught up with him and a root caught my foot. I stumbled forward but caught myself upright before I hurtled over into a wispy dry hedge. My boots skidded to a halt as I caught up with the giant rear end of Brenn.

He didn't say anything but sniffed in my direction.

"Where are we going?" I asked, looking around, chills travelling down my back like long spindly fingers. Everything about this place seemed eerie: I shuddered. Brenn's giant eyes flicked back to me and something like a chuckle emanated from his lips.

"Just a little exploration," he said. "Unless you're scared…"

I clenched my jaw. It was just some trees and a creepy forest in total darkness. What else could possibly happen? Brenn was here. I was safe.

"Trees don't scare me," I replied.

Something snapped underfoot and I nearly jumped out of my skin. The wraith chuckled.

The trees seemed to be swaying sideways, the sinister moonlight shining down on them. What happened here to make this place seem so devoid of life? It seemed that all that was left was the soggy mud, the skeletons of the foliage, and dried leaves.

"There's nothing here," I said. I hadn't spoken loudly, but the absence of all other sounds made my words ring. Brenn stalked off ahead of me.

"Not anymore."

I looked back; the path that had led us here, the path back to the black sands of the beach, somehow had disappeared, as if it had been eaten by the stretching trees, their roots clawing up from the ground. But if Brenn had noticed he didn't say anything, he just kept on walking. This land was dead. There was nothing.

My heart jumped into my throat. Every tree looked like the same corpse of its neighbour, but Brenn didn't seem to be slowing down.

"Are we lost?" I asked. I couldn't shake the feeling the ghosts who roamed this land were listening in and watching.

"Not at all," Brenn said. "I traversed this land years before your parents had even been conceived."

I grimaced.

"Thanks for *that* thought."

Brenn stopped a moment, his lion-like ears pricked up. I froze behind him. He twisted around and closed the distance between us, curling me inside his strange body. He looked one way and the next. "What is it?" I whispered. I couldn't see anything beyond fifteen feet at the most, my witchlight had been snuffed by Brenn's form, and my heart was pounding.

Brenn seemed to ease a little. He shook his giant head.

"I thought I heard something," he mumbled. "Perhaps it was just these lands playing tricks on us."

I wriggled out of his grasp. "Let's not stick around to find out."

Brenn paused a moment before he sniffed and turned around. I stuck close by to him this time.

We returned to the beach as if the path had been there all along. The crew had gathered lumber from the carcasses of the dead plants closest to the bay. Caden and Evan were not allowed to help due to their recovery, so they were dictating the actions of the others from the railing on the ship.

"Start stacking it in a pile, Regan," Caden called, rubbing his forehead, a pained expression on his face.

"This is a pile!" Regan called from the nest of trees, twigs and whatever tufts of dead plant she had been able to gather from the brush that grew up around her.

"You look like you're about to start laying for winter," came Caden's response. Regan's eye twitched.

We joined the fray, gathering what we could from the dusty dry beds on the front. Shards of old tree trunks could be salvaged to reveal slats of malleable wood; old, rubbery vines could be doubled as something that would work well as rope. After a suitable amount had been gathered, we regrouped on the Promise. The moon seemed to glow brighter as night drew on and we all sipped soup in mugs on deck.

I had seen no such creatures thus far, but the captain assured me that they were there; lurking in the darkness, keeping their distance because of Brenn's powerful aura. However, after our experience in the forest, I wasn't so sure.

"If only my presence didn't keep idiots away too," he said. He was still staying in his manticore form. It had been a bit strange to get used to, but I soon realised that due to his new size, he couldn't sleep on my bed. However, later, after the captain had re-tuned the wards up on the ship so we could sleep in peace, Brenn did attempt to sidle into my bunk.

It did not end well for him.

He grumpily resigned himself to the lower bunk.

"You could change back to the cat," I said, hanging over the edge of the top bunk. Brenn's dark face did not look impressed. His tail curled out from the bed at a weird angle. My hair had grown considerably since getting aboard here. I could even see it hanging next to my eyes as Brenn sniffed.

"I have no intention of being quite so vulnerable while we are here," he said with finality.

The magic was strong here – I could feel it in my chest. Yet, surprisingly, it filled me with a cold sense of familiarity and unease. When I tried to ask Brenn about it, he ignored me or would tell me to put on a jumper.

However, for once I would have the bunk to myself and I decided I would cherish it. Soon, the images of the dark waves outside my window lulled me to sleep.

I slept deeply. I was filled warmth I hadn't felt since being home in Kya: a night crouched by the fire at Randall's apartment, held in his arms; an embrace from Sorrel from when times were good; the summer sun streaming through one of the ancient stained-glass windows in the nursery – a woman in my peripheral vision was smiling. Long, blonde hair streaming down her sides – she looked happy…

"Bryony?" I looked down to see the green spirit in my hand. In less time than it takes to blink she had grown to the size of a candle. Her cheeks were pink and rounded. She was covered in freckles, dark ones that patterned along her cheeks, nose and down her neck. Her dress was made of long leaves that had been embroidered with beads. There seemed to be something regal in the angled panes of her freckled neck as she gazed up at me.

Her face was shaped like a heart; her full pink lips parted like she was going to speak but she shut her mouth as if thinking better of it. Her deep green eyes flicked behind me, but before I could turn back, she led me forward.

I was back in the dream. This version of the Wastes seemed just like Brenn's vision, full of life and beauty. So beautiful that I couldn't wait to tell Brenn about it when I woke up. I felt so happy, like my soul was radiating heat through me like the sun.

The colours were so bright and beaming – everything around me seemed to be glowing. The Wastes were thriving with loveliness and life.

Before the plants ceased to grow and the golden stretch of the sun failed to reach the dusty shores, this place was a beacon of everything good and right and magical…

The beach was busy! Filled with souls; nymphs, spirits, and

sprites gathered on the sand. Not one turned to look at me – it was as if I was invisible.

I saw the green light flash in my vision. The path was open again. The smell of lavender, bergamot, and salt from the sea filled my senses, and I instantly felt calm; then the green spirit stepped forward, letting go of my hand. She walked through the gap in the now blossoming brush.

"Highness," came a voice. It sounded so soft. Was the green spirit calling me? I heard it again. She must really need me. The path emerged from the brush; trees moving aside to let me through. "Highness!" This time it was more insistent. She needed me!

"I'm coming!" I mumbled, heading forward. It seemed the further I headed down the path, the more the scene seemed to darken. I crossed legions, but I never tired. The overgrowth stretched above, consuming me in a tunnel of leaves and green.

The lights of the forest, shining greens and bright sunshine yellows seemed to flash by as I dashed forward. The glade formed around me, and I couldn't seem to wipe a strange smile from my face. Everything was so beautiful, and I was nothing but joy.

Then my heart stuttered in my chest.

I saw him, Randall, standing there smiling, in the bright light of day. I raced towards him, wrapping my arms around him tightly. He smelled like the wood from his cabin, like hay, like my boy. I felt tears spring to my eyes.

I pulled back and reached for his face. I could feel the soft stubble around his jaw and the soft skin under his neck.

"Princess," came a feminine, wistful voice.

I turned and saw that the pool, once shimmering with gold, was now filled with murky black liquid, the altar covered in dust. Suddenly the voices ceased around me. Something was watching me.

I kept Randall's hand tight as I moved to the green spirit.

Leaning over the pool I stared down, only a pit of darkness awaited me. Her face was gone.

"Princess." Someone was saying. "*Bryony.*" Brenn?

"This is all gone now, Princess," the spirit said sadly. "Remnants of a life I once led. This spell shows the desires of your heart." Her voice went soft. "This is mine."

Her eyes flicked over to where Randall stood.

"I assume who you're seeing is yours," she said sadly. I smiled at Randall – she was wrong. He was here. Flesh and blood – my promised – my boy – my Randall.

I looked around. The glade had emptied apart from the three of us. No longer did the stones around the bottom of the pool glow. Instead, the tree that had glistened in the sunlight was dull and withered.

"This place used to run with magic – our magic," the spirit added. With a flash of green, she returned to being no bigger than one of my fingers. When she spoke, her voice seemed so sad. "I was sent to you, Princess."

She looked down in the pool. I couldn't see the face at all. Celine – the all-seeing now confined to darkness.

"You have to help us restore magic to this land," her voice was a plea. "Come home, Bryony."

I felt a brush of magic whip past me – a cool breeze, one I knew so well. Magic from warlocks, mages, wizards, sorcerers, and witches. My people's magic. I could feel it here.

It had been buried deep. Layers of age and decay had trapped it – but there it was.

"Kya…" I started to say.

She shook her head.

"When your people left, the magic here withered." Speaking about this made the spirit's face crease in pain. "The sun disappeared for us. The days had always been short here, but then they eventually ceased to be."

The shadow realm…

"How do I help you?"

Her eyes widened and began to shine.

"This land is part of you, you must return part of yourself to it," she said. Pleading. "You can have it all back."

There was a noise, like a blade whipping through the air, and then everything snapped back. I felt myself rush back into reality - the moon was bright and startling. The green spirit still lingered ahead of me. Her face was real and startled.

I was awake!

The coolness of the night made me shiver. The colours around me faded back into bleak normality. I looked down and saw my feet were ankle-deep in mud.

I turned and saw the magic fade away from where Randall had been standing. As his face faded into someone else entirely. I felt like someone had landed a punch in my gut. Gone was my stable boy; instead, a looming figure towered over me, dressed in darkness once more. His red eyes met mine, and I felt my breath catch.

The Bonekeeper general was standing there, holding my hand.

I couldn't read the expression on his face, but I couldn't stop the feeling that the floor had slipped away from me.

All the happiness I had felt returned fizzed away as I found myself struggling to breathe. My head was spinning as I let go of the demon's hand and felt myself fold forward. I pressed my hands on my thighs and breathed in deeply. Magic spilled over my tongue and made bile rise in my throat as the spell faded away.

He didn't move. He couldn't be here. Could he? Why? What were the spirits trying to tell me?

"You must help us," came a feeble voice. I turned to face the spirit, but she was gone. Instead, the Bonekeeper and I both stood next to the altar – I looked between the pool, the tree, the altar, and him.

I did my best to wipe my face, and then I cleared my throat as I straightened up.

My heart was racing, but he was still and made no movements. I cast a look around the glen. Brenn wasn't here. I called out to him using our pact, but the demon prince did nothing.

"Illusion magic," I said, both to myself and to him. I suddenly felt the realisation dawn on me. "Sorry, I grabbed you."

The Bonekeeper looked at me incredulously – his scarlet eyes wide. I couldn't help the nervous giggle that slipped from me.

"Just be glad I didn't kiss you," I added – the tension right now was too much. My hands were shaking, and I could feel it going up to my shoulders. I clenched my jaw, but my teeth started chattering. "It could've been way worse."

I couldn't stop envisioning Randall's face. It had been so real. I tried my best for an unperturbed expression, but I felt like I might bring back up my soup. I gripped my hands together hard.

"The spirit – she spelled you – your pupils were blown," he suddenly said next to me. His voice was low but the same familiar roughness I had met in that alleyway. Perhaps it was the shock, but I didn't feel frightened. "She was speaking Archaic Riachan." He clenched his jaw. "I haven't heard that dialect in many years."

I blinked hard, then released the breath that seemed to be bundling up in my chest.

"Strangely enough I understood her," I said. It seemed like my mother tongue – I hadn't even noticed. Usually, when I switched to another language, it felt like I had to concentrate hard so I didn't muddle the bunch of them in my head.

"You did more than that – you spoke as fluently as she did," the Bonekeeper said. Everything still seemed to be catching up with me. My bones ached and the chill was settling on my bare skin. Yet the general made no movement – all was still.

I looked at the altar. The dry stone that had been worn smooth with time was covered in dust. No glowing red stones and the pool was empty. No face. Just dirt.

"She kept saying I should help them, but I don't understand how I can," I sighed. I looked back at the general who was watching me carefully. "Maybe you frightened her off."

I ran my finger along the top of the font, which shone like silver at the tip. The stone grazed me, and I felt a cut nip, barely anything, at the top. A zap of pain, as quickly as it appeared, evaporated.

The red dot fell on the rim. The raw stone's edge had cut across my right finger.

"I don't see how I even came to be here," the general said, crossing his arms. "We've been searching the Wastes for days but haven't found anything. Then I felt the spirit's enchantment and portalled to shore. She must've used me in her spell."

That brought me back to reality. I looked down at my palm and saw the little cross there our pact remained strong. The ability of the green spirit to put Brenn to sleep was something that made the hairs stand up on the back of my neck. If she had she been a malevolent spirit I could've died. Or had we simply not got to that part yet?

I was in the bed shirt that Regan had lent me and besides my pants, I had nothing else on. The cold instantly made me shiver all over again.

I met the flaming eyes of the demon opposite me my face felt stiff from the tears, but I raised my chin.

"What happens now?" I asked him. "I know I'm in pyjamas, but I can still punch you in the face."

The general narrowed his eyes.

"You want to fight me?" he asked in a voice filled with disbelief.

I didn't lower my hands.

"Are you going to let me go?"

"No."

"Then I guess I am going to have to," I said. I changed my stance to give myself a better posture.

I saw his jaw clench in the darkness. His hood was up but the moon still caught on the tanned panes of his face.

"Why start a fight you can't win?"

"Who says I can't?" I replied. I felt the magic stir in me.

A moment later I felt a quick whip of wind. Then he was right in front of me. Looming over as if he expected me to cower.

"I do."

My breath caught in my throat, but I stared right back, sticking my chin up.

"There is a reason why lightning magic is banned," he said shortly. His hand grabbed my wrist and turned it to face the floor. The lines that had come up from the shock had never receded. I doubted they would. "You keep it up I won't need to kill you."

"I didn't really have much of an option, your Highness," I said, yanking my wrist out of his hand. He narrowed his eyes a little. "Wouldn't you rather be doing something of value instead of getting in my way?"

I stored up my magic in my chest and then in my hands.

"It's foolish to start something when you are at a disadvantage."

I released the magic in my hand and sent a smooth bolt out of my fingers. He easily dodged it, and I stepped back to make space between us.

"It is more foolish to gravely underestimate your opponent,"

I felt my magic travel up my arms and to my neck. It came to me

212

with ease – my practice must be paying off.

The Bonekeeper met my eyes once more. His lips were pressed together. I charged up my arcane senses and focused on him. He glowed with power – it came around him in red flames, never quite meeting the colour in his eyes.

I sent a bolt in his direction. He jumped back to avoid it, but then I sensed him move to come forward. My arcane senses easily picked up on his advance and I dived to the left. He pulled out the same onyx dagger from Draig.

He swung it right at me, but I ducked and sidestepped it.

"Don't do this, Princess," he growled in a low voice. "The Demon King is merciful when things go his way."

I kept the distance between us. I could feel the electricity in me build. My arms flooded with power - it seemed to be behaving well today. Perhaps all my practising was paying off, or perhaps it was down to this place.

"After his forces helped butcher my people, I doubt I would have much to say," I sent out charges around me. He came quickly towards me, blade swinging to the left and then the right. He seemed to be going to destabilise rather than kill me.

I went to charge again, but then he beat me in speed. Lunging downward, he nicked the outside of my thigh before I could fully dodge it. My bare legs did little to protect me from the slash. I hissed but quickened my attack, which I was happy to see kept him busy.

I thought about the healing book I had briefly looked at. My idea was that if I was the best at fighting, I would never need to heal. However, I could now understand why Brenn had not looked impressed by what I had called my "genius way of thinking".

The sharp slice in my leg must've shown on my face.

"Stop this, or I won't hold back," the general said. His back was to the dark pool that was still as quiet and dead as night.

I grinned at him, feeling the bolts gain more power along my arms. I felt my hair start to fizz with electricity. Suddenly, the force of the electricity hit me in the chest. My heart was racing, I could feel it in my mouth and along my tongue.

Everything rushed back to me – Kya – the tower – Hector – it all filled me with a feeling so intense I couldn't deny it any longer: rage.

"Then neither will I."

I let loose my bolt quickly. The light was blinding as it shot like a cannon through the glade. Perhaps I had been too quick for even him as it smashed into his shoulder. The light faded, and I saw that it had pushed him back to one of the watching trees.

It happened a moment later.

He charged forward with inhuman speed, but I moved aside. He tried to tackle me from behind. I used the opportunity to jab him in the stomach. He grunted but it didn't slow him in the slightest.

I had no idea how I was moving so fast, but I didn't dare stop. He moved so quickly that I could barely follow him. But as he landed another cut across my shoulder blade, I used my elbow to hit him across the temple. The girls' combat practice was paying off.

That seemed to stun him – the electricity gave the blow an extra sting. I took the opportunity to kick him in the knee and tackle him down. I loosed a final bolt into his chest which seemed to finish the job.

He fell backward and I pulled the blade from his hand and followed him down. I pressed it against his throat. I pulled my magic back in. I felt the heat of it recede into me. My magic had never felt more alive. I could call it at any moment – it didn't feel skittish in my chest.

The dazed look in his eyes faded as he lay on the mud.

I kept the blade right against the bob of his throat. My right hand was muddy and now my knees were as I straddled his torso.

"Give up. Stop following us." The feeling of the bound leather hilt in my hand made me feel powerful. The general under me did too. His glare steeled and he ground his teeth.

He raised his chin a little, and I had to be careful not to nick him.

"I'm done playing with you, Princess," he said through gritted teeth.

One hand of his went to grab the knife and the other clasped around my throat. Instantly I was void of breath, but I didn't drop the knife.

"That's cheating," I wheezed, trying to pry his solid hand from around my neck.

"Give up."

"Never."

I pressed the knife forward, but it did nothing to loosen his grip. Any further and it would cut right through the skin there.

"Are you going to kill me, Princess?"

My throat was on fire.

"I'm seriously considering it, jackass."

Suddenly I felt a rumble in the ground. I saw in my peripheral vision that the trees had swayed to the side. Their roots rippled through the sodden mud like it was nothing. A snake I knew well joined my side in an instant.

Brenn's ink-black scales glistened in the moonlight as he darted forward. Nudging my hand out the way he wrapped his long, lithe body around the demon's neck.

"What time do you call this?" I forced out – despite Brenn's form, the snake did not look impressed.

"The forest is alive, your Highness," he snapped furiously. The Bonekeeper's grip didn't loosen. "It kept me running round in circles."

I shrugged my shoulders; his fingers shook around my neck.

"Don't kill him – we don't want another war," I croaked out.

I saw Brenn squeeze around the Prince's neck and then, thankfully, the fingers loosed from around my neck as the demon passed out. His head thumped to the floor, his hood falling backwards – that intense face of his strangely peaceful for once. I heaved a breath – and started breathing as deeply as I could. I rubbed the space around my neck – it felt tight and hard to breathe for a moment – and I wondered if I would bruise. I felt a wave of nausea at first, but that quickly passed, and I drew myself up slowly.

Brenn released the general's neck. Slithering free he finally took in the surroundings.

"You saw this in your dream," he said, taking in the tree, the pool, and the altar. "But it probably didn't look this dire."

I nodded, climbing to my feet, careful not to tread on the general.

"The spirit brought me here – the green one," I told him. Her crestfallen eyes made my stomach fall. "She wanted me to fix it."

215

Brenn tutted which sounded strange when it was primarily made of hissing.

"She said that my people came from here." Brenn paused right next to the pool. "That's true, isn't it?"

He turned back and blinked at me.

"Why ask questions when you already know the answers?"

The magic felt so familiar. I'd thought that when we came. It felt strong, but this place was a graveyard.

"Why didn't you tell me?"

Brenn slithered forward, climbing up my leg until he landed on my shoulder.

"This was before, back before your family imprisoned me in the Tower," he said dejectedly. "I don't remember much of it, but I know your family was keen to distance itself from the uncivilised ways of the forest folk who dwelled there. Even though, they are, in fact, your kin."

My kin.

My people.

"How did it become like this?"

The trees parted again, forming a new path ahead. As we walked, I turned to see the demon prince stirring as the glade disappeared behind us. These lands were more living than our bleak surroundings would imply. Everything moved on its own accord and the glade where both the general and the altar lay were gone from view; the only evidence I had of him even being present were my wounds.

Questions filled my thoughts as we seemed to climb down a rooted path to a more even forest floor. I kicked away the dusty leaves to reveal stone that was worn smooth underneath.

"You've forgotten my real name, your Highness."

He spoke quietly. The trees pulled away to reveal ruins. What used to be houses had been laid to waste. There were barely any foundations left.

A stray wall. Burned rubble. Ruins upon ruins upon ruins.

The Wraith of the Wastes.

I stopped walking.

The forest laid out the deserted plains in front of us. Desolation had won here: death reigned. And everything fell into place.

"It was you, wasn't it?"

The world had gone quiet again. The Wastes seemed to absorb all the sound and I could hear my heart thundering in my ears.

Brenn nodded once.

I felt my stomach clench hard. All I could think about was what happened to Kya happening here. Bloodshed, flames, the smell of death and destruction, and then nothing. I felt my hand clench around something hard – it was the onyx dagger. The one from the general. I tucked it away in my pocket – there would be no more use of it today.

"Why?"

I looked down at the Wraith whose face was tense. He evaporated from my shoulder – in his shadow form once more. The same Wraith I had met in the Tower.

I knew it all. A part of me must have known that this was him. He wasn't even a "he" – it was a creature, a monster.

"Your thoughts are louder than ever, your Highness."

I couldn't stop the emotions flooding through me. The sadness; the bitterness; the rage.

"Why did you do it? This place was beautiful," I heard myself say. Brenn bared his teeth – his eyes were wide and dark.

"It's who I am, your Highness," he snapped. "Even before I destroyed it, your people had claimed Riach as their own. They *abandoned* their people for their own selfishness." I started walking forward – leaving Brenn behind me. The forest showed me the despair he had caused. My heart ached in my chest. How could I fix this?

"Stop walking away from me, Bryony – I had no choice! It's who I am." I couldn't stop and I couldn't look at him. "Wraiths devour and wraiths kill – that's what we do."

I pressed forward. The desolate scene in front of me receded until eventually, I was back on the shore. The trees that had guided us in seemed to have returned as they showed me the way out.

Instead of climbing aboard the ship, I looked at the water. It was all so peaceful – moonlight glittering off the surface as the waves lapped lazily. It all kept going blurry, so I sniffed hard. I looked up and down the beach – remembering the souls that had laid here and spent time enjoying the sun.

Now there was no joy.

The cut on my leg and shoulder were savagely sore and it couldn't be a good idea to get mud in them. Thankfully, I had a great deal of saltwater to hand.

Ignoring Brenn's glare, I waded out until the water was around my waist. My teeth chattered before I let myself drop. The impact slapped my back for the briefest of moments before I submerged. The chill went right up my back, but I needed the shock. I quickly climbed up to my feet – the sand was soft under my toes.

I ignored the cold sting coming from the cuts as I cleaned them and then my hair. I was filthy all over. I wondered how long I had walked with the spirit. I had a go at trying to swim by flapping my legs about. I remembered pictures of the sea and people using their arms.

I nearly drowned myself twice so settled for just floating on my back in the shallow waters near the shore. I found myself sending a prayer to the moon Goddess Serena. And then to the star Goddess Elektra, you couldn't possibly ignore them when they shined so brightly on you.

I thought of the dreams I had, so many smiling faces on the glittering black sand. When did my family decide to abandon them? Why did no one speak about it? Why didn't I learn any of this? In that moment, I wished for Sorrel so I could annoy him into telling me everything I wasn't taught.

I got up and checked I was all clean.

Hopefully, I would be able to heal myself or if not, at least I knew how to give myself stitches.

I climbed aboard the Siren's Promise. It seemed everyone was getting up. I spied Evan languidly lying across the banister by the helm.

"I wondered where you two had gone," he said, grinning. But his grin faltered as he saw my face and then the gash. "What happened?"

"It's complicated, but I will tell you later. I need to sleep," I said in quickly but hopefully not too rudely. However, my powers for dealing with people were low today. Evan's brows raised, but before he could say anything else, I quickened my step and flew below deck. I was in our quarters in a matter of moments.

I threw off the sodden clothes and hung them over the pipes that kept our room warm. Dabbing myself dry with a towel, I wrung my hair out and then climbed into bed.

"Are you going to see to that wound?"

I turned over.

I heard everyone start to get up next door. I had a feeling Brenn had told them to stay away as no one knocked. I heard him warn the captain of the general's presence on the shore, but Bennett was sure the cove we were hiding in was well hidden. I wondered if the Wastes themselves were hiding us too: who knew the depths of this land's power? My head was spinning from tiredness, and I was unable to sleep as I churned over everything in my head.

The day remained dark. Endless night. It was all connected – I could feel it. However, I couldn't bring myself to look at Brenn. It felt like something of a betrayal asking him.

Eventually, I drifted off to a dreamless sleep.

I awoke when the moon was full and high again. I headed back to the glade to investigate further. The Wastes guided me along the path once more. And I found the glade empty of all life, no Bonekeeper, no spirits, not even grass. Brenn lurked at the centre of the glade as I pored over the altar.

I cleared the dust away on the top of the stone rim. There were runes written there but I didn't recognise them. I spotted where my blood had dried last time and was careful not to snag my fingers on the sharp rim anytime soon.

I investigated the tree and pulled away a chunk of bark to see if any of it was still living. It crumbled in my hand, and I shook the splinters of bark away. I checked the pool too, but even when I dug with my hands my fingers met more mud.

I heard him hiss lowly. "You can't be mad at me forever."

"Hearing you butchered my people's homeland and drove them out would be enough for some people," I replied. He slithered next to me.

"Don't be so naïve," he snipped back. "It's not my fault you look at me in the same stupid light you look at everyone. Stop acting like I lied to you."

I sat upright, shaking the mud from my hands. The gash on my shoulder stung a little at the action. I ground my teeth together.

"I think the Goddess wanted me to know what happened," I said. Brenn scoffed at that. "That's what the dreams were."

Brenn didn't reply.

"Isn't it ironic how you only cared about the Wastes when you realised they were your people? If they were demons, would you have felt anything at all?" He said flatly.

My blood boiled.

"Of course, I would," I retorted. "The wound is deeper for my people too – what happened out there – it's desolation."

"I had no choice," he spoke through his bared fangs. "It's who I am. I kill and I enjoy it."

"You should have told me," I replied.

"I thought you may have figured it out," he admitted.

"You knew. You knew I was standing on the graves of my people," I snapped.

"That's what made the spirit flee – she feared you." Brenn scoffed. "The forest remembered you. You didn't just come from the Wastes – you *made* the Wastes."

There was a moment of quiet between us. Brenn's face was completely unreadable in this form. He kept his eyes low and slithered next to me.

I felt a muddle of things. But I couldn't bring myself to yell anymore.

Perhaps Brenn felt the same way as he just looked at the ruined pool for a while.

"I did come from the Wastes," Brenn spoke with finality. "So, I remember when the children of magic decided to abandon the nymphs, spirits, and sprites that made them." He looked up at me.

"I have snippets of my memory from back then. Before I was, who I am today," his voice softened.

Everything fell into place.

"You're Riachian, aren't you?"

One of my people.

"I was. I lived here. Back then it was Riachia. I don't remember much about who I was before I changed but I remember how our society fell apart." He spoke sadly. "Then one day the sun didn't rise – thus the shadow realm was born."

"It was falling apart before I destroyed it," he added. He seemed like the recollection was a difficult one – perhaps it was so far back.

I felt a weight grow on my chest. One of sadness that wrapped around my heart.

My eyes welled up.

"I'm sorry," he said. He changed back into a feline, four paws standing next to me. "For keeping it from you."

"I'm sorry for yelling," I said. "And everything my ancestors did."

He let a laugh as he launched into my arms.

"If we are doing apologies for that you'd be here all day."

I rolled my eyes as he twisted into a circle in my arms.

"Don't ruin the moment, wraith," I told him.

"Your Highness is warm – that is the only reason I am here," he said as I stroked his head.

"And I need protection."

"Obviously."

"Of course."

Seventeen

The following day we remained undisturbed. The forest was as empty and dead as it had been, yet I didn't see the darkly clad figures of the Bonekeepers stalking through to ambush us. Was the forest still keeping them at bay? It showed no sign of life as the moon hung low on the dying branches that reached over the dark sands.

I told everyone what happened over breakfast the next day – including the dreams and last night's adventure. Regan was staring open-mouthed at me. Caden, now on his feet once more, looked impressed as he fired up the stove, filling the cabin with heat. Soon, the smell of frying bacon and eggs wafted around the room.

Captain Bennett sat at the head of the table, eyebrows raised.

"Only you would go against a Bonekeeper alone," Aoife said in a voice light with disbelief.

I shook my shoulders.

"He seemed unnerved by the forest," I thought aloud. I explained that my magic seemed to be even more charged up than usual. I raised my damaged hand and willed my lightning. Instantly my fingertips were aglow and the veins down my arm sparked to life.

Evan spoke with a mouthful of yesterday's leftover egg as he hadn't been able to wait until today's breakfast had been served. Donna, who was sitting opposite him, looked disgusted.

"Your Goddess wanted to show you the truth," he said, bits of egg going flying. "Maybe she just wanted to drive the message home a little louder."

I sighed, Caden placed two plates in front of me – threads of magic had been spun from his fingers and carried the food on feather-thin tracks around the table. Evan had another plate placed in front of him, which landed on top of the previous one.

He grinned wider.

I let the lightning fade on my arm.

Brenn, who had decided not to occupy a seat today, was on my lap. I pushed his plate closer to us and used my knife and fork. As the others continued to speak, I saw Brenn's soft, clawed hand swipe out

222

and stab various bits of the breakfast before they disappeared into his mouth. Being a shifter, no food was too big for him. He would change his mouth so it could consume anything – thankfully, everyone around the table was used to it by now.

"But I didn't accomplish anything. Nothing has happened since," I sighed. I stabbed a sausage as the only noise around the table was that of cutlery scraping on plates.

"Maybe she couldn't tell you because she didn't know," Donna suggested.

"Or maybe she wanted to, but the Bonekeeper put her off," Regan offered up. She ate her breakfast with as much ferocity as she battled. Thus, she had already finished and looked at Caden expectantly.

Caden's nose wrinkled.

"We are on our last few loaves," he said, shaking his head. "Through our diversions; the cargo we lost in the demon attack; and people helping themselves to the cupboards whenever they feel like it," surprisingly, he cast a glare at the Captain and Evan. Evan looked comically offended at the accusation. The captain took up his cup of tea and sipped it, whereas, surprisingly, Aoife looked suitably bashful. "We are understocked until we reach Qicog. As it stands, we might have to have a few meagre meals unless we start getting creative."

Evan loosed a dramatic sigh, letting his hand smack the table with a thump. "I for one, am very disappointed in some of the people in this room."

"Shut your face, Evan," Caden snipped back.

Aoife looked at Caden with an apologetic look. "I will go fishing."

"We can all help," Regan said, crossing her arms.

"It'll be a challenge. Who can get the most fish?" the captain said.

"I still can't swim but I can forage," I offered. Brenn didn't say anything to oppose my suggestion, so I assumed he was in as well.

Round the table, the faces stiffened.

"And today we teach Princess Bryony how to swim," Captain Bennett added.

Everyone agreed instantly.

After breakfast, we all descended from the ship onto the damp shore. The glow from the ship's lanterns made it easier to see the dark waters. Suddenly, a surge of light started to glow from the shore. I turned my head and saw Brenn had cast a large orb of light. No longer a cat – he was wearing a different skin I had not seen before.

Short-haired, pixie-faced, with a pointed nose and a prominent mouth of pink lips. She was tall and wore a loose-fitting, blue-bagged dress that hung off her shoulders. Her skin was a cool neutral tone, her hair light brown, but her eyes – as ever were the same onyx black.

I gave Brenn a questioning look but he – she simply shrugged her shoulders.

"*It felt right,*" she said through our link. Her voice hadn't changed like I thought it would have. It was still, low, bored and unimpressed with everything when I asked if Brenn was going to come in the water.

If anyone else noticed Brenn's change, they didn't mention it.

After arguing for a moment on how it would be best to show me the ways of the water, Aoife had me wade out until I was waist-deep. The water now glittered under the orb that Brenn had set above us, and I was thankful as now I could see past the surface and see nearly down to my ankles.

"I think first it would be a good idea to float for a minute," she said. She came beside me and slowly lay on the water's surface. I copied her.

She moved her arms a little to help herself stay upright. I copied the movement, moving back and forth.

"I'm still surprised your father never wanted you to learn," she said. "My father practically took me from the womb and dropped me in."

"You are partly aquatic though, Aoife," Captain Bennett called from further down the bay.

I raised my head a little above the water to see the rest of the crew floating too. Heads bobbing on the water.

"I can't decide if my father cloistered me away so badly because he was afraid of what would happen to me, or maybe it was just because I was bad at being a princess," I told her. She laughed.

"Being your own person did not make you a bad princess, Bryony," Aoife said. "Parents do strange things in the name of protecting their children. But you're a progressive, Bryony. And it sounds like your father wasn't quite ready for you." I couldn't help the sigh that escaped me.

"He never treated the boys like that."

Aoife didn't say anything – she didn't need to. The truth was sharp and as salty as the water around us. The cut on my shoulder stung.

I was surprised the Bonekeepers hadn't tried again. There was no way that they had just given up. There was no chance of that.

Brenn had said something about the forest changing. Maybe, even though we couldn't see it, it was holding them back.

Aoife had me start moving my legs, the water pleasantly streaming between my toes, and I started to move. Next came my arms.

She stood up and showed me two ways of swimming – with small fast paddling at my front, like a dog and one with longer arm strokes that cut through the waves neatly. Of course, she was an amazing swimmer. I managed to do the first paddling one after a while, but I couldn't do it for very long before having to stop.

Soon enough I was paddling about like a pro. I kept to shallow waters but despite the burn in my arms I could feel the water moving under me, I tilted my head back as far as I could without straining myself.

There was something liberating as I gained more confidence and swam around the others. Once everyone was sure I was not going to drown if I fell from the edge of the boat, they commenced the hunt for fish. I saw Aoife abandon her clothes on the shore and the briefest emergence of her scales before she disappeared under the waves.

Regan did the same; nudity was something all of them seemed too comfortable with each other to worry about. Having been aboard for weeks on end meant that all of them were as open as family were. I had also seen Regan naked more times than I had fingers and toes. She claimed she was averse to clothes.

In her wolf form she sprinted up the beach, black and brown

patches zipping up the beach, no doubt to find a stream of some kind to find the most fish.

We split up, Brenn following me as I paddled along in the sea. Her new form sauntered forward, blue dress whipping in the wind. She looked over at me with a poignant look – her eyes were wide.

"Get out of the water!"

Instantly her new form sprouted wings, long and black but I couldn't see for a slimy arm had wrapped around my foot. I gasped but the next thing I knew I was submerged, and I was being dragged backwards. Water rushed up my nose and down my throat as bubbles streamed past me.

I opened my eyes for a minute and saw something was dragging me down and down – a creature with multiple legs, its skin a dark brown and its eyes big and bulbous.

"Hang on, Bryony!" Brenn's voice rang in my head.

The creature swam deeper and deeper, but it seemed to be getting brighter behind my eyelids. I felt the rush of bubbles hitting my face slow to a halt. My head was still spinning but I opened my eyes – the clearness of the water must've been due to magic – it was like looking through glass.

The underwater world sprawled out in front of me. Plants I had never seen before flourished outwards, some with leaves as wide as a barrel. And the roots connecting them all were glowing.

In front of me, the creature and its many legs receded, leaving me on the base of what seemed to be a thriving reef. It looked back at me as it disappeared into the pitch waters – for the briefest of moments, I felt like it might've wanted to stay. A look of longing appeared in its eyes.

Now I was upright, I envisioned a circle for motion magic. Perhaps if I moved the water, I may be able to create a sphere for air for me to breathe. Brenn flourished beside me, now a long and grey eel that glowed like a piece of witchlight with the familiar onyx eyes.

I saw the threads glow in the water, I strengthened them determinedly, watching them go a bright white colour in my hands. The magic caught a bubble – I focused and pulled the bubble wide and then wider still. I kept my focus, trying to ignore the burning need to breathe. It was big enough now. I placed my head in it and found myself coughing as I raked the air back into my lungs.

Brenn glanced back at me before resuming scouring the land over the reef. His long tail was flicking back and forth as he cut through the water like a knife.

"Krakens do not come so close to the shore," Brenn said into my mind, he didn't need to worry about the air. *"Well done on not dying,"* he said, diving lower into the reef below.

I kicked my legs at a steady pace like Aoife had shown me. I used my hands to flap in front of me to keep myself upright the best I could.

"Why did it steal me? What do krakens eat?" I replied.

"Big fish," he replied. *"But if they're hungry enough they will eat anything."*

I thought of how the Kraken had looked back for me.

"It didn't even try and eat me," I said. I checked over the place where the tentacle had wrapped around my ankle. Nothing was damaged.

Brenn rose from the seabed; his eyes were glowing an even brighter yellow.

"We thought everything here was dead," Brenn started to say, we looked around. There didn't seem to be anything more to say.

Life existed in the Wastes.

Here, at the root level, things still grew – life was thriving. Brenn was not the only fish here – I spotted a school of silver-backed fish heading off in the distance. And when I peered closer to the shell, I could see the smaller sea habitants – wobbling jellyfish, snails with heavy loads, and starfish that shone with a brightness that rivalled their family in the sky.

Then I thought of the Kraken.

"It showed me the truth."

Brenn hovered next to me.

The truth – Celine.

A joy filled my chest like a bubble had just blown there. I couldn't help the smile that bloomed across my face.

The Wastes weren't doomed after all.

It could still come back – the seabed was proof of this.

The eel zipped through the water. *"Hold my tail – I'll take us back."*

I kicked my legs indignantly.

"I'm swimming."

Brenn narrowed his eyes.

"Not drowning is not swimming, Your Highness."

I gave him my best saccharine smile.

"That's exactly what it is."

I realised then we were down quite far.

Brenn looked at me with a pleased expression.

I reached for his tail; a slippery rubbery surface greeted my hand. Brenn easily wove us through the water and back to the surface in a matter of moments. I let the bubble pop just before we emerged so I could enjoy the feeling of fresh air on my face.

I couldn't wipe the smile from my face as Brenn and I waded out onto the shore. The female form appeared next to me – just as sodden as I was. Yet in a blink, she was as dry as the rest of the sand above the shoreline.

The Wastes were empty and dead, as we had seen during our stay. But when Brenn returned to the ship later, she had a whole horde of dead fish. Many patterns and breeds must've been native to the area, as I had never seen them before.

"Lily Fish," Brenn explained, laying them out before me. The fish was fat and had a strange fin across its eyes – it was big and pink.

"Tiger's Eyes," she explained, showing me an orange fish with black and red stripes on its scales. But it had four eyes at its front.

There was a huge silver one next.

"And that one? Silverfish?"

Brenn blinked once.

"That's a salmon."

One by one, the rest of the crew returned to us. Each with a considerable catch of many fish of great shapes and sizes. I thought Regan had clinched the win with a huge cod-like fish that had one too many fins and glowed a bright yellow.

But then Aoife appeared in her serpent form next to the boat. There was a huge white fish in her jaws. She dumped it on the deck with relish as Regan's face fell and Evan began to chortle. Caden clapped everyone and proclaimed Aoife the winner.

Brenn didn't complain once about not winning; though later that night before we went to bed, she changed back into a cat, she grumbled something about if it were judged on quantity then she would've won.

Suddenly, I had a feeling wash over me all at once. A tingling sensation started at my feet and seemed to grow up my bones like a shiver, but filled with warmth. I reached for Donna to steady me, but Brenn had already changed back and caught my shoulder.

"Woah," I said, feeling it spread across my spine and down my shoulders. It felt warm – it was magic. I could feel it coursing through me like a wave sending my senses reeling. I looked up at Brenn's face and could see her eyes were wide. Everyone had stopped now around us.

"Are you alright, Bryony?" Donna asked.

I could feel the magic – warm and inviting like an embrace washing over me.

"Can you feel that?" I asked Brenn. She had gone still. I looked at the others.

Donna shook her head. But it was the Captain who spoke next.

"How is this happening?" his voice was soft, and I looked at him. He was looking up. Everyone did the same.

Silence fell among us. Across the shadow realm, the sun was coming up.